This book should be returned to any ~~~~
Lancashire County Library on or before the date shown

Lancashire County Library,
County Hall Complex,
1st floor Christ Church Precinct,
Preston, PR1 8XJ

www.lancashire.gov.uk/libraries

LL1(A)

30118 135 350 365

DYING DAY

Bill Day – former RAF Wing Commander, war hero and superb pilot. Did he really help fly five fugitive SS men – and their loot – out of Berlin during the 1948 airlift in his company's Dakota ... none of them to be seen again? Forty years on, Anglo-Italian private eye Ron Hogget is hired to find that missing aircraft but soon finds he is not the only one searching for it, its pilot and its cargo. All he has to do is follow the trail of bodies and hope one of them isn't his...

DYING DAY

DYING DAY

by

James Mitchell

Magna Large Print Books
Long Preston, North Yorkshire,
BD23 4ND, England.

British Library Cataloguing in Publication Data.

A catalogue record of this book is
available from the British Library

ISBN   978-0-7505-4304-0

First published in Great Britain in 1988
Published by Ostara Publishing Ltd. in 2015

Copyright © James Mitchell 1988

Cover illustration © Paul Bucknall by arrangement with
Arcangel Images

The moral right of the author has been asserted

Published in Large Print 2017 by arrangement with
Ostara Publishing

Magna Large Print is an imprint of Library Magna Books Ltd.

Printed and bound in Great Britain by
T.J. (International) Ltd., Cornwall, PL28 8RW

135350365

To Su and James Strettell

1

He came into the room without knocking, but he had long since given up worrying about things like that. Every visible part of him that could twitch was twitching. He worried the hell out of me.

'You're Ron Hogget,' he said, and I didn't deny it. The way I was placed, I was in no position to deny anything.

'That's right,' I said.

He was young, thin, not bad-looking, casually but elegantly dressed, but all that twitching scared me. Then he did something that scared me even more. He opened the camera bag he was carrying – and from it he took a gun. When I described it to Dave he said it sounded like a Colt .38, or maybe a European copy of the same. My visitor handled it as if he wasn't all that sure how it worked and twitched worse than ever, and I began to twitch a bit myself...

'You're Ron Hogget,' he said again. I still couldn't deny it.

'You're going to help me,' he told me.

'Of course I am,' I said.

It wasn't all that heroic, but then I'm not a heroic man, and anyway I was in an impossible position. And yet five seconds before that, just before the door opened and the twitcher came in, I'd been thinking how happy I was: how lucky I was: how life couldn't possibly be better. I'd been right, too.

I was staying in a hotel in a place called Abano Terme, which is a little Italian spa about an hour's drive from Venice. With me was my fiancée, a lady by the name of Sabena Redditch, who had strong views on the standards of food and wine and comfort in the hotels she used. The best, Sabena reckoned, was just about good enough for her. Mind you, it was an attitude she could afford, inasmuch as her father was Sir Montague Redditch, the eighth, or possibly ninth, richest man in the country. I was paying my own way, on account of my need to call my soul my own, so that I knew exactly how much a stay in La Residenza cost, but I could afford it, so I had fun.

We ate Italian food and drank Italian wine, and swam and lay in the sun, and drove sometimes to Venice, but before we did any of those things we got up early, and each of us went to rooms at the end of our corridor, and a man, or in Sabena's case a woman, prepared a bucket of mud so hot it was steaming, mud that had then been emptied on to a bed covered in linen sheets. Then he waited till I took off my robe, smeared some of the mud on my back, helped me lie down in the rest and smeared the surplus on my legs, then wrapped me in the linen sheet, put a blanket over the sheet, and left me for ten minutes to simmer. And I loved it. I really did. It's an unbeatable way to relax. And that's exactly what Guido had done to me just before my twitching friend came in and showed me his gun. There I was, tucked up tight in hot mud, my only companion a maniac with a gun seeking my help. Like I say, an impossible position.

My visitor said, 'You're going to find something for me.'

'Be a pleasure,' I said. It was supposed to sound amused, but in fact it sounded like pure terror. The man with the gun didn't even notice.

'It's an aeroplane,' he said. 'Rather an old one. It shouldn't take you long.' He moved closer, and so did the .38.

'Please,' I said. 'You're pointing the gun at me. If it goes off I'll never be able to help you.'

'Oh,' he said, and then to my astonishment: 'Oh, sorry.'

But he didn't put the bloody thing away, merely pointed it downwards.

'I want you to know I'm serious,' he said.

'I believe you,' I said.

'The gun is to warn you not to betray me.'

'I wouldn't dream of it,' I assured him.

'Then there's this.' He put the gun down for a moment, took out an envelope from the camera bag and tucked it in the pocket of my bathrobe, then at once picked up the gun again.

'We'll meet on *Il Burchiello*,' he said. 'Bring your wife.'

He must have meant Sabena.

'She'll love it,' I said.

'Probably not,' he said. 'But she'll hate it if you don't do what you're told.'

Then the gun disappeared into the briefcase and he was gone.

'Il Burchiello?' Sabena said.

11

'It's a pleasure boat that goes from Padua to Venice,' I said. 'Stops off at a few villas on the way.'

'How knowledgeable you are,' she said.

'He left me a brochure, *and* a couple of tickets. For Thursday.'

'In that envelope?'

'Right,' I said. 'He also left me some fifty-pound notes.'

'How many?'

'Ninety-nine. Only they were cut in half.'

'Funny sort of number.'

'I think he meant to make it a hundred but he was too nervous to count straight.'

'But he gave you a half of four thousand nine hundred and fifty quid?'

'In a way,' I said. 'But they're not worth two thousand four hundred and seventy-five. They're not worth a damn thing unless I get the other halves.'

'All the same,' Sabena said, 'he really must want you to find that aeroplane. A wad of money and a large revolver. Carrot and stick... Were you frightened?'

'I still am,' I said.

'But you said yourself he did it all wrong.'

'Well, so he did,' I said. 'Guido could have come in at any minute, he talked far too much, he gave me too much money – and he didn't look too happy holding that gun.'

'Not like Dave,' Sabena said.

'Not in the least like Dave.'

'Then why are you so nervous?'

'Not nervous,' I said. 'Terrified.'

'But why?'

'*Because* he did it all wrong,' I said. 'He might be new to the game but he meant every word.'

'What will you do?'

'See him,' I said. 'What else can I do?'

'You realise,' she said, 'that I'll be coming too?'

'You happen to be the one he threatened.'

'You think that's what he was doing?'

'I know that's what he was doing.'

'All the same you'll have to take me,' Sabena said. 'Otherwise you'll be disobeying instructions – and I'll be the one he takes it out on.'

We were eating breakfast in one of La Residenza's classier suites: all cream and blue, with a double bed Sabena had insisted on, and a view of the outdoor swimming pool and the Euganean hills beyond, indoors and out beauty, order, pleasure – but all I could feel was fear: the fear that I might lose her. It had happened once before. I didn't think I could endure it again.

'We'll have to go to the police,' I said.

'Do you think they'll believe you?'

'They'll believe your dad's money,' I said, and this was no slur on the Italian coppers. *Any* police force would believe Sir Montague's money. But all that meant was they'd be polite and considerate instead of just throwing me out, because there was nothing they could do unless and until my acquaintance with the gun made his move and tried to kill her. Or succeeded.

'He could be having us watched,' said Sabena. 'If he saw us go to the police–'

'You're saying we have to do what he wants?'

'I'm saying just that. No harm in playing it safe,

13

just for the moment. Besides–' She drank more coffee. 'I'm rather intrigued by this aeroplane.'

'Why?' I said.

'Because it's such a difficult thing to lose.'

She reached out and touched me, and grinned in that special only-you-and-I-know-about-this way, and it worked the way it always did.

'I'm having a facial at eleven,' she said.

'So?'

'That's more than an hour away...'

As she dressed she said, 'Do I still make you happy?'

'You mean you didn't notice?'

'I was too busy being happy myself,' she said, and went to have her facial.

I took out the brochure that told us what a wonderful time we would have on *Il Burchiello*. And it didn't look such a bad idea at that – so long as a .38 revolver wasn't featured. A river and canal cruise and a visit to a few villas – one that had been owned by Napoleon, another that Palladio had designed, and a bar on the boat. Culture *and* conviviality. Not a bad place for a meeting either. Guido had told me that *Il Burchiello* was a very popular tour. It would be packed. Who would notice three more Brits having a chat? It occurred to me that, besides a bad case of twitches, my visitor might also have a few brains. Certainly somebody had...

He didn't turn up. We were there, bright and early, all Baedekers and cameras and eager, questing eyes: Sabena and me and a couple of dozen other culture lovers: Germans and Swedes, French, more Brits, even a few Italians, but not my

14

twitching friend. It didn't exactly ruin my day. We set off down the Brenta Canal that links Padua and Venice, and cruised serenely past some of the most desirable residences I'd ever seen. They'd been built by the merchant princes of Venice any time between the sixteenth and eighteenth centuries as country places – very much as an English lord might have built in Sussex or Kent – but, Italy being what it is, a lot of them are still in private hands and closed to the public. 'A poor country full of rich people.' That was how an American ambassador described Italy, and how right he was. And believe me I should know. My mother was Italian.

Anyway we oohed and aahed and took photographs of the Villa Noventa and the Villa Pisani, and sat patiently while the canal locks filled, and drank cappuccino and kept our eyes open. But the carrot and stick man didn't show. From time to time we went ashore and inside a villa to look at pictures and statues and enormous, elegant rooms. At the Villa Pisani, which had once belonged to Napoleon, we even looked at the bathroom, I suppose because Napoleon had once sat in it. After all that culture I bought a couple of campari and sodas and we sat and looked at the men fishing, the masses of greenery, the myriad yellow flowers.

'Are you disappointed?' Sabena asked.

'That he didn't show? I must admit I could use the other half of that five thousand quid or whatever it was. Anyway he could show yet.'

'Don't be absurd,' she said. 'We don't take on any more passengers now.'

15

'We stop at a few more villas,' I said. 'And we have lunch at a restaurant. He could join us there.'

'No, he couldn't,' Sabena said. 'It's a block booking. The girl who gave me the facial told me. Also it's terrible.'

'Block bookings always are,' I said.

We passed another villa: small and elegant, neat garden, gravelled walkways.

'I rather think,' Sabena said, 'that that's the one daddy nearly bought.'

'But not quite?' She nodded. 'Why not?'

'It was too cheap.'

'Too cheap for what?'

'For it to be what it claimed to be. Crammed full of antique statues and eighteenth-century furniture and minor masters.'

I was intrigued. I do a bit in that line myself. Not buying: finding.

'You never told me your father knows about antiques,' I said.

'He doesn't,' said Sabena. 'What he knows about is money.'

And God knows that's true.

Lunch was every bit as terrible as Sabena's beautician had said it would be. I doubt if Sabena had ever eaten one like it before, but then I doubt whether she'd ever shared a boat-ride with so many other people before, not unless the boat was the *QE2* and daddy had booked a suite. Not that she was a snob or anything, just rich. That was her good fortune. Mine was that she loved me. Anyway we filled up mostly on bread and wine, and promised ourselves a damn good dinner, and

16

went back to looking at villas.

It was the last one where I found him. It's called 'La Malcontenta' on account of a girl who was crossed in love once lived there, a long time ago. It is memorable, the guidebook said, as being an outstanding example of the gifted sixteenth-century architect Palladio. But not to me. To me it is memorable as being the place where I met up again with the twitcher...

A lot of the villas appear in movies or on Italian television from time to time, and it was about to be La Malcontenta's turn. Already they'd moved in a generator and a load of lighting equipment round the back, and they'd fixed up a wooden dock to augment the one already there to unload the stuff, which made it a very easy walk ashore from *Il Burchiello's* companionway.

We'd been drinking coffee at the bar when the boat arrived at the villa, which meant that we were last ashore, and like the little gent I am I let Sabena go first, and she moved off quickly to catch up with the guide. I stayed behind to re-move a stone from my shoe, and it was my luck (good or bad I'll never know) to glance sideways after I'd done it, and see a leg sticking out from under the dock. I went to look further, and the dock swayed as a motor-boat moved past, and the leg floated out further, followed by a torso and what was left of a head. Twitcher's head. Parts of the top of it had been shot away, very possibly by a .38, Dave told me later. I asked him if that could have been a Colt or a European copy of one, and Dave said why not? But, like I say, all that came later. For the moment all I was

17

doing was looking at a corpse and feeling sick. The twitcher by the look of him hadn't been dead very long, but equally by the look of him there was no doubt at all that he was dead, which was why I was feeling sick. Then another boat went by and again the dock swayed, but this time the twitcher went back under the dock as a man might go into the dark, and then and there I stopped feeling sick and went to join Sabena and learn all about Palladio.

After that we went back aboard and off to where the Brenta joined the Giudecca Canal, and so on to the Basin of San Marco, and one of the most famous views in the world, as we went ashore at the Piazza San Marco to dawdle time away at Florian's then on to the Bridge of Sighs and a restaurant called the Graspo de Uva – which is Venetian for the Bunch of Grapes – and a fish stew which is as messy as it's delicious, so that you have to wear a bib to eat it. I ate every scrap and drank a lot of dry white Salaparuta, and Sabena did the same. After that we took a water-taxi to the Piazzale Roma and then a regular taxi back to La Residenza. The regular taxi was a Mercedes because Sabena doesn't like Italian cars, though I never let her say so aloud, not in Italy. Then we made each other happy.

Later she said, 'Such ardour. What are we celebrating?'

'You're complaining?'

'Of course not,' she said. 'I'm enjoying. But I want to know what makes tonight so special.'

Put that way it didn't sound very nice; in fact it sounded downright nasty, but I told her anyway.

'We're happy because he's dead?' she asked.

'We're happy because you're not,' I said, 'and he can't threaten you any more.'

'I'd have been all right,' she said, 'with you to look after me.'

'Me and Dave,' I said, 'but not in that order.'

'Why didn't you tell me sooner?'

'We were in a boat or a café or a restaurant,' I said. 'Somebody might have heard. Now there's just us.'

'Which is fine with me.'

She got out of bed and fetched the half-bottle of champagne from the mini-bar fridge, and a couple of glasses, and shoved the bottle at me.

'Open that, will you?' she asked. 'The way we've been going at it tonight we're due for a hangover anyway. May as well make it a good one.'

I opened and poured.

'You're absolutely sure he was murdered?'

My hand shook a little and we had a champagne-scented pillow. 'I'm sure,' I said.

'Yes, well... I'm awfully sorry, darling, but don't you see? Maybe we're not out of this yet... Not if whoever killed him knows he came to see you.'

'You've got brains,' I said. 'It's a pity in a way. If you were stupid like me we could still be happy.'

She put her tongue out at me, then we drank the champagne and made love again, and it was still good, but it wasn't the same.

2

La Stampa and *Giornale d'Italia* didn't have much on it, but the Venice press and local TV gave it quite a spread. It seemed that what was due to be filmed at La Malcontenta was one of those witty, upmarket TV whodunnit movies and finding a real murder victim right there on the spot all helped the production, and the fact that the corpse was a mystery man helped even more. Not just a mystery, but an unidentified mystery. No way of identifying him at all. No scars, no operations, no dentures, just a male of twenty-five or so, a bit skinny but no signs of ill-health, until somebody shot bits of his head off. Actually there was something wrong with him, but for some reason the Italian police were a bit coy about saying it was needle marks. They did say that no gun had been found, and no bullet lodged in the skull, but even that was good. It was part of the mystery...

Time to go home. More than time really. But it was hard to say goodbye to all that mud and sex and Italian food and trade it in for Fulham. Sabena said I lived in Fulham because of inverted snobbery (she lives round the corner from Harrods), and Dave says I live there because it serves me right, but there's something wrong with his logic. He lives in Fulham too.

Anyway I went to see him once I'd taken Sabena

back to her place and emptied my suitcase ready for the launderette and dry cleaners... It's never all that difficult to catch up with Dave. He drives a mini-cab, and when he isn't working he sits in a pub called the Bricklayers' Arms and stretches out a lager till closing time and reads. Not page three of the *Sun*, not even *Sporting Life*. What Dave reads is books: literature, you might say. *The Letters of Dorothy Osborne*, maybe, or *Crime and Punishment*, or Vasari's *Lives of the Painters* or something. A great reader is Dave. It's one of his best things, on account of him having been to Sheffield University and taken a degree in English Language and Literature, but then he found out that with the sort of degree he'd got all he could do with the rest of his life was be a teacher, so he joined the Paras instead on account of he pre-ferred fighting with people his own size.

He's good at it, too. He did his time in the Paras and saw a bit of action here and there, and once he was demobbed he joined a martial arts club and got even better. Dave's like those government warnings you get on packets of cigarettes: he can seriously damage your health. Lean, blue eyes, fairish hair. Nobody would ever mistake him for Robert Redford, but he's not bad-looking and a good mate. I found him in the Bricklayers and brought him over a lager and a gin and tonic for myself. He put down his book. *Adam Bede* it was, by some geezer called George Eliot, except that Dave said George Eliot was a bird, and who was I to doubt him? I wasn't going to read the book to find out.

'Ta, Ron,' he said. 'Have a good holiday?'

21

'Most of the time,' I said.

He put the book down. You never have to draw pictures for Dave.

'How's Sabena?' he said.

'She's fine,' I said. 'Thank God.'

Dave sipped at his lager. 'Want to talk here?'

'Why not?' Apart from me and Dave there was only the barmaid and three blokes watching snooker on telly. I told him. That's when I found out the gun was most likely a .38. But that wasn't what grabbed him. Not even the corpse under the dock grabbed him. He's seen enough corpses in his time.

'An aeroplane,' he said. 'Rather an old one.' He took another sip of lager. 'Pity he didn't go into more detail.'

'Isn't it though?' I said, not believing a word.

'Still, we're bound to find out,' said Dave.

'Who's going to tell us?'

'The blokes who killed him.'

I wondered if Dave had been talking to Sabena. He looked at me, then got up and bought me another gin and tonic.

'Ron, boy,' he said, 'face it. He was killed waiting for you. It can't have been a coincidence.'

'I know,' I said.

'Course you do,' Dave said. 'You've got brains. So if he was killed to stop the two of you talking ... they must know who you are. What you do.'

'You mean finding things?' I said.

'The best in the business, you are,' said Dave.

'Not everybody knows that,' I said.

'No, but he did. Which means he's a bit dodgy, wouldn't you say?'

22

I didn't argue. The kind of geezers who come to me because they want things found and pay big money for finding them usually are a little bit dodgy. Or more than a little.

'And the bloke who knocked him off must be as dodgy as they come... I reckon I'd better move in with you for a while, Ron.'

'It may not be the way you say,' I said. 'After all, this bloke was killed before we got together – to stop us getting together. The killer must know we didn't have time to talk.'

Dave lit a cigarette. It isn't a thing he does very often, and when he does he takes his time about it. At last he said, 'It's a possibility. No more.'

'You are a ray of sunshine today.'

'I'm trying to help you,' he said.

'Help me? *Help me?*'

'Well, of course,' he said. 'Because there's another possibility and you know it. There's the possibility that the killer isn't sure how much you know. And if that's the right answer he'll do one of two things: either he'll come and ask you or he'll kill you. You'd better let me have the spare room, Ron. Just for a week or two.'

'Thanks,' I said. 'But no.'

'You think I'm past it?'

'Of course not.' Dave isn't the sort to be past it this side of his Senior Citizen's Bus Pass. 'But, when they see you, whoever it is will lay off – and then when you're busy doing something else they'll come and get me. And you will be busy sometimes, Dave. You'll have to be. If you're right I need round the clock surveillance or else don't bother.'

He sighed, and blew out smoke.

'You'll chance it alone then?'

'I think it's the best way,' I said.

And I did too. The way I looked at it, if they couldn't get at me they might try the Twitcher's idea and use Sabena as bait.

But nothing happened, not for three weeks, except that I retrieved a rock-star's wife's diamond necklace for her and she paid me a thousand quid for doing it even though it was paste and worth maybe a couple of hundred because her husband must never know. So the thousand helped me cover my overheads as my brother-in-law says, and in my spare time I sat in Fulham and waited for the phone to ring, and tried to figure out if there was any way known to man that the Queen's head half of a fifty-pound note can be converted into money without joining it to the other half. There isn't, believe me.

There were other interludes of course. Sabena saw to that. Like using my talent for finding things to get tickets for Wimbledon, and how many days should we spend at Ascot, and should we go to the villa at Antibes again this year or fling caution to the winds and hire a yacht at Puerto Banus. These after all are important considerations... My struggles with the fifty-pound notes became less like an intellectual exercise and more like a frantic necessity as my savings dwindled, and nobody lost anything they'd pay me over the odds to get back. Until I got the phone call: or rather the message on the telephone recorder.

'Would I care to meet Bertie Benskin for a

drink at the PAAA club?' a male voice asked. It was a voice that had more than its fair share of gin and tonics. If I would I was to report (that was the word so I knew it must mean money) at Number 9, Astley Gardens W8 at 6.30 sharp. If not, I was given a number to ring and explain my reluctance to do the decent thing. I reported.

Astley Gardens is just off Kensington High Street and wedged into the angle between Earl's Court Road and the Cromwell Road. 'Thou still unravished bride of quietness', Dave called it when he drove me there, which appeared to mean that it hadn't changed all that much in the last hundred and twenty years. A white stucco box stood on its end with big, shapely sash-windows, and a glowing mahogany door, one of a matching set that stretched the length of the street. I told Dave I'd see him in the Bricklayers next day and he scarpered. Later I'd arranged to see Sabena. That would mean a taxi – or more likely a bus the way she was planning our summer. The parking round that part of Kensington is murder and anyway I run a Datsun. Astley Gardens is all Mercs and Jags and BMWs.

I looked at my watch and it was 6.29, so I walked up the steps and looked at the row of bells by the door. Each house in Astley Gardens had been built for one family and its servants – say fifteen or sixteen people when you allow for the size of a family and the number of servants in the 1860s – but now it was flats. The PAAA club was on the ground floor and I was glad of it. Conversions like that don't often run to a lift. I pushed the button and a voice on the entryphone said 'Yes'.

'My name's Hogget,' I said. 'To see Mr Benskin.' A pause, then, until at last the voice said, 'Come in, Mr Hogget. You're expected.' There was a buzzing sound and the front door opened a little and I pushed it and went in.

A hallway in dark lincrusta and a carpet, nothing special, and a couple of oil-paintings that could have been anything, the kind you can buy by the square foot at the shops round Camden Passage. There was an ageing geezer in a pair of slate-blue trousers and a blue shirt and a blue tie by an open door across the hall, and he motioned to me to come in. It was the club bar, and it was something else. You couldn't have got that in Camden Passage or even Harrods: not even Sotheby's if you bought it a piece at a time. If you'd managed to distil the essence of the RAF museum at Cranwell and the RAF March Past and *Picture Post* articles on the Battle of Britain and a wartime documentary about a thousand-bomber raid on Hamburg you might have come near, but what you really needed was a time-warp that would take you back to the 1940s and an RAF flyer's way of life.

I'd never seen anything like it. There was an RAF greatcoat and caps on the coatstand – there was even a flying jacket – and on the floor a couple of life-jackets, the kind they called Mae Wests, had been somehow moulded into a seat. Hanging on hooks was a row of steel helmets and respirators with a flying helmet as a centrepiece. There was a propeller on one wall, and a stripped-down .303 Browning machine-gun, the kind they used to arm Spitfires and Hurricanes. There were

26

the red, white and blue circles they'd used to identify their planes, and a line of swastikas to record the number of kills they'd made: Heinkels, Dorniers, Messerschmitts. And everywhere that there wasn't some piece of machinery, some arte- fact, there was a photograph of an aircraft: Spit- fires, Hurricanes, Wellingtons, Boulton-Paul Defiants, Lancaster, Beaufighters, Dakotas. And if it wasn't the aircraft it was the men who flew them: names I'd scarcely heard of then, but I made up for it later: Douglas Bader, Johnny Johnson, Guy Gibson, Sailor Malan, Cats' Eyes Cunningham, G. L. Cheshire, Screwball Beur- ling, and a whole lot more who never made the papers, but all young, all valiant, and by now nearly all dead, and most of them young when it happened. There was even music, I remember. What looked like an HMV portable gramophone circa 1938, scratching its way through Geraldo and his orchestra's version of 'A Nightingale Sang in Berkeley Square'.

A man came in from another room, holding out a hand and spoiling the illusion.

'Hallo,' he said. 'I'm Benskin'

He was tall, but at least three stone overweight, grey hair growing thin, grey eyes that needed their spectacles. I shook the hand.

'Ron Hogget,' I said.

'Good of you to come.' He herded me to the bar. 'Drink?'

'Thanks,' I said. 'Gin and tonic.'

The geezer who'd let me in had acquired a white jacket and become a mess waiter. White on top of all that blue, I thought. Then it hit me. He

27

was in period costume too. All that blue was the wartime uniform of the RAF.

'Gin and tonic, Billings,' Benskin said, 'and a gin and lime. Large ones.' He turned to me. 'Somehow gin and lime's the only drink I enjoy in this place.' He offered me a Player's cigarette, untipped.

The gin and lime would be almost mandatory I thought as I refused the cigarette. But then so would the Player's be for a smoker, according to my dear father, and in World War II almost everybody had smoked when they could get them. Gin and lime and a Player's cigarette and you had the war in each hand... I waited, but he seemed to have run out of words, just nuzzled the gin and lime and lit the cigarette with a petrol lighter: an antique.

'You were in the RAF during the war?' I asked.

Not the most perceptive remark I'd ever made, but I had to get him started somehow. He looked at me as if I ought to be certified.

'Joined in 1939,' he said. 'Pilot. I was in Hali-bangs – what you would call the Halifax.'

I wouldn't have called it anything. To me the Halifax was a building society.

'Later on I transferred to Lancasters,' he said.

And that did get through to me. I'd seen a docu-mentary once about Lancasters: big, four-engined bombers that just about demolished Hamburg and Berlin and other places, including Dresden.

'Happy days,' he said, then nodded at a photo-graph on the wall and smiled as if it was a Betty Grable pin-up. 'That's a Lancaster,' he said.

Compared with one of today's jets it looked

28

crude, even clumsy. It also looked brutal.

'Nice kite to fly,' he said, and put down his empty glass. Billings filled it without being asked, then moved away.

'Almost forgot,' Benskin said. 'You got anything to show you really are Ron Hogget?'

I took out my driving licence and the visiting card I keep specially for the times when I'm asked that question. Benskin read them without moving his lips then handed them back.

'Sorry about that,' he said, 'but it is rather a confidential matter.'

'Perfectly all right,' I said. 'I've got used to it.'

'Good Lord,' Benskin said. 'I suppose you must have.'

Then he seized up again, and there was more silence: Geraldo had long since given up the struggle. Benskin went over to a pile of 78s and pulled out another one, then cranked up the gramophone. This time it was Glen Miller and 'Chattanooga Choo Choo'. I'm very fond of Glen Miller, but he wasn't what I'd come for.

'Do you think you'd like to tell me about it?' I asked.

Benskin had been making vaguely jitterbugging movements, with his gin and lime for a partner, but then he stopped dead.

'Certainly not,' he said, and I blinked at him. If I looked bewildered I wasn't acting.

'We have to wait for the CO,' he explained.

'The CO?'

'Squadron Leader Palliser,' Benskin said. He had the same tone of voice a parish priest might have had saying 'His Holiness the Pope'. 'All I

29

can say is there's something missing and he wants you to find it.'

But I'd expected that anyway. Like I say, finding things is what I'm for.

And then the phone rang. It was a loud and old-fashioned sort of ring, but then it was an old-fashioned sort of phone, the kind that rang in the ops room just before bells began to ring and young men came running, lugging flying jackets and parachutes, to where the Spitfires stood lined up waiting, their Rolls-Royce Merlin engines revving. And the next shot would show them climbing hard and high into the sun, till one of them spotted the Heinkels below, and 'Bandits at 8 o'clock' and 'Tally-ho, chaps', and one by one the Spitfires peeled off and went in screaming... And, if that's a hell of a lot to get from one telephone bell, all I can say is it was a hell of a room the phone was in. Benskin picked it up. 'Yes,' he said, then listened. 'Wilco.' He hung up and turned to me. 'The CO will see us now,' he said. Even the thought of it awed him.

We left the club and went up one curving flight of stairs, then Benskin pushed ahead of me to open another gleaming door. A drawing-room this time, and one that had nothing whatever to do with the RAF or World War II. Aubusson carpet, Regency furniture, heavy wool green and russet curtains with a bird design the like of which I'd never seen before, but they looked expensive. Later I found out they were Tibetan, and even more expensive than they looked. And in the middle of it all Squadron Leader Anthony Francis de Vries Palliser, DFC, looking rather like a bird design himself.

About average height, I thought, but so thin he looked taller. Hair silver and brushed close to the skull, eyes brown and restless and glittering, thin mouth, a curving beak of a nose: white shirt, blue trousers, Gucci loafers, a tie that was just a tie – nothing to do with the services or clubs or schools. He looked at once fit and clever and ruthless.

'Mr Hogget,' he said. 'I'm Palliser. I suppose my friend Benskin here told you?'

'Yes,' I said.

'You had a drink?' His voice was sharp, almost shrill: rather like Field Marshal Montgomery's: far removed from Benskin's fruity rumble.

'Yes,' I said.

'Want another?'

'No thanks.'

It seemed I'd given the right answer. He smiled for perhaps two seconds.

'Help yourself, Bertie,' he said to Benskin. 'Mr Hogget and I had better get on with it.'

Benskin went over to a drinks table looking rather like a naughty boy being stood in a corner, and Palliser led me over to a couple of carved rosewood numbers by Hepplewhite, their silk coverings imported from Paris about a hundred and sixty years ago.

'What did you make of our club?' he asked.

I hedged. I'd no idea what I was supposed to say.

'It looked – authentic,' I said.

'Oh, it is,' Palliser said. 'Every piece. As an exercise in nostalgia I'd say it's just about unbeatable. Even the name.'

'PAAA?' I said.

'Per Ardua Ad Astra,' said Palliser. 'The motto of the Royal Air Force. "Through Danger To The Stars".'

Benskin came over and joined us, and sat on another Hepplewhite masterpiece. He sat very carefully, as if he'd been warned many times that Hepplewhite is vulnerable. This time he had a gin and tonic.

'We all had the danger,' he said. 'Quite a lot of us reached the stars as well.'

'Bertie means the club's membership is restricted to aircrew,' Palliser said. 'Chaps who served between 1939 and 1945. My guess is it'll last about another twenty years. After that we'll all be in the stars.' He turned back to me. 'A lot of chaps won't come near the place,' he said. 'Gives them the willies just to think about it. Other chaps can't keep away. Like Bertie here. They think life was never quite the same after the war ended. Mind you so do the chaps who keep away. But Bertie – he was good, you see. In fact he was bloody marvellous.'

Benskin lit another Player's, and I wished he hadn't.

'What you want me to find – it has something to do with the club?' I asked. But already I knew what it was.

'Well, yes and no,' Benskin said, but Palliser had no time for vagaries.

'We want you to find an aeroplane,' he said. 'Rather an old one.'

'An aeroplane?' I said, and even to me it sounded like aeroplanes were something I'd heard of vaguely, but I'd never thought of them as something that people might lose.

'They can get lost you know,' Palliser said.

'We lost fifty-nine on a thousand-bomber raid on Hamburg in a single night,' Benskin said.

Palliser turned to Benskin and his voice was patient. My guess was that if it hadn't been Benskin there'd have been no patience in it at all.

'But even Mr Hogget here couldn't bring those planes back for us,' he said.

Benskin sucked at his gin and tonic then said, 'True, O King,' as if he meant every word.

'Bertie was in bombers,' Palliser said. 'I was in fighters – Spitfires actually. We didn't actually meet until after the war.'

'We went into business together,' Benskin said, and got up to fill his glass. That surprised me. Palliser didn't look the type to go into business with a lush, and then I remembered that to them after the war probably meant what it said – a time more than forty years ago, when for all I knew three pints of bitter could have meant a heavy night to Benskin.

'Bertie and I and a chap called Bill Day and a chap called Frank Denville,' Palliser said. 'Bill was in fighters, like me. Frank had been in Transport Command.'

'What sort of business?' I asked.

'We started an airline,' Benskin said, and Palliser laughed. If an eagle could laugh, that was more or less the sound it would make.

'Sounds awfully grand, doesn't it?' he said. 'But we weren't exactly Pan Am – or even British Caledonian.'

Benskin laughed then: a laugh I could recognise;

33

rumbling, human.

'Not exactly,' he said.

'We pooled our resources – that meant our gratuities and whatever we happened to have in the bank – I had sixty-three quid I remember – and we bought this Dak.' My face must have said it all, because he said, 'I take it you know very little about aeroplanes?'

'I know you catch them at Heathrow,' I said, 'and that's about it.'

'Then I'll explain.'

I eased back into my chair; I was about to receive a lecture.

'The Douglas DC3, otherwise known as the Dakota – hence Dak – is a twin-engined job with Pratt and Whitney engines. I say "is" because there are a few of them still flying, though the first ones came off the production line in 1936. She's an ugly brute, no glamour at all after Spitfires–' his glance flicked to Benskin '–or Lancasters – but she's an angel to fly – pilot's best friend we used to say – and she could take off and land on a cart-track.'

'Quite often did,' Benskin said.

'She's a workhorse, the Dakota,' Palliser went on. 'Stick seats in her and she's a passenger plane – take 'em out and she's a freighter. Pilgrims to Mecca, drilling machinery for an oil-rig, it was all the same to the Dakota. Just load her up and she'd go.

'So as I say, we bought one. Not a very good one because we hadn't much money, so the one we got was a bit knocked about – taken a swipe from a Focke-Wolff 190 – German fighter in France.

34

When we got a look at it we found we had to buy another one – even bigger wreck – to cannibalise for spares. All the same it was cheaper than buying them from Douglas.

We hired a couple of fitters and the four of us – Bill, Frank, Bertie and me – supplied the labour, and inside three days we had a Dak that could and did fly all six of us back to the UK.' He shook his head: the memory still warmed him. 'I tell you that was the most amazing kite that ever flew. It made Douglas's fortune. The world needed that plane, whether there was a war or not.'

'Did it make your fortune?' I asked and Benskin chuckled again, but not Palliser. To him the question was a serious one.

'Not immediately,' he said, and continued his saga. We called ourselves Ad Astra Airlines. We were very sentimental in those days.'

Not you, mate, I thought. Benskin almost certainly, but you haven't been sentimental since your second birthday.

'We were all good pilots,' he said, 'but Bill Day and I had flown single-engined stuff from the day we joined, and two engines are different, believe me. Bertie was more used to four engines, but he'd done a bit in two-engined jobs in the early days.'

'Wellingtons,' Bertie said. 'The dear old Wimpey.'

'But Frank Denville had flown almost everything we had, short of a barrage balloon. He'd flown bombers, fighters, even flying boats – and he'd spent a lot of time in Daks. Now – to win the coconut – who flew our Dak best?'

I gave him the obvious answer, knowing it must

be wrong.

'Denville? He would have been second,' Palliser said, 'if it weren't for Bertie here. Frank had the experience with Daks, but Bertie's one of the best pilots I ever knew.'

'So which of you was it?'

'Bill Day. He was absolutely *the* best pilot I ever knew.' He turned to Benskin. 'Wasn't he?'

'He was as good as they come,' Benskin said. There might have been four – maybe five – who could give him a game. There wouldn't be more.'

'Brave too,' Palliser said. There was neither warmth nor envy in his voice, he was just stating a fact. He could have been saying Day had a wart on his nose.

'But surely to God you were all brave?' I said.

'It's what we were paid for, certainly,' Palliser said, 'but we didn't all achieve the same levels. How could we? But Bill Day had the lot.'

'DSO and bar,' Benskin said.

According to what Dave had told me that was the equivalent of winning the DSO – the Distinguished Service Order – twice, and as the DSO ranks immediately below the Victoria Cross I believed them when they said Bill Day was brave.

'What rank did he hold?'

'Wingco,' said Benskin. 'That's Wing Commander. Denville was a flight-lieutenant like me.'

'What happened to him?'

'All in good time,' Palliser said. He was a man describing his first love-affair, and most likely his only one, with the airline he'd helped to build, and he wasn't going to be rushed. What it boiled down to was this:

It hadn't been easy, right from the beginning. There were an awful lot of ex-RAF pilots who thought they'd buy a second-hand aircraft and make a fortune, but hardly any of them did. The competition was too strong. But Ad Astra Airlines hung on. For starters they had two above-average pilots. One who was remarkable, and one who was incredible. They would go anywhere, literally anywhere, that a plane could go. Benskin hadn't been joking about landing on cart tracks, though a lot of the time it was desert landing strips, smuggling arms to North African Arabs who thought it was time the French went back to France. There were pilgrims to Mecca too, body-searched before the Dak took off to make sure they weren't carrying weapons after the time when Day and Benskin had to sort out a knife fight in mid-air.

There were the more normal jobs too: ferrying urgently needed machine parts mostly, or Scottish salmon for London hotels, but it was the exotic jobs that provided the loot, so much that they found in 1947 that they'd accumulated capital, and invested in another Dakota – just in time for the partition of India. And when that came they really cleaned up. Rich Hindus in Moslem states, rich Moslems in Hindu states, suddenly found an urgent need to be elsewhere, the faster the better and money no object. The Ad Astra Dakotas were the answer to many prayers. Of course the four pilots took chances, cut corners – they'd been doing nothing else since they first flew – and eventually they were invited to leave by both India and Pakistan, but in the meantime they'd been making the stuff in sackfuls. And when they got back the Berlin Airlift had begun even before they had time to buy another plane.

3

The way Palliser told it, India and Pakistan had been wild, but the Berlin Airlift was insanity. It had to be. Without a hefty injection of madness it could never have happened. In 1948, as now, Berlin was entirely surrounded by Communist East Germany, and, as now, was divided into Communist East Berlin and Allied West Berlin, though the Reds hadn't got around to building their wall yet. What they did do, in 1948, was cut off all West German road and rail links with West Berlin, which is to say they put it under siege. No assault with troops, just a stranglehold on supplies: no food except what was already there, and no hope of getting any. The winter was coming on, too, and Berlin was in a hell of a mess, and when winter did come it would be a hell of a cold mess, with blankets and coal as important as food, and no trucks or railway waggons to bring it in. A very bleak state of affairs for West Berlin, which looked as if it was about to be swallowed up by East Berlin and become part of the people's republic – until some bright spark among the planners thought up the airlift. At least that's what Palliser called him. To me it sounded more like the work of a fairy godmother.

Everything West Berlin needed, every sock, lump of coal, tin of sardines, was flown into Tempelhof Airport. Millions of people, for the first time ever, depended on the aeroplane for survival, and with aeroplanes the size they were then that meant dozens of aircraft, maybe scores, flying round the clock. And not just any kind of aircraft, these planes had to be transports: any company that owned a Dakota had it made. Ad Astra Airlines had it made twice over.

'It was weird,' Benskin said. 'There we were over Berlin, time after time, no searchlights, no ack-ack, no night-fighters, the whole place blazing with lights and the Krauts on our side working like demons. It was weird.'

It was also money in the bank.

For the first time they had a workload guaranteed every day and it was cash on the nail: a government contract.

'Nothing to it,' Benskin said. 'Go out full, come back empty.'

A lot of chaps didn't even do that, it seemed. They came back with a few extras at least, and not much of it belonging to Germans. There was a big force of Allied soldiers in West Berlin in 1948, and some of them had acquired what Benskin called 'souvenirs', though he used the word as if it had been an unmentionable disease. Jewellery – quite a lot of jewellery – and gold and silverware, paintings and statuettes, clocks, fine china. And nobody bothered when you flew it home, neither in Berlin or in whatever landing-field you'd been routed to, because everybody had been too damn busy getting stuff out, the food and blankets and coal that would keep Berliners alive.

But Palliser seemed to have been against the smuggling lark, and it was apparent that Benskin agreed with him. I asked them why and they looked at me as if I wasn't very nice.

'What do you mean, why?' Benskin asked

'I mean you did pretty much the same with those maharajahs in India and Pakistan,' I said. 'You smuggled both ways there. Guns in and jewellery out.'

'Not the same thing at all,' Palliser said. 'In India we were just helping some people to hang on to what was theirs, either by arming them – or putting their valuables where they could reach them. Nothing wrong in that. A bit unorthodox perhaps, but there was nothing morally wrong.'

'Hear hear,' said Benskin, and Palliser flicked a glance at him. The booze was getting to Benskin at last. All the same, Palliser said nothing when his mate set off for another glassful.

'But Berlin was dreadful,' he said. 'Really dreadful. All that loot that was brought out – it was made by selling food or medical supplies to poor devils who would die if they didn't get them.'

'That or vice rings,' Benskin said.

'That too,' said Palliser. 'Berlin was a cesspool in those days. A lot of Germany was. Petty officials made small fortunes just by looking the other way. We wouldn't touch it.'

I believed them, but I wanted it clear.

'You mean all four of you, or just you and Mr Benskin here?'

Benskin said, 'You're not just a pretty face, are you, old boy?' then snorted as if he'd said something funny. Maybe he had.

'I was pretty certain it was all four,' said Palliser. 'I mean Bertie and I usually flew as a team – one of us flying, the other navigating – and Bill Day and Frank Denville did the same. We didn't exactly check up on each other. I mean why should we? We were partners after all – we trusted each other – but all the same we were together an awful lot – in and out of each other's planes and so on. If they'd been up to something we'd have known. Right, Bertie?'

'Oh, absolutely,' Benskin said, but I wasn't sure he'd even heard the question.

'I would say that was true until the very last flight that Arthur made,' said Benskin.

'Arthur?' I asked.

'We had two planes,' Palliser said, 'and we named them alphabetically. A for Arthur and B for Boadicea. Bill and Frank flew Arthur.'

I wondered if it was significant that once again Palliser had copped the second position. He didn't look the sort of man who'd find it easy to come in second.

The last flight was the one where the aircraft disappeared,' said Palliser. 'And so did Bill Day and Frank Denville.'

'Well, as I told you before,' Benskin said, 'aircraft do disappear, but not the ones Bill Day flew.' He looked at me earnestly: he was now good and drunk. 'Bill Day was the best. I tell you if he was to come back now this minute he could take off in a four-engined jet without even looking at the manual.'

'I don't think he'll come back,' Palliser said.

'You think he's dead?'

'He could be. But alive or dead he won't come back.'

'Why not?'

'Firstly because he intended to steal that Dak and we can prove it. He was never on the flight path he should have been.'

'He and Denville,' I said.

'I understand what you mean,' said Palliser, 'but Bill Day was the leader. Denville was a follower all his life.'

'Do you have photographs of them?' I asked.

'Not any more,' Palliser said. 'Not after what happened.'

'Please go on,' I said.

'By that time we had more than sixty thousand quid in the bank,' Palliser said. 'The price of two more second-hand Daks and a bit left over.'

'Except that the other two took out their share,' Benskin said. 'Fifteen thousand each.'

'Except that it wasn't theirs to take,' Palliser said.

'Damn it, Tony,' Benskin said, 'it was their money. They'd earned it.'

'It was company money,' Palliser said. 'Money for investment. They stole from the company.'

'How could they?' I asked.

'Any two partners could sign a cheque,' Palliser said.

'Whose idea was that?'

'Bill Day's.'

'And who was company treasurer?' I asked.

'Me,' said Palliser. 'And normally I'd have been on to it like a shot – but they timed it well. I'd been flying every hour I wasn't sleeping for weeks

42

and weeks. I couldn't read a headline, never mind a balance-sheet.'

'So they took the money and ran?'

'They did rather more than that,' said Palliser. 'They lifted five blokes out of Berlin.'

'Refugees?'

'Nazis,' Palliser said. 'Ex-SS men.'

'When I heard it I couldn't believe it,' Benskin said. 'It didn't seem possible that *anybody* could do it. Not then. This was just three years after the Belsen pictures had been shown.'

'They did it for money?'

'Of course. Something to add to their fifteen thousand quid.'

'You think an SS man would have money – after they'd lost?'

'Well, of course,' said Palliser. 'They'd been winning for over five years. They only lost for one. Five years to loot from all the Jews in Europe – and a lot of other people too.'

I couldn't argue. Instead I asked, 'How did they reach Day and Denville?'

'For that you'll have to talk to a man named Joachim Kessler.'

'In Germany?'

'Oxford,' Palliser said. 'He's a don there. In 1948 he did rather a different kind of work.'

'What kind?'

'General labourer, black marketeer, thief.'

Benskin looked unhappy. 'He used to work for us,' he said. 'Helped with the loading and unloading. Nice chap. Never stole as much as the others.'

I asked more questions, but the only answers I got were 'Don't knows'. They didn't know who the SS men were or where the Dak had left the flight plan, or whether Denville or Day had ever been sighted again. And so on and so on. You ask it, they didn't know it.

I said at last, 'Well, gentlemen, we haven't a lot to go on, have we?'

'We've got sod all,' said Benskin, in a voice near tears.

'You realise – that being the case – that it's going to cost you?'

'Well, of course,' said Palliser, but he didn't look happy. What it was going to cost was his money.

'But before we go into that there is one other question.'

'Why we've waited so long?' Palliser said.

'That's the one.'

Benskin opened his mouth but Palliser cut in quickly. 'Let me answer this, Bertie.' He turned to me.

'There was only one time to go after Bill Day,' he said, 'and that was immediately after he ... left us. But we couldn't. Not then. Bertie and I still had half an airline to run, and even after the Berlin airlift was over we had to work round the clock to repair the damage he'd done to us: find new planes, new pilots. There just wasn't time.'

'Or even energy,' said Benskin. 'When a day ended then, all I could do was sleep.'

'Until we got lucky,' said Palliser. 'That was in the mid-'50s, when BEA took us over.'

'They made us redundant,' said Benskin. 'But they made us rich too.'

'We thought of starting up again – in the Middle East this time, but by then we were just a little too old to enjoy it. So I went into property instead.'

'With Mr Benskin?'

'With my money,' said Benskin. 'Tony didn't need me.' He looked at him admiringly. 'He doesn't need anybody. What I did was count the money Tony was making for me and start the PAAA club.'

'And wonder about Denville and Day?'

'You have rather a neat way of bringing one back to the point, Mr Hogget,' Palliser said. 'Bill Day had been married – but his wife was killed in a buzz-bomb raid in 1944. They had a daughter, Betty. She married a chap in the Foreign Office – only they were both killed by a car-bomb in Beirut a few years back.'

'Not the luckiest family you ever came across,' said Benskin.

'Betty also had a daughter,' Palliser said. 'Her name is Angela. Angela Rossie. I'm her godfather as a matter of fact. I was rather fond of Betty...'

'We both were,' Benskin said.

'She's grown up now,' said Palliser, 'I don't just mean adult – eighteen's grown up these days – at least the law says it is, but she's twenty-four. And bright. She rather wants to know what happened to her grandfather, and I've done rather well over the years and I'm in a position to oblige her. And as I say – her mother and I were friends. Bertie and I thought the best way to find Bill Day would be to find the Dak. What do you say?'

I didn't believe a word of it. Whatever else he wanted that Dak for it was money, but I didn't say that. Instead I told him that the cost of the

45

job would be ten grand plus expenses, two thousand up front, and another ten if it lasted more than a month, and he didn't even wince. So it looked as if I could indulge in the merry social whirl with Sabena, provided I could find the Dak before Ascot.

I went back to Sabena's place. After all that nostalgia, all those wizard prangs and tally-ho, chaps and bandits at twelve o'clock, it would be good to be contemporary again, and they didn't come much more contemporary than Sabena. She'd had a very busy life for one so young.

Once she'd jumped off Tower Bridge on one of those bungie ropes that turn you into a sort of human yo-yo, once she'd landed by helicopter on Lord's Cricket Ground when England were playing Australia to remind O'Mara, their fast bowler, that they were engaged and proceeded to prove it, she'd had a brief flirtation with Women's Lib and ended up picketing a monastery, then taken a nutrition course and worked for six months on famine relief in Africa. She'd married a boxer, a better than average middleweight, Jacko Hudson, then divorced him in eight months to marry a Hooray Henry Viscount and got rid of him in six. Very wild, our Sabena had been, until, God knows why, she took a fancy to me. One of the reasons her father approved of me was that I never resented what she'd done in the past but I didn't encourage her to go on doing it.

Her Filipino maid Rosario let me in to the flat that was so handy for Harrods and said she was pleased to see me. She was too. She thought I was a good influence on Sabena, whom she adored. Rosario also told me that Sir Montague was there, which was another way of saying watch your language, and in I went. Sabena was in jeans, and Sir Montague was in full evening dress. Not even the most brilliant tailor (which was the one he used) could disguise the fact that Sir Montague Redditch was too short and too fat, but then he didn't have to. My father-in-law-to-be looked like power the way the late Marilyn Monroe looked like sex. Maybe it was the eyes: grey and narrow and glittering; or the hard axe-blade of a nose and the mouth's crude slash. Whatever it was the power was always there. I wondered if it showed while he slept, but I didn't know who to ask, didn't dare find out.

Sabena didn't look like her dad. To begin with her eyes were brown and her hair was dark, whereas his was grey now and had once been yellow. Neither was she fat, but no one in their right minds would call her thin. She had the cleverness though, and a bit of the power... Dave said she had a combination of physical and mental elegance that was immensely attractive. I said that she was wonderful. I went and kissed her cheek.

'Hail, O Mighty One,' she said.

Sir Montague said, 'Good evening, Ron.' He'd only ever called me Ronald once, after I'd explained to him that Ron Hogget was bad enough, but Ronald Hogget was a bit more than even I could stand. It doesn't mean a pig, by the way. Hogget, I mean. I looked it up in the dictionary years ago. It means a year-old lamb. It also means five years of misery if you're at a South London elementary school and small for your age.

'Excuse daddy's grandeur,' Sabena said. 'He's off to dine in splendour.'

'City dinner,' Sir Montague said. 'Better food than the club, but that's not saying much.' He sipped at a whisky and soda. 'Are you working?'

'Just stopped,' I said.

'Then you'll want a drink,' said Sabena. I took a glass of her white wine.

'Anything interesting?'

'Could be,' I said. 'It's early days.'

'Does that mean you won't be able to go to Puerto Banus?'

Well, at least that was one problem solved. Antibes was off. 'Hope not,' I said.

'You can see what a chatterbox he is,' Sabena said to her father. 'Did you ever hear such a flow of words?... And yet he does have some very interesting jobs, you know. Only the other day a man wanted him to find an aeroplane.'

I looked at the wine bottle, but she hadn't had much. All the same it wasn't like her, rabbiting on about my work. Not even to her father.

His reaction was typical of him. 'What kind of aeroplane?' he asked. If there was information going he wanted it. And him being him and me being me I couldn't withhold it. Then again, the twitcher wasn't work. Or was he?

I said, 'Could be a Dakota.'

He took another sip of scotch and soda.

'I once knew a man who lost a Dakota,' he said. 'Chap called Palliser.' The wine slopped in my glass. 'You ever met him?'

'Yes,' I said.

48

'Best thing that ever happened to him,' Sir Montague said. 'Got him out of air transport and into property. Last I heard he was worth nine million.'

Suddenly my fee didn't sound quite so handsome. Sir Montague put down his glass. 'Better be off,' he said. 'They dine pretty promptly at these do's, and the soup's usually the best thing.'

He kissed his daughter, gave me a half-inch nod, and was gone.

Sabena took the glass from my hand, kissed me on the mouth, then lay back in my arms to look at me.

'I goofed,' she said. 'Isn't that what the Yanks would say? That I'd goofed?'

'You sure did,' I said, speaking Yank.

'The trouble is I'm so proud of you,' she said. 'You're the only man I've ever known that I can show off to daddy.'

'All the same you shouldn't do it,' I said. 'I'm supposed to be a confidential enquiry agent. *Confidential*, love.'

'But you can tell me.'

'Not if you tell daddy,' I said.

'I'll try not to do it again,' she said. 'Honestly... Tell me I'm forgiven.'

But I never got the chance to, because she began kissing me again and one thing led to another.

There are an awful lot of Rossies in the London telephone directory, but only one called Angela. Plenty of As, but at least with the full name like that you had something to go on. The address was Chelsea, Milbourne Court, which sounded like one of those purpose-built blocks. Seemed like a nice little job for Dave. He does work for me sometimes. Minder mostly. A real good minder is Dave when he doesn't get too enthusiastic. He's not bad at being nosey, either, when he puts his mind to it, provided he doesn't go all soft on me and start feeling sorry for the subject. Funny bloke, Dave. Real Jekyll and Hyde. When he starts duffing blokes he's a monster, and yet he can feel sorry for people...

Before I went to see him I phoned Sir Montague Redditch. It might be more difficult to put a call through to the Queen, though I doubt it. But I'm persistent – it's another reason he likes me – and in the end I got him, and an invitation to dine. At his club. It was a chance to ask about Palliser, and I took it. Then I went after Dave, which was a lot easier. All I did was call the mini-cab firm he worked for and ask for car 23. He was with me in half an hour. I sat in the back of his mini-cab and told him what I was after.

Dave listened carefully, the way he always does, and when I'd finished he said, 'And that's all I have to do? Find out about this bird?'

'That's all,' I said.

'No rough stuff?'

'She's a *bird*,' I said. 'A young bird. Twenty-four.'

'The geezer who walked in on you with a .38 wasn't a bird,' said Dave. 'Or are you trying to tell me the two planes aren't connected?'

'I don't *know*,' I said. 'How can I?'

'You can guess though,' Dave said. 'And so can I. I hope they're paying you enough, Ron.'

'Just about,' I said.

'That's all right then,' said Dave. 'Because if things do get rough my fees go up. Now then... What number Milbourne Court am I going to?'

But first he had to drive me to Fleet Street, to one of the few surviving dailies that hasn't moved out to dockland. On the way I thought about a twitching geezer, and Squadron Leader Palliser, and why Dave couldn't treat that mini-cab of his to a new set of shock absorbers.

The bloke I was after was a gossip columnist called Michael Copland and I went to his paper because there wasn't any answer at his flat, or either of his girl-friends', and it was just possible he might have stopped in to file something or have a drink with a mate or something. He wasn't there when I went in, but I sat and waited anyway, because a) he was my best bet for my next move and b) I couldn't think of anything else to do.

Half an hour later he came in, when the commissionaire had just reached the exciting part about exactly where his sciatica got him when the wind was in the east. Michael had brought some copy with him, and a friend who needed a drink, but he took one look at me and stalled the friend and asked me to wait, then disappeared into the lift. When he came back the commissionaire had moved on to his wife's sister's attack of shingles and I needed a drink myself. Michael took me down the road and ordered champagne.

Generous with the firm's money is Michael, and always has been, but it isn't just that. I'd put a few very nifty little items his way in the past, and who knew but what he might be in line for

51

another one? So champagne it was, and none of your sparkling Italian either.

'I'm afraid I can't give you lunch today, old boy,' he said. 'I'm giving it to that rock-star – you know – what's his name... The one who claims he's a quarter Red Indian and runs amok to prove it.'

'That's all right,' I said. 'I came to ask you a favour anyway.'

He didn't quite take the champers back, but it was touch and go.

'Mind you,' I said. 'There could be a story in it and, if there is, naturally you get first crack at it.'

He ordered another round.

'What can I do for you?' he asked.

'I need to see your back numbers for the winter of 1948,' I said.

'They're all on microfilm,' he said.

'No problem – so long as you can arrange for me to see them.'

'Of course,' he said. 'Any particular story?'

I said nothing.

'Only asking,' he said. 'Maybe I can help.'

'You can,' I said. 'By letting me see that micro-film.'

'You really mean it?' Michael said. 'You'll let me have whatever there is first?'

'Didn't I just say so?' I said, and wondered if I'd have to make the same rash promise to my journalist contacts in dockland if Michael's paper didn't deliver...

If that newspaper was anything to go by, life in Britain in 1948 was a pretty dreary business: rationing and freezing and power-cuts, and recipes on how to cook whale-meat. Queues for the cinema had never been longer, I read. And could you wonder? In the cinema you could escape reality and get warm at the same time...There was a lot about the Berlin Airlift of course. Pictures of Tempelhof and planes landing, pictures of Stalin looking grim, and Truman and Attlee looking determined. There were even pictures of pilots, but not of any that flew for Ad Astra Airlines. I supposed they'd all been up among the clouds earning money. Nothing about a missing plane and nothing about a crash, but then if there'd been a crash he'd have gone to see, busy or not, and missing planes don't become news till someone talks about them, and I doubted whether Palliser would want to do that. Or Benskin.

Then I went through the whole lot again, and nearly missed it a second time. Low down on page five – newspapers only ran to eight pages in those days – and used as filler copy at the bottom of a column. 'Dead Island Wakes?' it was headed.

'The lonely uninhabited island of Moyra in the Hebrides was disturbed last night by an explosion, according to reports from the neighbouring island of Culm. HM Forces investigating reported no change.' That was it, and there wasn't even that in the later editions. They'd replaced it with a story about a beer shortage in Tyneside. And no wonder, I thought. Lonely islands – explosions – and then a non-event. Some sub-editor would have copped it for that one. Besides it was two days after Bill Day had gone missing... And that was another thing that puzzled me – why did Palliser always call him Bill Day? Never Bill. Well, that was understandable. He would hardly be his best mate after that lot. But never just 'Day', either. Always Bill Day...

I went back to my brooding. 'An explosion,' the piece said. Bombs explode, and shells and mines. But internal combustion engines explode too, in cars and boats and planes. And the Dak could have spent one night somewhere and taken off the next and crashed and gone bang. And in the sea nearby, not on the island at all, but then there would have been wreckage, surely? And oil? Or wait a minute – the island was uninhabited. Maybe there was a reason other than the harshness of the Hebrides ... HM Forces, it said. A cover-up, maybe? It wasn't much, but it was all I had got, so I took the microfilm back, and after a long and bitter haggle I managed to get another one out of the librarian. You'd have thought I was asking for her virginity – or even her life-savings.

The next microfilm I got was for the summer of 1940. It was time to take a look at Bill Day. He wasn't hard to find. There'd been a lot of pictures of pilots taken in the summer of 1940, the summer of the Battle of Britain. The Few, they were called, because of the phrase Churchill had used: never so much owed by so many to so few. And so I looked at them and knew them for what they were: the bravest and the best. They had to be to do what they had done: knock the world's most efficient fighting machine clean out of the sky. They'd taken terrible punishment of course, many dead, many maimed, many scarred for life with burns, but they'd done it. And they were so young. Most of them looked no more than twenty-three, quite a few could have passed for fifteen.

Bill Day had been twenty. I knew that for a fact because it said so on the caption beneath the photograph. Twenty years old and shaking hands with the King who had just given him the first of his DSOs. He was twenty and he looked twenty, fit and thin and bursting with life, with a smile that was almost a grin because – I felt sure – he was having the time of his life, doing what he did best and being paid for it, and being told by the great men of his country that the more he shot down and blew up the better, because he was saving civilisation...

Then I told myself to go easy on the intuition, because that was far too much to get from a smile. It was a nice smile though, because he looked a nice man, clear eyes, straight nose, firm chin. I wondered what he'd have looked like if he'd survived. Well into his sixties by now, and either looking it, like Benskin, or fighting it, like Palliser. But it seemed he'd joined the ranks of those in the poem I'd learned at school, the ones in an earlier war:

They shall grow not old, as we that are left grow old;
Age shall not weary them, nor the years condemn...

But there again maybe he was alive, and living off the proceeds of what he'd got by ferrying the SS to safety, though it must have been a hell of a lot to keep him going for forty-odd years.

I took one more look at him. There was no way I could get a copy of that microfilm, and anyway, alive or dead, he wouldn't look like that now, though it might be useful for jogging people's

55

memories... I shut up shop for the day and handed back the microfilm and thanked the nice lady for her co-operation and assistance. She didn't even bother to snarl at me.

4

I took a taxi over to the Bricklayers because it was on expenses, and anyway I had to go home and change after I'd seen Dave on account of my dinner date with Sir Montague. Dave was there all right, with his lager and his book. This time it was *Anna Karenina*. I bought a round and joined him.

'How d'you get on?' I asked.

He put the book down. 'You never told me she was beautiful,' said Dave.

I looked at him. 'Are you in love again?' I asked.

That's another thing about Dave. He falls in love a lot.

He nodded. 'I've never seen anything quite like her,' he said. 'You weren't thinking of harming her, were you, Ron?'

'Who said anything about harming her?' I said. 'All I want to do is suss out what happened to her grandad.'

'She's about five foot three,' Dave said dreamily. 'Elegant and graceful, but with that young look. You know – that special kind of innocence, I suppose you'd call it. Black hair, hazel eyes, and her mouth–'

On and on he went. It was like he was describing

56

the Romney portrait of the young Emma Hamilton. Well, at least I knew why he was reading *Anna Karenina*.

'She sounds like a good-looker all right,' I said.

Dave looked at me reproachfully. 'She's beautiful,' he said. 'I told you.'

'All right then. Beautiful,' I said. 'But did you get to speak to her?'

'No,' he said. 'But I heard her voice. That's beautiful too.'

He looked like he was going into a trance remembering, so I hurried him on. 'How did you hear it?'

'She was coming out just as I arrived. She said "Good morning" to the postman.'

'And then?'

'She got into her car. Mini-Metro licence EDX 35C – pale blue bodywork. That shade of blue's the wrong colour for her.'

'Oh, get on with it,' I said.

'She went to another block of flats. Notting Hill... Nice part though. Quiet. Went to see her boy-friend.'

From his tone of voice Dave didn't think much of her boyfriend. But then he wouldn't. Not even if it had been Robert Redford. 'How d'you know?' I said.

'I got chatting with the porter,' Dave said. 'He's ex-army. Not the Paras–' by the tone of his voice he was sorry for him '–but he'd been to Northern Ireland a couple of times.'

'What'd you get?'

'Her boy-friend's George Watkins – only she calls him Georgie. Lives at Number 43. 43,

57

Kelham Mansions that is.'

'What's he do?'

'Money futures. You know what that is?'

'Sure,' I said. 'You look in your crystal ball and decide that the dollar's going to go down, so you sell all your dollars and buy Japanese yen because your crystal ball says that the yen's going to go up. If you're right you make maybe twenty per cent net. If you're wrong you make the obituary column.'

'What do they use for a crystal ball?'

'A computer,' I said. 'What else? How old is Mr Watkins?'

'Twenty-seven or so, my mate thinks.'

'Don't worry,' I said. 'He'll never make twenty-eight. Not unless he changes his line of work.'

'Harry – my mate, the porter – reckons he's rich.'

'Well, of course he is,' I said. 'That's because he hasn't lost one yet. Usually one is all it takes. And, anyway, he can't be all that rich.'

'Why not?'

'He lives in Notting Hill.' I let Dave enjoy the thought for a moment, then I asked him, 'Anything else?'

'They're not – you know... Lovers.'

'How d'you know?'

'Harry, the porter. He's nosey. It's a bit of a turn-on for him, I think. He reckons he'd know.'

I filed that one. 'What's she do?'

'Model,' he said. 'She's with the Soames-Poynter Agency.'

'That was quick,' I said.

'After I finished in Notting Hill I went back to her place,' said Dave. 'Walked in with the milk-

58

man. The postman had left her letters stuck half-way in the letter-box.'

'A habit they have,' I said.

'One was from this Soames-Poynter mob. They had a couple of jobs for her.'

'You opened it?' I'd taught him how to do that long since. He nodded.

'Took its picture,' said Dave, 'then put it back. Did the same with the rest of the stuff.'

'What else was there?'

'Couple of bits of junk-mail – Diners Club bill – she owes seventy-four quid for a new dress – and a letter from a bloke who says he'll kill himself if she won't let him when he gets back.'

'Let him what?' I asked.

'You know,' said Dave. He's a terrible prude when he's in love.

'Was the letter from Italy?'

'No,' he said. 'France.' I must have looked glum because he said, 'I got something else though.'

'What?'

'Her picture,' he said.

'Let's go home and take a look at your happy snaps.'

Dave's camera is a nice little Nikon which I bought for him for just such opportunities as these, just as I gave him the gear for opening the letters. But, when it comes to developing, that's my department. That way if things go wrong it's my own fault, and whatever happens I always get first look... So I left him in the kitchen making a bacon sandwich and went into the bathroom and got to work.

For once Dave had pressed the right buttons in

the right order, and I had some nice stuff to look at. Especially Angela Rossie. She looked like very nice stuff indeed, and Dave had scarcely exaggerated at all. The Diners Club bill was just a bill – though seventy-four quid seemed pretty cheap for the shop it came from. Maybe she got some sort of discount on account of being a model...

The letter, though. The letter was something else. Typewritten, but hot enough to fry eggs on. Not too explicit if you follow me, and certainly not dirty, just one long wail of frustration and despair. The poor geezer ached in every corpuscle. I took another look at Angela Rossie, and understood, sympathised even. But I didn't share his need, thank God. I took the blow-up into the kitchen, where Dave was eating bacon and fried bread and catching up on Russian romance. The smell of the bacon reminded me that I'd missed lunch. It also reminded me that soon I'd be dining in the West End.

'What did you make of that letter?' I said.

'For a bloke with a head of steam on he was pretty anonymous, wasn't he?' said Dave. 'No signature – only B., was it? – and no address. Not even a date.'

'Could you read the date on the envelope?'

'Twenty-eighth,' Dave said. 'Two days ago.'

'And the postmark?'

'Smudged,' he said. 'All I could read was the date. I only knew it was France by the stamps.'

'What d'you make of the letter?' I said.

'Let's have another look.' I skimmed it to him and he read it through.

'Educated bloke,' he said. 'Uses a lot of long

words and spells them right. Bit of a pedant, too. Look at his grammar: "Had I but known." Ninety-nine geezers out of a hundred would have written "If I'd only known."'

'A writer maybe?'

Dave looked at the letter again.

'If he is he's a bad one,' he said, and went back to Tolstoy.

Still saving up for my hols, I went by Tube to Green Park and walked to St. James's. He was waiting in the bar, which was sunk in its usual gloom, and bought me a gin and tonic, which was terrible. He was having a whisky and water, and it made me wish I liked the stuff. There isn't much even that club's barman could do to a scotch and water if the whisky was good and you added the water yourself.

'How was your City dinner?' I asked.

'Pompous.' He sipped his whisky. 'Got any British Aerospace shares?'

'No.'

'I should buy some,' he said, and looked around the room. It was full.

'Busy?' he asked.

'So so.'

'Maybe we'd better go in and eat,' he said, and finished his drink. I left mine. The food was as awful as it always is. Potted shrimps, game pie, spotted dick with custard, but with it we had a Pomerol, a Château La Fleur Pétrus '66, that sang on the palate like a choir of angels. How could anyone match such terrible food with such incredible wine? I wondered, as I always did.

61

'You're not eating much,' he said.

'I'm not hungry,' I said.

I lied, but I'd promised myself a bacon sandwich just like Dave's when I got back.

'You're thirsty though,' he said.

'Who wouldn't be?'

He chuckled, and I found the courage to ask him the question that bothered me. 'Why do you eat here?' I asked.

'Because I eat very well everywhere else I go, and this food helps me to appreciate the rest.'

'But why do you always bring me here?'

'Because you do pretty well yourself these days too.' He was talking about Sabena and I knew it.

'Besides,' he said, 'you're one of the few people I know who appreciates the wine here.'

He looked about him. The nearest member was yards away.

'Do I take it you're working for Palliser?'

'You do,' I said. There was no sense in being coy. He'd find out anyway.

'He wants you to find that Dakota.' I nodded. 'Did he say why?'

'To oblige his goddaughter. She's the grandchild of the man who flew the Dakota when it disappeared.'

Sir Montague snorted. 'Tony Palliser had the nerve to tell you he was willing to spend good money to oblige someone?'

'That's right.'

Sir Montague made a kind of wheezing sound which I took to be laughter. 'Did he take you for an utter fool?'

'I doubt it,' I said. 'He's going to pay me a lot

62

of money and he's already paid me some.'

'So he can please himself what reasons he gives you?'

'That's right,' I said.

'Palliser's after money,' he said.

'What makes you think so?'

'Because he always is. Palliser can smell money the way a pig smells truffles. Be careful, Ron.'

'I always am,' I said.

'Be extra careful,' Sir Montague said. 'If Tony Palliser drops you into anything shady he won't try all that hard to pull you out.'

'What about his boyhood chum?'

'Benskin? Worth about a million, I suppose. No more than a million three.'

'As a *person*,' I said. 'Is he as greedy as Palliser?'

'No idea,' Sir Montague said. 'I only discovered his existence this morning when I ran a check on Palliser. But I doubt if he's as greedy. Nobody is.'

'Why did you get into this?' I asked.

'I didn't promise any goddaughter a favour,' he said. 'Couldn't. I haven't got any. But I have got a daughter and she's fond of you and so am I. I don't want you hurt.'

'Palliser's on my side,' I said.

'He is so long as it suits him. That may not be for long. I'll tell you again. You be careful. Better still, get out of it.'

'I can't,' I said. 'It's my job.'

'I'll give you a job,' he said.

'Maybe when I've finished this,' I said, and he sighed and ordered port, the Graham's '47.

While he drank I said, 'Can I ask a favour?'

'Possibly.'

'Could you introduce me to anyone who knew Palliser?'

'Cattle,' he said: at least that's what it sounded like. He explained. 'Air-Vice Marshal Cattell,' he said. 'Started off as a pilot. Shot down and wounded, and transferred to Personnel. Now he's on one of my boards. I'll give him a buzz.'

'Thank you,' I said.

'Don't mention it. I'll help you all I can. And, Ron – when it's over and done with, I think you ought to marry my daughter.'

'So do I,' I said. 'But she says definitely not before Ascot.'

Still taking care of the pennies I walked back to Green Park and the Tube. It was as I was feeding coins into the ticket machine that I knew I was being followed. It's a gift some people have and I'm one of them. Somebody, I knew, had picked me up outside Sir Montague's club and tailed me here. No. Not some one. Some ones. Whoever had taken on the job must know that tailing people in London, in any big city, can't possibly be a one-man operation. There are too many ways of losing your subject even when he doesn't know he's being followed. You need a minimum of three, but four is better, and even five wouldn't be over-doing it.

I strolled on to the escalators, willing myself not to look round. It took a bit of doing. But Green Park Station was crowded and I'd have no chance of spotting who was after me and if I started looking around it would be a dead giveaway. Let them think whoever it was had me fooled and I might learn something. My best bet would be the platform...

It was, too. Piccadilly Line I was after, change at Earl's Court, then on the District to Fulham Broadway. There were a lot of people waiting for the train, and I started walking down the platform, looking at the advertisements on the other side of the line, pretending to read a bit, then moving on, getting further down towards the entrance to the Victoria Line. Whoever was tailing me would have to make a move in case I had one of those rushes of blood people sometimes do have when you're tailing them and they decide they'd sooner go to Pimlico.

I got the elegant geezer first. Oh, very elegant he was. Designer jeans, shirt that looked like silk, airline bag, trainer shoes. He kept edging after me, not rushing it, but stopping when I stopped, which is bad technique. Then I moved as if I was going to go through to the Victoria platform and the other two broke cover. They had no choice. But instead of going through I stopped at a notice by the archway: a list of forthcoming ballets at Covent Garden. They weren't doing *Les Sylphides,* I saw. A pity. It's the only ballet I ever really liked...

Then I turned back to take a look at the other two. Young lovers, and so alike they looked like unisex. He was a blond, she was brunette, and they were both casually and inexpensively dressed. His hands were empty, she carried a handbag, and snuggled against him, his arm around her. Ah, young love, not seeing anything but each other, except the only thing those two were seeing was me. And a very nice little set-up they had, too. Nobody takes a ha'porth of notice of a couple of kids having a cuddle, but when necessary they could split and work as two separate parts of the team. The boy-friend, like the elegant geezer, looked as if he did his share of weight training, and if the girl looked a bit on the lean side, it was an athlete's leanness rather than a model's. They were altogether too much for me and I didn't have to look twice to know it.

Ah well, the sooner the better, I thought, and waited for the train. When it came, the elegant geezer followed me, the lovebirds used a door further down the same carriage. I grabbed the last seat facing the door: the rest of them had to stand. After a bit I yawned, and settled back in my seat: Ronald Hogget, finder of lost property, knackered after a hard day's slog. Hyde Park Corner came and went, and Knightsbridge, but at South Kensington I got what I'd been praying for: bodies; a solid phalanx of Australians on their way back to Earl's Court. They moved in down the carriage, herding the elegant geezer with them. From the other end a fat man and his fat wife and two suitcases sealed off the door nearest the lovebirds. All in the timing, I thought, still laid back, still worn out with working for nine million quid, then at the last possible moment, just before the doors began to move, I was up and out and away, and none of them had the chance to follow me.

Not that I was home-free. No way. If they knew me they knew my address, and all they had to do was get off at Earl's Court like the Aussies, change to the District Line, leave it at Fulham Broadway, take a five-minute walk, and wait for me. They could even have a fourth party waiting there already. A bloke – or maybe a bird – with a car. A bird would be my bet. Two couples snogging to pass the time until I showed up and they could rebuke me for being coy.

I caught a bus to Kensington High Street, found a pub, and used their phone to dial Dave's minicab service. Car number 23 was on its way back from the airport, they told me. Twenty minutes or so, they said. Actually it was twenty-nine: some of the longest minutes I've ever spent. I knew, logic assured me, that there was no way that my three could figure out where I was, but persons of my nervous disposition don't go by logic. We go by fear. Then Dave arrived, and I began to feel better at once. The odds had evened up. I would take care of the girl and Dave would take care of the weight-trainers, provided the girl wasn't a weight-trainer too.

'You look bothered,' he said.

'I am bothered.' I bought him a lager and told him why.

'You must have hopped like a rabbit when you left the train,' he said.

'More like a kangaroo,' I said, remembering the Aussies.

'Now what?'

'There's a good chance they'll be waiting for me at my place,' I said.

'And you'd like a bit of company?'

'Please,' I said.

'This isn't your line of work, Ron,' said Dave. 'Never has been. Why don't I just run you over to Sabena's and take a look on my own?'

But I wasn't having that. Sabena was to run no more risks, and not because her father said so.

'We go together,' I said, and he grinned at me.

'Suits me,' he said. 'I'll lend you a tyre iron.'

He did too, but when we got back to my place we didn't find a living soul waiting for us. We found a corpse.

5

It was Benskin. He lay huddled in the darkness of the porch like a pile of old clothes, which for whatever stupid reason was what I thought he was. But not Dave. Dave knew him for a corpse the moment he saw him: but then Dave has spent a lot of his working life in Ulster: the Falls Road, South Armagh, where you learn to spot a corpse quick or else become one yourself. He got a torch from the mini-cab and I told him who it was.

'A bit early in the case to lose your client,' he said.

'Palliser's the client,' I said. I was beginning to feel sick.

'His throat's cut,' said Dave.

'So I see,' I said.

Dave took a look at me and switched off the torch.

'Sorry, mate,' he said. 'It was a very efficient job.'

'You mean it killed him.'

'I mean it killed him before you and him had a chat.'

'Who we have a chat with is the police,' I said.

Dave sighed. 'Do I have to?'

Dave doesn't like coppers, and who can blame him? They take the view that because he did a spell in the Paras he spends half his time duffing people: all the same I've got nosey neighbours.

''Fraid so,' I said.

We went round the corner to the nearest phone booth, which turned out to be between vandalisations, so I used it to call Palliser first, but he was out. I left a message on his answer machine, and after that I made a free one and dialed 999.

'Emergency,' the British Telecom voice said. 'Which service do you require?'

'Police,' I said.

What we got eventually was a couple of detectives, but first off was two geezers in a patrol car who acted as if they'd been bored rigid all day and a nice juicy murder was just what they yearned for. They started in on me as if their names were Hercule Poirot and Sexton Blake... First they asked me if I knew the deceased and I said I did and they thought *that* was suspicious, then they asked if Dave knew the deceased and he said he didn't, and they acted as if that was suspicious. Then they asked me what I did for a living and when I told them they very nearly put the handcuffs on me. For them it was an open and shut case. I was glad when the CID came – at first.

The CID was Detective Inspector Sutton and Detective Sergeant Cairns, and at first what they did was tell each other the poor bastard's throat had been cut, and it couldn't have been suicide, not the way the poor sod was lying and in any case where was the weapon? And after that they started to ask us the same lot of questions as the patrol boys, and the situation deteriorated. Mind you, it would have deteriorated a hell of a lot further if they'd known I'd seen another corpse, the result of another violent death, outside the Malcontenta villa on the Brenta Canal a few weeks back. But they didn't, and I wasn't going to tell them. Apart from anything else they'd just found out that I was a private detective and Dave had been in the Paras...

Then the next lot arrived: photographs and fingerprints, and the doctor from forensic, and by that time the nosey neighbours were there in packs, with the patrol boys keeping them back, and looking as if they'd need a whip and a chair apiece any minute.

I said, 'How about going inside for a cup of coffee?'

Sutton looked wistful, like he'd had a rough day, but all he said was, 'We can't. Not till the lab boys have finished.'

'We could use the back door,' I said. That made me a genius.

Anyway we went in round the back, and I took them through the kitchen and into the living-room, that still looks as if my ex-wife's just popped out for a minute.

I said, 'Give the gentlemen a drink, Dave, while I put the kettle on.'

Dave opened up the drinks cabinet that plays 'Parlez-moi d'Amour', then I shot into the kitchen, ran the tap, and looked at my answer machine that stands on a shelf by a cupboard with a vegetable rack in front of it. The red light was on: I'd had a caller. So I pulled out the jack plug and put the answer machine in the cupboard and a pot plant on the shelf, then filled the kettle and got out cups and a jar full of instant.

When I got back the inspector and sergeant were stuck into the Johnny Walker Black Label and Dave was having a lager. They took their time getting round to the coffee.

Sutton said again, 'So you knew him?'

'Name of Benskin,' I said. 'First name Bertie. World War Two flyer. Flight Lieutenant.'

'Client, you said.'

'Him and a chap called Palliser,' I said. 'Another ex-RAF type. Squadron Leader.'

'What's he do now?'

I shrugged. 'Maybe nothing,' I said. 'Except count his money. From what I hear he made a killing in property development a few years back.'

'Where did you hear that?'

And there you have it: my dilemma. Any private snooper's dilemma. He's neither doctor, lawyer nor priest. Nothing he is told is confidential: not when the police are asking. And just at the moment I didn't feel it would be wise to shop my father-in-law to be. Instead I looked nonchalant, or tried to.

'I looked him up,' I said. 'You know. Registrar of Companies.'

He didn't know, but he wasn't going to admit it, not to me. Instead he looked even more nonchalant than I did.

'Quite,' he said. 'Quite,' and drank about 40p's

71

worth of my whisky. 'Pays well, does he?' he asked.

If he pressed I was going to lie about it, divide my fee by two or even three – no sense in antagonising him – but that would have been going too far, even for a detective-inspector. He let it lie.

'What sort of a job had he got lined up for you – him and this Benskin?' he asked.

I took a deep breath: there was no way to soften the blow.

'They wanted me to find an aeroplane.'

'You're saying they *lost* one?'

'About forty years ago,' I said.

And then the storm burst. Not just Sutton; Cairns too. They took it as a personal affront that I should try to fob them off with such a terrible story. But in the end of course they had to calm down: start listening. I mean who in his right mind would try to pass off a load of codswallop like that unless he believed it to be true? They asked for more, and I gave it to them. Ad Astra Airlines, Bill Day, Frank Denville, the Berlin Airlift, embezzled funds.

But nothing about Kessler, or the missing SS men, or the Isle of Moyra. The Dakota A for Arthur was my business, and my money. The coppers would have to stick to solving murders for a monthly pay-cheque. We moved on to the reason why. Why wait forty years, why spend money anyway on such a hopeless quest, why – or so it seemed by the look of it – embark on a course of action that got you killed? I tried to look manly, frank and cooperative all at once.

'I've no idea,' I said.

It didn't go down well: I didn't expect it to. The

second storm broke. When they ran out of names for me I said, 'Look. Those lads are rich, especially Palliser, and he was the one who seemed to be running the show.'

'What's that got to do with it?' said Cairns.

'They're paying me quite a lot of money even by their standards,' I said. 'That means that what I get is orders, not explanations. All I know is it's got something to do with Angela Rossie. Maybe that's because she's Palliser's goddaughter – or maybe it's because she's Bill Day's granddaughter. I don't know, and I'm not being paid to find out. I'm being paid to look for an aeroplane.'

'Just like we're being paid to look for a murderer,' Sutton said. For the first time he looked formidable, as if the scotch had helped him over his fatigue and he had started to function properly again.

I began to wonder if I should tell him about the bird and two geezers who were following me, but that would have increased Dave's involvement and I didn't want that. And anyway the fingerprint man and the photographer and the MO came in, and I had to fetch another bottle of whisky... A really neat job, the MO said. Either the bloke knew his stuff or he was extremely lucky... No fingerprints, no handprints in the blood, no footprints, knives or handkerchiefs, no cigarette-stubs blended from rare tobaccos. In fact all they had was a corpse and a lot of photographs. The next lot of experts would outline its position on the porch in chalk then take it to the mortuary.

Sutton said, 'Be all right to see what he's got on him now, Doc?'

73

'He won't feel a thing,' the doctor said, and finished his drink. 'If there's nothing else–'

'No. You push off and get some rest,' said Sutton. He used the word 'rest' as if it was one he'd heard a long time ago and couldn't quite remember what it meant. 'Go and take a look, Arthur,' he said.

Cairns sighed as he left, and I didn't blame him. Searching Benskin would be messy.

He was replaced by one of the patrol-car men. They'd been doing a canvas of the neighbours while they held them back, but none of them could tell them a thing. Hear no evil, see no evil, speak no evil, was what it amounted to. It didn't sound like my neighbours at all. Sutton sent him out to try further down the street, then I asked Sutton if he'd like a sandwich.

'I'd like dinner in the Riverside Suite at the Savoy,' he said, 'then a line of page-three girls to tuck me up in bed. But if I ate even a packet of crisps I'd be fast asleep. So don't try to bribe me.' Then the other patrol-car man came in to say that the press had arrived and they'd like a few photographs.

'All in good time,' said Sutton.

'They want Hogget mostly,' said the patrol car man.

'God knows I don't,' Sutton said.

Then the phone rang, and Dave got that wary look he gets when he's thinking. I got up to answer it, but Sutton blocked me off.

'Is there an extension?' he asked.

'In the hall,' I said. 'Dave'll show you.'

Dave led him out and looked more relaxed, and I knew why.

74

The phone had given more than five rings, which meant I'd switched off the answer machine. I picked up the phone. 'Hogget,' I said.

'This is Palliser. I've just played back your message.' His voice was grim. 'I take it – there's no possibility of a mistake?'

'None,' I said. 'I'm sorry.'

'Of course not,' he said. 'Damn silly question. Do the police know?'

'There's one listening on my extension now,' I said. 'Detective Inspector Sutton.'

'Who called them?'

'I did,' I said.

'Before consulting me?'

'You were out,' I said. 'And time's vital in a murder case.'

Sutton's voice came on. 'Mr Hogget is right,' he said. 'I'd like a word with you as soon as possible, Mr Palliser. I'm Detective Inspector Sutton.'

'It won't be this evening,' Palliser said.

'It really is urgent,' said Sutton.

'No doubt. But I've been advised by my doctor to relax whenever I have anything approaching a trauma. The news of Bertie's death was very traumatic indeed, so I've just taken rather a powerful sedative. Good-night, Mr Sutton. I'll phone you when I'm fit to be spoken to.'

He hung up, and Sutton swore rather a lot: nothing memorable, but all deeply felt. Then Cairns came back with his hands full of Benskin's possessions, and took his mind off things. He jibbed a bit when he saw Dave and me sitting there, but Sutton waved him on.

'Let 'em look,' he said. 'Hogget knows more

75

than we do anyway.' Cairns sifted through the pile.

'We tested for fingerprints in the kitchen,' he said, and I wondered how close they'd come to the answer-machine.

'Goatskin wallet and card-holder,' he said. 'A hundred and eighty-five quid cash and six credit cards. Want a breakdown?'

'Anything weird?' Sutton asked.

'All standard,' said Cairns.

'Leave 'em,' Sutton said. 'What else?'

'Pocket diary.'

'Look at the last few days.'

'I have,' said Cairns. 'There's a note that says "Hogget – Club" – two days ago, but nothing about coming here tonight.'

'Anything else?'

'Not in the diary part,' said Cairns, 'but in the front there's a bit about personal details. You know – VAT number, size in shoes, all that.'

'Get on with it, Arthur,' Sutton said.

'There's one that says "Who to notify in the event of an accident". Somebody's filled in "Jo Benskin".'

'Joe?' said Sutton.

'Must mean Josephine,' Cairns said, 'because underneath it says, "Wife". In brackets,' he added.

I got the feeling that Arthur Cairns was a very conscientious man who would never rise beyond sergeant. Sutton glowered at me.

'You never told me he was married,' he said.

'I didn't know myself,' I said.

Sutton said, 'I don't like you and I don't like this case and I'm absolutely knackered and so is Arthur. Give me Benskin's phone number.'

I gave it to him and he began to dial.

Dave said, 'I thought you blokes were supposed to tell the next of kin straight away.'

'In the first place we've been working since ten this morning,' said Sutton. 'In the second place we only just found out there was a next of kin. And in the third place this is straight away – unless you want to say it isn't.'

'Nothing to do with me,' said Dave.

'You'd better believe it,' Sutton said, and let the phone ring ten more times then hung up. 'Nobody home,' he said. 'Somebody'll have to go round and wait.'

By the way he said it, somebody meant Detective Inspector Sutton. He rose to his feet. 'Better get on with it,' he said. 'Face the press. You mind if I take a look round before I go?'

'You got a warrant?' I asked.

'I'm at the scene of a crime,' he said.

'No, you're not. The crime is outside. This is inside. Behind two locked doors.'

'I'll get a warrant,' he said.

'Let me know in advance and I'll put the kettle on.'

That must have got to him, because when we reached the back door he said, 'Thanks for the whisky.'

Then I opened the door to where the reporters were waiting in a pack. Flashes started popping straight away.

I went back. Dave was still in the kitchen. He was smoking a cigarette the way a well brought-up little boy would take a spoon to a jampot. Like he knows what he's doing is wrong but he just

77

can't help himself.

'He had a good look round,' he said.

'Coppers always do.'

'Where d'you put it?'

'Put what?' I asked.

'The answer machine. I knew you must have got to it when the phone went on ringing.'

Dave Baxter, the thinking man's tearaway.

I got the machine out of the cupboard and plugged it in and the red light came on, so I ran the tape back and played it.

Benskin's voice said, 'Oh... Oh, I see. It's that machine thing again.' He didn't sound all that sober. 'Well look here, old boy, I've been thinking. Got a lot of time for it these days. Different when I was flying. They make you pass a lot of exams if you want to fly – mug up a lot of books and lectures – but once you do it it's mostly instinct. I rather suspect I'm good at instinct... Where was I?

'Oh yes. Thinking. About our little bit of business. And what I was thinking was it isn't on, you know. Not really. Bill Day *couldn't* have been that bad. Or Frank Denville. I mean I'd flown with them both. You know instinctively–' He broke off then to cough very hard, as if he'd choked on cigarette smoke, but even through the coughing he wheezed. 'There. You see? I even *know* by instinct.' He sounded triumphant, as if he'd made an important debating point. Perhaps he had. There was more coughing, then a sound that could only have been a gin and tonic sliding down, smooth and tingling and cool.

'So my point is,' Benskin continued, 'that we should stop this thing now. In its tracks. Tony may not agree – no reason why he should. After all, he's been pushing this one for years – but he could be wrong, damn it. After all, he's been wrong before. He's not the bloody Pope for Chrissake.' More gin and tonic noises, then, 'I say, Hogget, I do apologise for that. I'm not a blasphemer, not usually. I do hope you aren't a Catholic.' I am, as it happens, on account of my mum having been Italian, but it was nice of him to apologise.

'Thought I'd best fill you in first,' Benskin's voice went on. 'Tony will see it my way I'm sure, once we've had a chat. Trouble is I chat too much – or so he says. But anyway I know I do. Ask any popsy I ever met... Tell you what, I'll come on over and sort something out, eh? Not ten thou. Can't run to that. But something – you know – reasonable. Acceptable to both sides as they say I'll come over now, before I lose my nerve. After all it's ten-sixteen. You can't be all that long, unless there's some popsy... Which I do hope there is, old boy. You're the type that deserves a nice popsy, but not tonight. Anyway, whatever time you get back I'll be waiting.' There was a sound like ice-cubes clinking, then he said as one who'd remembered the drill only just in time: 'Oh, by the way, the name is Benskin. Bertie Benskin. Over and out.' The line went dead.

'Well well,' said Dave.

'Well well indeed,' I said, and waited, but there were no more messages.

I ran the tape back, took it out, and put in a new one, then placed the answer machine on its usual shelf and left the pot plant beside it. After all, Sutton had promised me he'd be back with a warrant.

'What now?' said Dave, but he needn't have bothered. The reporters had squeezed the last drop of juice out of Sutton. Now it was our turn.

The last one left after midnight, when there was no more scotch. All they'd got was our pictures and the fact that I'd been investigating a confidential matter for the deceased. And the fact that Dave was a mini-cab driver. Not that would stop them. Dave and I had made headlines before. Suddenly it dawned on me that I'd be hearing from Michael Copland shortly and he wouldn't be best pleased. I hadn't called him. Then I found I didn't give a damn because it also dawned on me that drunk or sober I'd liked Bertie Benskin, and I was as mad as hell he'd been murdered, and even madder because it had happened on my doorstep. Mine.

Dave said, 'You didn't say he was the nervous type.'

I blinked at him, not with it. 'Benskin?' I said.

'Certainly Benskin. You heard him. "I'll come over now before I lose my nerve."'

'He was about as nervous as a Chieftain tank,' I said. 'He had a DSO.'

'Benskin?'

'Flight Lieutenant Bertram Benskin, DSO,' I said. 'Bestowed by the late King George VI himself.'

'Dear God,' said Dave. 'The way you told it he was just another old drunk.'

'My father is just another old drunk,' I said. 'Bertie Benskin was an old drunk who'd served his country faithfully and well. He was also a man who had thought over what was going on,

80

and decided that the only possible thing to do was to come here and sort it all out with me even if it killed him. And it did.'

'The DSO,' Dave said. 'It makes a difference. They didn't exactly come up with the rations.'

I remembered what Sir Montague had told me.

'He got his up in the air,' I said. 'In a Lancaster that had a hole in it the size of a London taxi. He was over Bremen when an anti-aircraft burst got him. Killed the co-pilot. He flew the thing home and put it down and saved the lives of the rest of the crew. He had a broken leg and a lump of shell in his chest.'

'You don't get many like that,' said Dave, and then: 'You going to tell Sutton about the tape?'

'No,' I said.

'Why not?'

'He'll handle it wrong,' I said. 'He'll go and yell at Palliser, and Palliser will go all stern and noble and say he hasn't the faintest idea what he's talking about and in the meantime his oldest and dearest friend has been murdered and why doesn't Sutton go and do something about it. I can just hear him.'

'You'll be suppressing evidence,' said Dave.

'*We'll* be suppressing evidence,' I said. 'So if you don't want to do it say so and I'll play that tape to Sutton.'

'I should have known it'd be my fault,' said Dave. 'All the same, you're probably right. Go ahead and suppress.' He yawned. 'What now?'

'Get some kip,' I said. 'It's turned one in the morning. Pick me up tomorrow and I'll go and see Palliser. So far as he's concerned I'll be looking for

81

a Dakota – since that's what he's paying me for – but you and I know we're after a killer.'

It was only after Dave had gone that I realised I hadn't phoned Sabena, and by then it was too late.

It is police practice to leave a copper on duty at the scene of a crime like murder, and I'm blowed if I know why. I mean you can't murder the same person twice, and anyway the corpse has usually been removed by the time the bobby starts hanging about. All the same, that was one time I approved of the idea. The rozzer might not be keeping an eye on a corpse, but he was keeping an eye on me. Even so I put the chain bolts on, front and back, and fastened the deadlocks. Unlike Bertie I am the nervous type, but all the same I needed no rocking that night.

What I'd been through, being followed, finding a corpse, with all that implied, were frightening things, and fear is exhausting. And so I slept as deeply as if Sabena were beside me. The knocking and ringing must have gone on for minutes before it got to me, and even when it brought me to the edge of wakefulness I had to think hard to realise what it was. I said a few words of a vulgar nature, a thing I dislike doing usually, but this was different, then I found my dressing gown and slippers and went downstairs, walking like the starring role in a horror movie. The double act on knocker and bell went on till the moment I opened the door to the limit of the chain. The duty copper was handling the knocker, and he had the muscles for it. A woman, a blonde, youngish, pretty, handled the bell. Lighter work, the bell. All she had to do was push with the thumb and hold it. I looked at them in disgust. I'd rarely hated two people more in my life. I was exhausted.

'Yes?' I said. It came out a croak.

'This lady would like a word, sir,' the copper said.

I took another look. Blonde hair, as I say, that looked as if it had been expensively cared for, but not recently. Yellow dress and coat that both looked like money, blue eyes that popped a little, but would have been pretty even so except for the puffiness around them. I still hated her, but by then I was wide enough awake to know I'd never seen her before in my life.

'Are you sure you've got the right house?' I said.

'Of course I am. I'm Jocasta Benskin.'

For a moment I didn't get it, then at last I did. Not Josephine. Jocasta. I was looking at the widow. There was nothing else for it. I took off the chain bolt and let her in. The rozzer was reporting on his walkie-talkie before I'd even shut the door but, ever the little gentleman, I took her into the living-room and sat her down and went on hating her. She looked around the room, and took her time, and I hated her even more. I mean I know Melanie had designed the room and her taste was awful, but even so she hadn't exactly been invited. I mean it was after four in the morning.

At last she said, 'Do you really live in this room?'

'I live in the whole house,' I said. 'That's why I bought it.'

'And it's all like this?'

'Not all of it,' I said. 'Some of it's in rather poor taste.'

'Oooh,' she said, at least it sounded like that, and then, 'You must allow for the fact that I'm in a state of shock.'

'I am allowing for it,' I said, and she made the 'Oooh' noise again.

Then we had a bit of silence, and I started to nod off until she said, 'Could I have a drink?'

'Certainly,' I said. 'What would you like?'

'What have you got?'

'Almost everything except scotch.'

'Why no scotch?'

'We've had rather a lot of policemen here,' I said.

'Oh, God,' she said. 'Oh, my poor darling Bertie.'

She began to cry. She did it beautifully. The rounded, slightly popping blue eyes oozed tears the way a muscat grape oozes juice, but even so she never lost her good looks, and they really were good. I mean it was perfectly obvious that she'd started out her love-life as a sex kitten and still looked the part here and there, but the rest of her had matured the way a good claret does. She was, and looked, a remarkable woman: not beautiful, but pretty, and very very sexy. And all the time the tears flowed juicily, and it's a funny thing but I knew from the start that they were genuine, that she really mourned her man; yet even so, as she wept and I waited, it began to seem for ever, her eyes peered through all that shimmering grief to stare thoughtfully, almost you could say analytically, at my crotch.

I mean to say it's ridiculous. I'm not like that. True I'd been fairly lucky with Melanie, and once

84

I'd hit the jackpot with Sabena, but that's twice in a lifetime. I mean it's not a gift of the gods. I can't go switching it on and off like the telly... And yet there she was, staring. Eyes like lasers. It didn't make sense.

Suppose it was Dave, for instance. Good looker, talks well, and with just that hint of danger – girls often get excited if a bloke looks dangerous – no wonder he pulls them. And he does, too. There's times you'd think he can't go wrong; but it's not every time, even with him. He's had his failures as well as his successes, and he told me straight he wouldn't fancy his chances much with a bird who'd lost the husband she dearly loved. Wouldn't want to, come to that.

And yet – there was me. And there was her, looking. She said, 'The police were waiting. When I got home.'

'They told you what happened?'

'Yes.' She nodded: the blonde hair bounced. 'They said it wouldn't be necessary to – to identify. Not yet.'

I'd already done that for her, I said. 'But they'll want corroboration later.'

'Is he ghastly?'

'No,' I said. 'He's not. I know it's a cliché, but he can't have suffered.'

Her eyes still stared unwaveringly where they shouldn't.

'He told me he was coming here,' she said. 'I'd signed up for a theatre party, then Annabel's. You know how it is.'

I made a noise that said I might or might not know how it was.

'Then I went home and there was this police-man.'

'Detective Inspector Sutton?'

'I expected you'd know. He told me Bertie was dead. Where's my drink?'

'You haven't told me what you want.'

'No scotch, you said. Do you have any wine? White wine?'

I went into the kitchen. There was a bottle of Sud Tiroler Pinot Grigio in the fridge. I'd been saving it for an occasion. Well, whatever else a wake is, it's an occasion. She sipped and liked it, and said so, still rudely staring.

'Why did he come here?' she asked.

I could see no reason to tell her about the message on my machine.

'I'm sorry,' I said. 'I just don't know.'

'It would be about the Dakota.'

'He told you about that?'

'Of course,' she said. 'I was his wife. Now I'm his widow. Are you still going to look for it?'

'If Mr Palliser still wants me to.'

'The Squadron Leader,' she said, and drank more wine. Apparently that was the end of the message, but there was nothing in it for me. I needed more data.

'Do you want me to go on?' I asked.

'Of course I do. It was what Bertie wanted.' It wasn't, but I couldn't tell her so. 'It was his idea,' she said. Nobody had told me that.

'Did your husband tell you why he wanted the Dakota found?'

'Yes,' she said, then cut off communications again. Somebody should have told her that conversation involves a certain amount of give and take, but it wasn't going to be me. I poured more Pinot Grigio and settled down to wait.

At last she said, 'Would it help you to find the Dak if you knew what Bertie and the Squadron Leader were up to?'

'It certainly wouldn't hinder,' I said. 'I don't ask questions like that for fun.'

'You look tired,' she said.

What that had to do with anything I had no idea and was too weary to find out.

'I am tired,' I said, and looked at my watch. 'It's four thirty-seven. In the morning. Of course I'm tired.'

'Let's go to bed then,' she said, 'and afterwards I'll tell you why they want that aircraft found.'

I gawped at her as if she *was* a freak. Damn it, she was a freak. She was mourning her husband.

'I like you,' she said. 'Honestly.'

Then the doorbell rang, and that meant the end of that particular round, which was as well. She had me on the ropes. I was up and moving before she could offer to buy me a mink coat. Anybody would be welcome, I thought. Anybody at all. It was Detective Inspector Sutton, but I still continued to smile.

'Good Lord,' I said. 'Don't you ever sleep?'

'Given half a chance,' he said. 'I don't often get it.'

'You come to see my visitor?'

Telling him about Jocasta instead of letting him choke it out of me stole his big moment, but I wasn't feeling that benevolent.

'That's right,' he said. 'I'd like a word with you both.'

'Come on in then,' I said, and took him into the living-room.

'Let me get you a glass of wine,' I said. 'I'm afraid we're out of whisky.'

'Don't bother,' Sutton said. 'Thanks anyway. I just thought maybe–' I waited.

'Maybe what?' said Mrs Benskin.

'That you'd remembered something.'

'I remembered my husband's dead. You told me.'

Sutton sighed. For a policeman he did a lot of sighing.

'I thought maybe you'd come to give Hogget some information.'

'You've been spying on Mr Hogget?' She hit the 'mister' hard.

'Not spying, no.'

'What else would you call it?'

'Surveillance,' Sutton said. 'There's been a murder here. The police have a right to know what's happening. Isn't that so, Hogget?'

'That is absolutely so, Sutton,' I said.

It was childish, I admit it, but I was whacked.

For a moment I thought Sutton was going to take a sock at me, but he was even more whacked than I was, and at last he forced himself to face the fact. The skin beneath his eyelids was stained dark with fatigue.

'I'm going to bed,' he said. 'We'll talk tomorrow – after I've rested.'

'Certainly,' I said.

'It'll be an in-depth discussion,' he said, and I

didn't like that, but I saw him out anyway, just to be sure he didn't slam the front door from the inside then sneak back to eavesdrop outside the living-room.

Mrs Benskin said, 'He doesn't like you.'

'Of course not,' I said. 'I make more money than he does.'

'Show off,' she said. 'Are you really rich?'

'Not yet,' I said.

'I'm rich,' she said, and the tears came again. 'Oh, dear God – I'm a millionairess.'

She fumbled for her handbag and failed to find it, and I knew what she was after and gave her my handkerchief to dab her eyes. When she was done she offered it back to me and when my hand reached out she took it and rose, graceful as a dancer, to press herself against me.

'Don't look so worried,' she said.

'I'm not worried,' I said, nor was I. I was appalled, because I was enjoying it, Sabena or no Sabena.

'I shan't rape you,' she said. 'I shan't even indecently assault you. Not tonight. I've gone off the boil.'

I hadn't and she knew it. She put her arms around my neck and kissed me. She knew everything there is to know about kissing. When she'd done she let me go and stood back to look at me again. There. Then she giggled.

'One for my side,' she said. 'Don't you think that's funny?'

'Your husband's dead,' I said.

'I loved poor Bertie – and I wept for him. You saw me. For you I giggled.'

89

'Why?'

'Because you're alive.'

'I'm trying to find out who killed him but you won't help me.'

'Not till you do something for me... It won't take you all that long either.'

'That doesn't make sense.'

'Women like me don't deal in sense,' she said. 'And anyway I won't tell you a thing till you've had your chat with Sutton. He might get it out of you even if he is poorer than you are.'

She went to the door and I let her out. She turned to me and began to move.

'Don't kiss me again unless you want Sutton to know,' I said. 'His copper will be watching.'

She put her tongue out at me instead.

'What do your friends call you?' she asked. 'Ronald or Ronnie?'

'Ron,' I said.

'And what do your girls call you?'

'The same.'

'Ron Hogget.' The way she said it sounded like she was reading her favourite dish off the menu of a very good restaurant. 'Goodnight, Ron Hogget.'

She walked over to her car: it was a brand-new two-door Jaguar XJS in powder blue. Just the thing for a blonde who took risks. I waited till she started up and moved off, and the copper wished me goodnight from the shelter of the garage, so I wished him the same and looked up at the sky. It was already blue. All the same I went back to bed.

6

The phone woke me at eight-thirty. Somebody seemed to have passed a new law saying Hogget must never, under any circumstances, have more than four consecutive hours of sleep. This time it was Palliser. He had news for me: he'd been burgled. He seemed to find the fact more important than I did. I told him the police hadn't left my place till after four-thirty, which in a way was true, then promised I'd be over as soon as I could, which meant after I'd showered and shaved and eaten breakfast.

I was still chewing toast when the phone rang again.

'Hogget,' I said, and the voice at the other end said, 'This is Cattell.'

I wondered just how far Sabena's father would go in pursuit of a joke.

'Air-Vice Marshal,' I said. 'How kind of you to call.'

'Your pal Sir Monty seems to think I could help you. Suggested I give you a buzz, in fact. Ask away.'

'I'd rather see you personally,' I said.

'Certainly. Urgent, is it?'

'Somewhat,' I said, feeling rather proud that I could find such a word at such an hour.

'Come and see me in the City,' Cattell said. 'The Belle Epoque Wine Bar in Sly Court. Know it?'

'I'll find it,' I said.

'Good man. Twelve forty-five suit you?'

'Fine,' I said.

'See you then. Just ask for me at the bar.'

He hung up and I marvelled at the power of Sir Montague. Even Air-Vice Marshals were as wax in his hands. Then I phoned Dave to tell him our schedule and he was asleep. It made my day.

Palliser's place had been turned over with vigour, enthusiasm even. Whoever had broken in had been looking for something, and had sworn not to give up until they found it. The drawing-room was a mess. So were the bathroom, the dining-room, the study, the kitchen, even the bedroom, where presumably Palliser had been anaesthetised by his sleeping pill. Dave and I walked from room to room, trying not to react to the ripped chairs and sofas, the smashed ornaments, the orgy of destruction, because that's what it really looked like – an orgy. Even to battered old pros like Dave and me, even when the victim is a pillock like Palliser, there's a brutality about it, and a sense of obscene pleasure, too. An orgy.

Palliser said, 'Well?' He was looking at Dave as he said it. He approved of Dave: the way he looked. All that. Dave shrugged and looked at me.

'How much is missing?' I said.

'How the blazes do I know?' he said. 'You've seen the place.'

'Is there money missing? Credit cards? Jewellery?'

He marched out on me, and I took another look at the kitchen: eggs tipped from the fridge to the floor, cream and butter on top, a bottle of hock poured over the lot to enrich the mixture.

'They were feeling frustrated when they got to here,' I said.

'What makes you think so?' Dave asked.

'No sense to it.'

'No sense to any of it,' Dave said.

'Oh yes, there is,' I said. 'There has to be.' Palliser came back.

'Money's all there, and credit cards,' he said. 'The only jewellery here is my watch – it's a Patek Philippe – and some cuff-links. They're here too.'

'What about your wife's jewellery?'

'How the devil did you know I was married?' he said.

'I asked.'

'Then you should have asked further. You'd have learned that for the last three years she's lived in a nursing home.'

'Sorry,' I said. 'What's wrong with her?'

'Nothing,' he said. 'She likes being nursed. Her jewellery's in the bank. Now for God's sake stop asking bloody silly questions about things that don't concern you and get on with what I'm paying for.'

'I haven't been paid at all yet,' I said, 'and if you're going to start yelling every time I ask a question I don't want to be.'

He started spluttering like a Guy Fawkes' firework, but got it under control at last. 'I'm sorry,' he said. 'This has been the worst time of my life. My best friend killed, my home smashed... I'm sorry.'

His words moved me, but I didn't like the way

he kept watching me to see what effect they had.

'You still want me to go on?' I said.

'I want that Dak found.'

'This break-in–' I said.

'It's relevant?'

'You think so,' I said. 'Otherwise you wouldn't have sent for me before you called the police.'

'How do you know I haven't called them?'

I sighed: a habit I'd caught from Detective Inspector Sutton.

'Because they're not here,' I said. 'Asking the same questions I'm trying to ask. But they will be here soon.'

'Oh, God,' he said.

'Do you know what they were after?' I asked, and he shook his head. 'Will you look to see what's missing and let me know?'

'All right,' he said.

'Do you want me here when the police come?'

'Will it help me?'

'No.'

'Then bugger off,' he said, but added almost at once: 'I didn't mean that. I don't know what the hell I do mean. Shall I tell the police I called you?'

'You might as well,' I said. 'They'll find out anyway.'

We made the long, grinding journey across London to the City, and every traffic light was against us. Dave had to leave me at the bottom of Sly Court, and find a place to park. Across the road was a pub, the Ring of Bells. 'I'll be in there,' he said. Him and a book and a long, slow lager. I left him to it, and scuttled off to the wine bar.

94

There are wine bars and wine bars, and I was glad I wasn't picking up the bill in this one. It reeked of money, that sweet-sour satisfying smell of the kind of money that knows there's plenty more where that came from. I asked the necessary question of a young lady behind the bar, who looked as if she mixed half-pints of Black Velvet in silver tankards in between modelling Jean Muir dresses. She told me politely and with a smile where to go. My guess was that the Air-Vice Marshal tipped well.

He was a small, spare man with a balding head on which two great wings of white hair still survived. His nose and chin were determined, and his voice was not a small man's voice. It boomed like artillery.

'Delighted to meet you,' he said. 'As you see I've taken the liberty of ordering a bottle of Bollinger. I hope that's all right.'

I said it was, and he poured me a glass, then passed me the card.

'Order what you like,' he said. 'It's all pretty good here.'

I decided to take him at his word, and ordered gulls' eggs and the foie gras salade tiède just to see what happened. He didn't even blink, and I wondered who was paying.

'Sir Monty said you wanted to know about Palliser?'

'And the others.'

'The Ad Astra Airline crowd?'

'You knew them all?' I said.

'The Berlin Airlift,' said Cattell. 'I was an Air Commodore then. They were my responsibility.'

95

'I see,' I said. 'Were they good?'

'They were the best,' Cattell said, and meant it.

'Bill Day?'

'A freak,' he said. 'A one in God knows how many. A thousand? A million?' He shrugged. 'Also a hell of a nice man.'

'The best of the best?' I said.

'A nice way of putting it.' The Jean Muir model came and he ordered for us both, asking for Gevrey-Chambertin with the salad. Sabena's father had briefed him well.

'Bertie Benskin was good too,' he said. 'You'd never have believed it to look at him.'

'Why not?'

'He looked like Billy Bunter on a diet,' said Cattell, 'but he didn't fly like it.'

'You've heard, I suppose. About Benskin?'

'I've heard precious little else,' Cattell said. 'My phone's been ringing all morning. People liked him, you see.'

'Like Bill Day?'

'Not really,' Cattell said. 'Bill Day was a shrine you worshipped at. Bertie was the one who made you laugh and ordered the next round.'

'And Palliser?'

'He wasn't a natural flyer,' Cattell said. 'He was good because he was a born achiever but he couldn't live with Bill, or Bertie. They were born flyers.'

'Did he resent that?'

'Not specially,' Cattell said. They were making money for him. For themselves too, of course. But Tony was the one who needed money.'

'Why?'

'Because he had to be rich. And now he is – thanks to Bill and Bertie. And Frank Denville too of course.'

Poor old Frank Denville, I thought. He always comes last if he's allowed in at all.

'What about Frank Denville?'

'Eh?' The gulls' eggs arrived, and Cattell brooded on the question till the waitress left.

'He's always the one left out,' I said. 'Yet he flew the Dakota as well as Benskin.'

'He was – serious,' Cattell said. 'No jokes, no chit-chat. Worked hard and saved his pay.'

'Like Palliser,' I said.

'In a way,' said Cattell. 'But the other three all had one thing in common that Denville hadn't.'

'Which was?'

'They'd all killed people,' Cattell said, and ate his first gull's egg. 'Frank was in Transport Command, you see. They didn't shoot – or drop bombs.'

'Was he married?'

'No,' Cattell said. 'He had a girl. Wendy – Lawrence, was it? Pretty little thing. Not fearfully bright, but pretty.'

'I suppose you don't know what happened to her?'

'Of course I do,' said Cattell. 'She married Palliser. I was at the wedding.' He munched another egg. 'Next question.'

'Bill Day,' I said.

'What about him?'

'Was he really such a paragon?' I asked. 'So loved and admired by all?'

Cattell took his time thinking about it. At last he

said, 'Yes. He was. I know what you're after of course. He sounds too much like a cross between Sir Galahad and Rupert Brooke. But he wasn't. He – how shall I put it? – he could beat you at almost anything you cared to mention and you'd never resent it. He could walk off with the girl you were after and you'd shake your head and laugh. But up there, where it counted'– his eyes looked up at the ceiling then came back to mine – 'in a dogfight, Bill would never let you down. Never. And believe me I know. I was in his squadron.'

'And his wife?'

'Sheila? She adored him, like everybody else.'

'Was he faithful to her?'

'Is that relevant?' He was angry.

'I don't know,' I said. 'But I'm reaching back over forty years. Help me please.'

'Of course he wasn't,' Cattell said. 'He lived far too close to death.'

'But you said he was wonderful.'

'And so he was,' said Cattell. 'But so many things could go wrong. No. He wasn't faithful. And then she died.'

'Buzz bomb.'

'Just after D-Day,' Cattell said. 'Bill was flying sweeps over France. When he got word he just sat there in the mess for an hour, then flew another sweep, shot up some German infantry, went out for a few gins as if nothing had changed. But it had.'

'In what way?'

'It had never occurred to him that she'd be the one to go first. How could it? And despite all his shenanigans he adored her.' He pushed his plate

98

away and the model brought the burgundy, waiting till he nodded approval. 'Next question?' he asked.

'There were all kinds of illegal things those blokes could have done in those days,' I said. 'Smuggling, taking stolen goods out of occupied countries, all that. But I gather they never did.'

'It would certainly be out of character.'

'Out of Palliser's character?'

'We all have our price, I suppose,' Cattell said, 'but Tony's would be pretty high.'

'And Bill Day's?'

'He wouldn't even have understood there was a price involved.'

'He was that moral?'

'Morals wouldn't have entered into it,' Cattell said. 'He was having far too much fun being honest to worry about crime.'

The foie gras arrived. He was having it too. After the girl had served, he said, 'A lot of people were like that in those days.'

'So, when the Dakota disappeared, you don't think there was anything criminal involved?'

'Not with Bill.'

'How about Denville?'

'Not with Frank either. But anyway the question doesn't arise. Bill would be in charge.'

I began to think I was looking for Superman. Cattell poured burgundy, sipped, and said, 'Mm.' It was a noise of approval. I sipped and said the same.

'I can never understand why the French drink Château Yquem with foie gras,' he said. 'It just doesn't go with sweet wine.'

'It goes with the burgundy,' I said. 'It's delicious.'

Cattell said, 'Anything else I can do for you? I don't want to rush you but there is a meeting I have to attend later–'

'Just one thing,' I said. 'I need to go to an island in the Hebrides.'

'Getting away from it all?'

'Business,' I said. 'Urgent.'

'You going on your own?'

'No,' I said. No way was I going to go without Dave. 'Two of us.'

'Your best bet is the shuttle to Glasgow then rent a helicopter. I can recommend someone if you like.' I said I would like. I also told him the gear I'd need, and he nodded. 'Choppers Ltd. Small firm – but reliable. London-based but Glasgow's no problem. They'll look after you. I'll give them a ring. When d'you want to go?'

'Thursday,' I said. Two days' delay, but there was a lot to do nearer home.

'I'll tell them so,' he said and I thanked him. I noticed he didn't ask which island I was going to, but then he didn't have to.

After that we talked about cricket – he knew a lot about cricket – and horse-racing. He knew a lot about that, too, especially Ascot, and I wondered if he'd met Sabena, but I didn't ask him. Life was complicated enough without that. He paid the bill with a Diners' Club Gold Card, and I thanked him again for his hospitality.

'A pleasure,' he said. 'I didn't think it would be but it was. Always a pleasure to lunch a man who enjoys the best.'

I wasn't sure how I was supposed to react to

that, so I let it lie.

'Besides,' he said, 'Cattell and Hogget... No wonder we ate gulls' eggs and goose-liver.' He offered his hand and I took it, and we both said we hoped we'd meet again soon. Both of us lied, but we were nice about it.

Dave was in the bar of the Ring of Bells, with the remains of a cheese and chutney sandwich, one and a half inches of lager, and volume 3 of *À la Recherche du Temps Perdu*, by Marcel Proust, translated by Scott-Moncrieff. The look he gave me told me I'd interrupted a really juicy bit.

'Can I get you something?' he said.

'God no,' I said. I mean champagne *and* burgundy.

'Where we going?'

'Home,' I said. 'To pack. Thursday we're off to bonny Scotland.'

On the way back I stopped and bought more whisky, which was just as well. There were three messages on my answering machine, all from Detective Inspector Sutton. When I called the number he gave, all he said was 'Stay where you are', so I made myself a cup of coffee and called my boss. Palliser didn't think that anything had been stolen, and I didn't think he was lying. He sounded too relieved. I asked him if he'd talked to Sutton and Cairns and he said he had. He didn't make it sound like one of the highlights of his life. Then the doorbell rang and it was Sutton. Cairns was with him. Cairns too fat and Sutton too thin, but when it came to wrath there was nothing to choose between them. I offered them coffee or scotch or both, but they refused. They

101

were too angry to swallow.

It seemed that I had been doing naughty things, like disappearing for a whole morning.

'But you told me you wanted to rest,' I said.

I gathered that one should never tell policemen they want to rest. It damages their self-esteem.

'Then there's Palliser,' said Sutton.

'What about him?' I asked.

'What about him?' Cairns screamed. *'What about him?'* He was close to foaming at the mouth.

'He was burgled,' Sutton said.

'I know that,' I said. 'He sent for me.'

'And you went. To the scene of a crime. But you didn't send for us.'

I thought about using the resting gag again, but decided against it after another look at them.

'I told him to do that,' I said. 'Did he?'

'Eventually,' said Sutton.

'What was pinched?'

'We thought maybe you could tell us that,' said Cairns.

'Me?' I said. 'I'm looking for an aeroplane. I thought I told you.'

'You did tell us,' said Cairns, 'and so did Palliser tell us. But it doesn't make any bloody sense.'

'No more it does,' said Sutton, and this time his voice was silky. 'Let's talk about telephone answering machines instead.'

'By all means,' I said. Considering the way I felt, it came out almost nonchalant.

'So you admit–' Cairns began, but Sutton shushed him. Pity. I'd like to have known what I was admitting.

'You've got one,' Sutton said. I took a moment

to remind myself that I was in the clear, but Cairns couldn't wait that long.

'Don't deny it,' he said. 'Palliser told us he'd talked with Benskin, and Benskin said he'd left a message on your tape.'

For a moment I was sure that I was deep in the river and that Sutton was about to make the nastiest waves of all, and then I looked at him. He was furious, but not with me. With Cairns. And suddenly I knew why.

'Why should I deny it?' I said. 'I've still got the tape. I'll play it for you now if you like.'

'You will?' said Cairns.

The way he said it this was totally the wrong answer. It was like the innkeeper telling Joseph that there were rooms on all floors and to forget about the stable.

'Certainly,' I said, and led the way to the kitchen. We all stood and looked at the tape-recorder with the pot plant beside it, and I knew what was worrying them. They both remembered the pot plant and the recorder – after all, they'd seen them when they first came into my house, and they'd been trained to remember things – but they couldn't be absolutely sure whereabouts in the kitchen they'd been.

Cairns stretched out a hand, but Sutton stopped him.

'Just a minute, Arthur,' he said, then turned to me. 'I told you I'd be back with a warrant.'

'Do you mean you haven't got it?' I asked.

He struggled for words, found they wouldn't come, and showed me the warrant in silence. I looked at it, but quickly. I push my luck just so far.

'The tape in the player's blank,' I told Cairns. 'The one you want is in that plastic box.' The one they really wanted was in Dave's car, but we all learn by our mistakes.

I waited for them to swop the tapes over, but of course they didn't, not on my say-so. Cairns played the one already in, and we stood and listened to its slow silence, till Sutton put it on fast forward and got it over with. Then I reached for the tape in the storage box, but Cairns grabbed it first and played it through. Calls from a client, from Dave, from Sabena – these last of an all too personal nature, but it helped with the authenticity – and then the one thing they thought they were waiting for: 'Eh... What?... Oh, I see... It's a *machine*... Look, old chum, this is Bertie Benskin here to... You don't know me and I don't know you, but if you could find your way to the PAAA club, there might be a job of work in it for you.' And so on and so on. The first time I'd heard Bertie Benskin's voice.

When it was over, Sutton said, 'And that's it?'

'That's it,' I said. It hadn't made his day.

'But Palliser said–' Cairns began.

Sutton lost his cool.

'Never mind what Palliser said,' he yelled. 'Just forget what Palliser said. I'm up to *here* in what Palliser said.'

'What did he say?' I asked.

For the second time since I'd known him Sutton took a vote on it and decided, by the narrowest of margins, not to hit me. He gave Mr Nice Guy one more try.

'Palliser said I might learn something useful,'

104

he said. 'He was wrong.'

He turned and started his walk-out. Cairns followed.

'Is that it?' I said.

'Yes,' he said, then turned for another yell. 'Don't leave the country.'

He didn't say which one, and I didn't ask him. Instead I waited till the door banged, checked that they were outside it, and phoned Palliser.

He told me he was busy.

'I won't keep you long,' I said. 'All I want is the answer to one question.'

'Very well.'

'How do you spell "resign"?' I said. 'If you don't know, "quit" will do.'

'Oh,' he said, and there was a silence, then: 'You've been talking to Sutton.'

'Obviously,' I said.

'Did he ask you about Bertie's message on the tape?'

'You still haven't answered the question.'

'I have to *know*.'

'Not from me,' I said. 'I've resigned – or I will have as soon as you tell me how to spell it.'

'What Bertie put on tape – it could be vital,' Palliser said.

'It didn't sound that way to me.'

'Or the police?'

'I played them the wrong tape,' I said. 'The one when he called me to fix a meeting.'

'Did you, by God. Good man.'

'If I'm so good – why did you shop me?'

'Because I had to know,' he said.

'Above all else?'

'*Yes* ... How many more times?'

'In other words you've got vital information I need to do your job?'

'I've got it,' he said. 'And I must keep it. You can still do the job.'

'And another thing – how did you know that Mr Benskin phoned me?'

'He sent me a note – to let me know he wanted a chat with you.'

'He warned you?'

'I wouldn't tell Sutton if I were you,' I said. 'That gives you a motive.'

'Damn your impudence–'

'And damn your stupidity,' I said. 'I resign.' I hung up.

I thought he'd call me back before I'd counted a hundred, but I was up to two hundred and seventeen before the phone rang. I suppose he thought he was tough.

'Well?' I said.

'I want you to go on,' said Palliser.

'No,' I said.

'Listen,' said Palliser, and then, *'Please. I know there's something I haven't told you, but I can't. And maybe it's as well for you that I can't. You can still go after that Dak, I promise you. If it's a question of more money–'

'How much more?' I asked, and then he knew he'd got me. All the same I got another five grand out of him. It would be money earned, and Palliser and I both knew it. He wanted Bertie Benskin's tape too, and I said I'd post it to him. I wasn't going to call in person. Sutton would be having me tailed round the clock. Besides I had to edit it first.

Next I had to go and see Jocasta Benskin, and the earlier the better, before she started thinking about bed – if there ever was a time when she didn't start to think about bed – so I rang up Dave and told him we were off to work. He grumbled a bit because he hadn't finished his novel – it ran to a lot of volumes he told me – but he turned up on time on account of being a mate – that and the money I was paying, and just as well he did. Punctuality had its rewards. Parked outside the Benskin residence – which was a mansion block in South Kensington – was a pale blue Mini Metro, licence number EDX 35C. Dave didn't need any prompting either.

'She's here,' he said. 'Now you can judge for yourself.'

And so can you, I thought. Only I didn't tell him about Jocasta Benskin. He might have thought I was showing off.

7

There was a porter on duty in the hall, and a security man, which meant the flat-owners counted their money by the sackful. The porter made a phone-call and said that Mrs Benskin would see us. He sounded surprised...

The woman who opened the door was neither Jocasta nor Angela. Tallish bird, about thirty-five, thin but not skinny, in a Bruce Oldfield suit that had never been cheap, dark hair, very shrewd brown eyes. She gave me one look and Dave two as I told her who we were.

'This way,' she said. Her movements were like her manners: brisk and sure. We left the hall that was mostly leather chairs and pictures of World War Two aeroplanes, then into a drawing-room: parquet floor, washed silk Chinese rug, more leather chairs and a sofa-table that might well have been Sheraton. On the walls were a few repro pictures of girls: Titian's 'Venus with a Dog', and a Fragonard of a girl on a swing, I remember, and a little Renoir original: 'The Girl with the Straw Hat'. About twelve inches by seven, say, and insured for fifty thousand at least. But I didn't waste time on the pictures: not with the real thing so much in evidence.

The dark and the fair, simplicity and sophistication, innocence and experience. No matter what you cared to call them, they were sensational: the one enhancing the other so to speak. To begin with Angela did show a kind of simplicity, if not innocence. But that may have just been because of the high-voltage sophistication my old chum Jo was spreading around. Angela wore a grey dress with a few touches of white – the nearest she could get to mourning, I guessed – and Jocasta was in the full black silk and top quality Italian. I risked a look at Dave and hoped I wasn't goggling quite as much as he was. The brisk brunette asked if there'd be anything else.

'Coffee?' Jocasta asked and I said yes. Dave still wasn't up to making noises. The brisk one left to get it and Jocasta asked us to sit down.

108

'It's kind of you to see us,' she said, and at once she looked at my crotch, but this time thank God she looked away again. Just checking.

'I'm glad of the company,' she said. 'You don't know Angela, do you?' And of course we said we didn't, and she introduced us, and I said Dave was my partner. It sounds much better than assistant, and anyway Dave isn't anybody's assistant.

'Angela came over as soon as she heard,' Jo Benskin told us. 'She's an old friend of the family.' She turned to Angela then. 'These two gentlemen have been doing some confidential work for Bertie... The smaller one's rather nice. I haven't had time to make up my mind about the big one yet.'

'Jo, for goodness' sake,' said Angela. She sounded the way I felt: at once shocked and delighted. Only with me there was worry as well. I was due to get married after Ascot. Anyway Miss Brisk came in then with coffee and we changed the subject. Jo for some reason was very wary of Miss Brisk, whose name, I gathered, was Beverly. She didn't look like a Beverly somehow. When she'd dished out the coffee and left I said I had questions.

'We'll go to the study,' Jo said, then turned to Dave.

'You stay and talk to Angela,' she said. 'Get her to tell you about Bertie. I honestly don't think I could cope with the pair of you.'

All it meant was that she was grieving, but all the same Dave blushed.

I took my coffee with me to another smaller sitting-room: furniture in silk brocade, telly against the far wall, more good repro stuff and a Sickert of a barmaid: blonde and busty and cheerful, as indeed she should have been. She was worth thirty grand at least. This, I knew at once, was *her* room. She took the coffee-cup from me, put it down beside hers, and kissed me again. It seemed to take about four hours. When she let me go she said, 'What is it about you? It can't be your manly beauty, can it?'

'I doubt it,' I said, then realised that I was holding her in a way I shouldn't. Not if I was engaged to another. I let her go, and she shrugged. Watching her shrug could become my favourite hobby, I thought, then told myself to behave and reached for the coffee. What I really needed was a fig-leaf. She was looking again. 'Please,' I said. 'I have a few questions—'

'Yes, of course,' she said. 'Your body can wait. For a while. But not too long. You're absolutely scrumptious, you know. Damned if I know why.' She sipped her coffee. 'I cried for Bertie. All night,' she said. 'Do you believe that?'

'Yes,' I said.

And it was true. I did.

She nodded at the Sickert barmaid.

'If it hadn't been for Bertie that would have been me. But he married me and made a lady out of me,' she said. 'I was an orphan. In care. Not that anybody did much caring. Except me... I grew up very quickly. Got away as soon as I could. When Bertie met me I was a waitress in a coffee bar. Soon as I got old enough I was going to be a barmaid. Do you remember coffee bars or are you too young?'

'Of course I remember them,' I said. But she

wanted to talk not listen.

'Bertie made a lady out of me, then he married me. And I made him happy, whatever I did. *And* I loved him. Everybody liked him, but *I* loved him.'

'Somebody didn't like him,' I said.

She was on her feet, screaming, and I had to yell at her. I was surprised when it worked.

'Oh, God,' she said. 'I do hope Beverly didn't hear. She's such a *prude*.'

'Tell her to lump it,' I said.

'How can I? She irons and cooks and sews and cleans. She's brilliant. All the same you had no right–'

'You want them caught, don't you? Whoever did it?'

'Well, of course,' she said. 'But isn't that the rozzers' job? Aren't you supposed to find the Dak?'

'The two things are linked,' I said.

'But how?'

'Because of when and where,' I said. 'Outside my house. Don't you see?'

She saw all right. Despite her looks and the blonde hair, she was no fool.

'You were right,' she said. 'He did have an enemy.'

'At least he was in somebody's way,' I said.

'And you want me to tell you whose? But I can't... He owed nobody. He cheated nobody. He had a host of friends.'

'Maybe they owed him?'

'You don't understand,' she said. 'They liked him too much to cheat him – even the dodgy ones. And besides–'

'You were there to see that they didn't?'

'I think I go for your mind as well as your body,' she said. 'I bet it's a very sexy mind.'

'Not when it's working,' I said. 'It's working now. Tell me about it being Bertie's idea to look for the Dak. What did he say?'

'Just that?'

'He didn't say why he wanted it found?'

'Not really. What he said was: "They say it's best to let sleeping dogs lie, old girl, but these are dead dogs. Dirty dogs too. Better have them out in the open before there's trouble. Be all my fault if there is."'

Her voice had become exactly that of a gorgeous blonde imitating Bertie Benskin. Then it went back to normal.

'I asked him why and he said he'd tell me one day, once he'd sorted out a few things. And I honestly believe he would, except that–'

If she cried again she might not recover. I tried another question.

'Did he keep a diary, letters, anything like that?'

It was the right question. She even managed a smile.

'Bertie kept everything,' she said. 'He hoarded like a squirrel. Come and look.'

She took me down a corridor to a room with a vast Victorian desk, three filing cabinets, a table and a bookcase. Every space was covered with books, magazines, files. No pictures on the walls, not this time: just photographs of aeroplanes. Jo opened the drawers of the cabinets. They were crammed full.

'My poor darling Bertie,' she said. 'This is all that's left of him.'

112

She wept as she did everything else. Beautifully.

'Do you really want to go through all this stuff?' she asked at last.

'Would you mind?'

'I would if I was here,' she said. 'Tell me when and I'll go out.' So we arranged it, then I asked her if she would make a phone call for me, and she said it would be okay. And then I told her to expect a visit from Sutton and Cairns.

'What do I tell them?' she asked.

'Not the truth,' I said. 'Just say I called to see how you were.'

'They'll never believe that,' she said.

'Of course not,' I said, 'but how can they call you a liar?'

We went back to Angela and Dave. Dave didn't look at all pleased to see me.

Then we went back to Dave's place, on account of Dave's got a very good Jap music-centre with two tape-recorders, and I edited Bertie Benskin's tape while Dave made us an omelette. All I did was record the bit where Bertie said he knew by instinct that Bill Day and Denville were innocent – at least that's what it sounded like – then add some bits from the end saying he'd come over straight away, but omitting any references to money or being afraid to come. Also omitted was his reference to the fact that Palliser wasn't infallible, and to popsies he'd chatted to. What was left was harmless enough even for Palliser. I borrowed an envelope then went at the omelette. It was good. Dave's always are.

'How d'you get on?' I asked him.

'She's very upset,' said Dave. 'She liked him.' He made it sound as if people Angela Rossie liked shouldn't go getting themselves killed and upsetting her.

'Tell you anything?'

'She collects book matches,' he said.

'Anything *relevant*.'

'Sorry,' he said. 'She's fond of the Benskins – both of them – and didn't like Palliser. Sorry for his wife though. Just like her mum and dad.' I gave myself a very black mark for not asking my new chum about Mrs Palliser.

'Did she say why?'

'He keeps putting her down. Did the same to her mum.'

'And Mrs P.?'

'Hypochondriac,' said Dave. 'Lives in a nursing-home. Or maybe she's just getting away from Palliser. Not that Palliser cares. He's too busy chasing crumpet.'

'Any names?'

'Her for a start. *And* her mum. Not a nice man.'

'Not nice at all,' I said, 'but his cheque's in the bank.'

Dave sighed. 'I suppose so,' he said, whatever that meant, and reached for Proust.

I rang Michael Copland at the paper, but he was out, it being lunch time. Well, of course he was. At San Lorenzo or Langan's or somewhere with whoever was climbing the charts. I said I was sorry I'd missed him, which was a lie, and that I'd have something for him soon, which could well be a lie. Then I told Dave I was going to call Sabena and he took the hint and went to do the washing-up.

'Where the hell have you *been?*' she said. Charming.

'At the scene of the crime,' I said. 'I just about am the scene of the crime.'

'Oh.' She was thinking. She's good at thinking, when she can be bothered. Then at last: 'You might have phoned.'

'My friends will be pestered,' I said. 'By the rozzers. And the closer the friend—'

'They couldn't watch you phoning.'

'I am phoning,' I said. 'First chance I've got. I was with the police till three' – liar – 'and up again at eight-thirty.'

'Your picture in the paper looked awful.'

'I was feeling awful.'

'Oh.' More thought. 'Was he nice – that Mr Benskin?'

'Very nice. Also a hero.'

'Oh dear. Married?'

'Yes,' I said.

'What's she like?'

'Shattered,' I said.

'Oh come on, Ronaldo. You can do better than that. Shattered and pretty? Shattered and ugly?'

'Shattered and blonde,' I said. 'But none the less shattered.' Then before she could start anything I said, 'I miss you very much.'

'I was beginning to wonder.'

'You're the only fix I need,' I said. 'But I don't want you mixed up in this.'

'What's so awful about finding lost aeroplanes?'

'Nothing,' I said. 'What's awful is nice men being killed.'

115

At once she said, 'I hope Dave's with you.'

'He is,' I said. 'And he's staying with me right through the job. It's not all that easy to hurt Dave. He's not like you.'

'But why should anyone—'

'In Abano a young man with a gun thought it might be the way to make me behave.'

'But he's dead.'

'He wasn't all that good,' I said. 'Not like the one who killed Bertie Benskin by cutting his throat – slick as a surgeon.'

'Damn you, Ronaldo, do you have to be so graphic?'

'And another thing,' I said. 'Your father's still on my side – but he won't be if I get you mixed up in this.'

'All right,' she said. 'All *right!* Go and be a hero, but don't keep me waiting too long.'

'You could help me,' I said. 'To get back to you, I mean.'

'How?' For Sabena she sounded wary.

'Did you ever meet a man called Kessler when you were at Oxford?'

'Dr Kessler?'

'His first name's Joachim,' I said.

'That's the one.'

'What can you tell me about him?'

'He's a fellow of Leicester College. You know what a fellow is?'

'More or less,' I said. 'He gets a whack of the college income and teaches a bit. What they call a don.'

'My little know-all... Well, Joachim's a philosopher. His field is post-Wittgenstein analytical

116

theory, whatever that is. Maybe three other men living would know.'

'Sounds like a million laughs.'

'Oh, he is,' said Sabena. 'Believe me. He's the sexiest man in the city – apart from a golf pro I used to know. Only he lives out at Cowley so he doesn't count. Do you know, we girls used to go to his tutorials in threes – two wasn't enough. He thought it was just an excuse for a party.'

She knew I hated reference to her sex life before she met me: she was punishing me.

'I thought you said you studied history.'

'Read,' she said. 'At Oxford one doesn't study things: one reads them. Perhaps that's what's wrong with the place. And I did read history. I switched after two terms. Before that I read PPE – politics, philosophy and economics to you.'

'And the same to you,' I said. 'With knobs on. Why did you switch? Because of Joachim?'

'The tenacious Teuton...' Her voice was dreamy with remembering. 'That's what we called him. He was altogether too much. What's he got to do with aeroplanes?'

'Maybe nothing,' I said. 'Maybe a lot. I have to go.'

'Take Dave with you,' she said.

'And your love?'

'Yes, goddamit,' she said. 'My love as well.' Then she banged the phone down and Dave came back in.

'Do we need the car this afternoon?' he said, and I nodded. 'Where we going?'

'Oxford,' I said.

'I wouldn't go there if I was you, Ron.'

117

'Why not?'

'You know what they call it, don't you? The home of lost causes.' But it was where Dr Sexy Kessler lived, so we had to go.

We had company on the way out – an unmarked Granada, but nobody can tail a vehicle in London with only one car. We got rid of him before we got to Shepherd's Bush, and he didn't even know he'd been got rid of, not with Dave driving. When we got to the motorway Dave opened up a bit. He was driving a Vauxhall Cavalier that year, that still had a bit of poke in it.

'Nice sight the two of them made sitting in that drawing-room,' he said.

I muttered something – I had to – but I didn't want to know.

'You told Sabena about yours?' said Dave.

'Let's have some music,' I said, and switched the radio on to Radio Three. It was a geezer called Hindemith, but at least it shut Dave up.

To get to Leicester College you drive down the High Street past Magdalen and Queen's, then sort of veer round on to the New Road and there you are, nice and handy for the Westgate Shopping Centre. Leicester itself is Jacobean mostly – nothing more modern than its Hawksmoor Chapel, – and a bit bewildered by the shopping centre. And so too was I...

The porter on duty made a phone call, and said that yes indeed, Dr Kessler was expecting Mr Mills and Mr Boon and we were to go to New Quad, straight on through the arches, staircase four. And so we did. Not that the porter noticed.

His eyes stayed the whole time on a page-three girl whose tangible assets defied credence, never mind gravity.

'Mills and Boon,' said Dave. 'Who on earth dreamed that one up?'

'Mrs Benskin,' I said.

'She would,' said Dave.

New Quad was nice: big, airy, enough turf for a bowling green, plane trees, window boxes and mellow grey stone. All the best, most expensive clichés, and worth every penny. It didn't seem at all fair and just that the man whom Sabena had found so memorable should live in such National Trust surroundings. Lucky bastard, I thought. Rags to riches. Tempelhof loader to post-Wittgenstein what's-its-name.

Dave said, 'I applied for a post-graduate scholarship here once.'

'What did they say?'

'They said they liked my ideas but I hadn't got a first... The Paras weren't so fussy.'

We reached staircase four and there he was. Dr J. Kessler, ground floor, so we knocked and a voice said, 'Come in.' No accent. But then he'd been in England a long time.

We went in. I had what was for me a fair head of steam up by then, but I never get all that angry. Dave says I haven't had enough practice, but I reckon it's a knack, and I haven't got it. All the same, whatever puny rage I had evaporated as soon as I saw him. He was in a wheelchair, a rug tucked round him, a book on his lap. The whole of the left side of his body looked rigid, as if it had been deep-frozen. But his right eye still glittered, the voice that came from the left side of his mouth stayed strong.

'Mr Mills? Mr Boon?' he said. 'Which is which? Or can't you remember?'

'We're never quite sure,' said Dave. 'Usually we take turns.'

Kessler chuckled: 'I somehow felt that Jocasta Benskin chose to call you so. It is very much her kind of whimsy. Please sit down.'

The room was furnished like a good club's library: books all over, and heavy, comfortable leather to sit on. Wherever there was space, on table tops, or between bookcases, were pictures of girls. All his pupils by the look of them, and somewhere in the midst my very own Sabena. But she hadn't been then. I willed myself not to look for her.

'Tell me how I may help her,' Kessler said.

'It's – difficult,' I said. 'To tell you how, I mean. She just wanted you to answer some questions that might tell us about Bertie's death.'

His right hand moved as if I'd struck a reflexive nerve, and his book fell to the floor. Dave got up and retrieved it for him.

'Bertie is dead?'

'He was murdered,' I said. 'Last night. The papers were full of it.' And me, and Dave, and Jocasta Benskin, I thought.

'I do not read the newspapers often. Or listen to the radio. Or watch television. I have no time, you see.'

'What do you do?' Dave asked.

'I read,' said Kessler. 'Or mostly I re-read. All the books that I enjoyed the most. Of all the joys in life, reading was one of two that gave me most pleasure.' He chuckled. 'Now there can only be reading. Sad, wouldn't you say?' He had a shock of black hair growing grey, gleaming blue eyes, a mouth that only a stroke could prevent from smiling, and then only half-way. 'I loved so many, but I think I loved the books even more. So maybe I am lucky even now... How did Bertie die?'

'He was stabbed,' I said. 'He wanted to find out about the Dakota and he was stabbed to death.'

'The Dakota?' Kessler said. 'After all these years?'

'Maybe I should have said Palliser wanted us to find it,' I said. 'But Mr Benskin thought of the idea. Also he knew things. That's why he was killed.'

'Poor Bertie,' said Kessler. 'Of all men I think he was the one I liked most... Per Ardua Ad Astra.' He smiled. 'Poor Bertie.'

'You worked for Ad Astra Airlines?'

'It is the reason I am here,' he said. 'You remember that young President from Boston – what he said? "Ich bin ein Berliner." But he had food, a warm coat, a warm house – even his car was heated. I was a real Berliner. A corner of a cellar to sleep in, potatoes to eat when I was lucky. No coat and such a winter – the worst we could remember. I was dying then as I am dying now. But that time Bertie saved me.'

'How?'

'He came out of a bar. He was smoking a cigarette and I thought maybe he will throw it away before it is finished, and I wanted so much to taste tobacco. It was a cold night – all the nights were cold – but for a while I forgot because the tobacco was important... And then he threw it away. Almost a whole cigarette. A Player's it must have been. He always smoked Player's.'

'Till the day he died,' I said, but he didn't hear me.

'I bent down to pick it up and that's all I remember,' he said, 'because when I bent over I fainted... And when I came to I was wearing a flying jacket and there was a blanket around me, and Bertie had found me some soup and Palliser was cursing him for behaving like a damn fool, and Bertie was saying I had a job.'

'What sort of a job?' Dave asked.

'Loader on a Dakota. I said yes thank you very much, and Palliser swore some more. In fact I was more of an unloader. A lot came in: almost nothing went out.'

'Almost?'

Kessler shrugged, but only his right shoulder moved.

'Cigarettes, whisky, gin, a few nylons.'

'Nylons?' I said. 'In West Berlin?'

'From the American pilots,' Kessler said. 'They were as good as money. But not to sell – only as presents. It was all for their own use – and presents. Of course I sold mine.'

'You were in on it too?'

'Bertie said I must be. I turned out to be – useful. I spoke good English, they made me foreman and I hired only men I could trust, I kept the books, I made the schedules. Of course I was never a partner, but in the end I became general manager, so to speak... So I got a little too, and sold it. In West Berlin I was rich. Did Palliser not tell you this?'

'He said you were a black marketeer.'

'That is hardly brilliant on his part. In Berlin everybody was a black marketeer.'

'Also a thief,' said Dave.

Again Kessler shrugged his lop-sided shrug.

'Sometimes he would not give me my share of the presents,' he said. 'So I took them.'

'And that's all you ever loaded?' Dave asked. 'For any of them? Day and Denville too?'

Kessler nodded.

'Never any people?' Dave asked. 'Never any Gestapo or SS men?'

'You understand, Dr Kessler,' I said, 'we have to ask you that?'

You can see the way we were playing it: Dave the heavy and me Mr Nice Guy. It didn't faze Kessler.

'Of course,' he said. 'I realised as soon as Jocasta called me. That tired old story.'

'It isn't true then?' Dave asked.

'It may be,' said Kessler. 'But it's not true of Day and Denville. They could not.'

'Palliser says they did,' said Dave.

'Of course. Palliser believes in money the way a Trappist believes in silence,' Kessler said. 'He thinks it cures all pain, all problems. But the other three – they were not like that.'

'Were you in the war?' Dave asked.

'In the army,' said Kessler. 'Rank of lieutenant. I fought in Russia – in Germany too.'

'Not the SS?'

'No,' said Kessler. 'Not the SS – though I knew they existed – just as I knew the camps existed.

But of course in those days I would have denied it. One had to eat.'

'Dr Kessler,' I said, 'can you tell us anything about the night the Dakota disappeared?'

'It was not a good night,' he said. 'Snow, much cloud, and very cold.'

'A bad night for flying?'

'Bad,' he said. 'But not impossible. Not with Bill Day flying.'

'Did you see the take-off?'

'No,' he said. 'I did not work that night.'

'Why not?' That was Dave; hard, and almost too nasty. After all, we'd been invited. But Kessler didn't even notice.

'I had a cold,' he said, 'It turned to flu. I was given the night off.'

'Who by?'

'Bertie, of course. All the kind things came from Bertie.'

'Not Denville?' I asked. 'Not Day?'

'They were kind too, certainly,' Kessler said. 'But Bertie – he had almost certainly saved my life and we both knew it.'

'Can't you tell us anything that can help us?'

'You might ask Müller,' said Kessler. 'Heinrich Müller – if you can find him. He was my assistant foreman. He was an architect – rather a good one. He should not be hard to trace – unless he went back to his family.'

'Where does his family live?' Dave barked.

'In Dresden. There would be a lot of work for an architect in Dresden when your bombers had done with it.'

'Dresden's in the Eastern Zone,' said Dave.

124

'I fear it is,' said Kessler. 'It is most unfortunate.'

'And is that really all?' I asked. 'About the two men who vanished? Are you saying you can tell us nothing?'

'Oh no,' Kessler said. 'I can tell you that Denville loved his girl, and that Bill Day still mourned for his wife... That Denville saved his money to give to his girl... That Day didn't smoke, and sometimes would give me cigarettes... That Denville was a cuckold...'

'How do you know?' Dave snapped.

'Because the others knew and could not keep it hidden. Not from me. In those days I survived by knowing things.' Suddenly he was off, remembering. Dave wanted to speak but I shushed him.

'Bonny Bessie's house in Palmerston Street,' Kessler said at last. 'Roses round the door... Bill Day said that... It was one of the times they'd come over together. He was talking to Bertie. And Bertie said, "Messing about in boats... What a shame. What a bloody shame."'

'What on earth was all that about?' Dave asked.

'They'd been talking about Denville,' Kessler said.

'In front of you?'

'I was adding up figures,' Kessler said. 'To them that made me non-existent.' He straightened up a little in his chair.

'I am sorry I can help you no further,' he said.

'You want us to go?'

'Please,' he said. 'I am a little tired, and also I have a pupil coming.' He smiled. 'My last. I retire this year... I wish very much I did not.' He blinked, surprised by his own words. 'Now why did I tell

125

you that?'

'If you're saying you don't want to talk to us again, I can't blame you,' I said.

Dave nodded a goodbye and left. Hard men never commiserate.

'Not exactly that,' said Kessler. 'If I could help you I would – at least I think so. Mrs Benskin phoned me on your behalf as you know. But it was you she talked about. A wonderful woman.'

'Yes indeed,' I said.

'I have always liked women,' Kessler said. 'To me they were a challenge, each one, like a mountain to a mountaineer. But I never attempted Everest. I wish you good luck, Mr Boon.'

On the way out I spotted Sabena's picture. It was between two birds in bikinis but she was wearing cap and gown. It made me feel better, apart from the worry of what Jocasta Benskin had told Dr Kessler. Then, as we left staircase four, an undergraduate came in, and I found I was feeling glad for Kessler's sake, because it was a girl. I didn't see her face, but my guess was she was pretty.

8

'You've no idea how much I've missed you,' Sabena said.

She was leaning against me, and we fitted together as snugly as we always did. 'Maybe I have,' I said.

'You mean you've missed me, too?'

'Well of course.'

'Ah,' she said. 'But you've been busy. Interrogating suspects. Looking for clues.'

'Looking for Dakotas,' I said.

'And did you find any?'

'Not yet.'

'Didn't that poor Mr Benskin tell you anything?'

'Benskin was dead when I found him,' I said.

'Yes but before?'

'Nothing that helped... I liked him. Very much.'

'Daddy says he's met Mrs Benskin. He says she's gorgeous.' I said nothing. 'Is she?'

I lied because I didn't want a row. There was too much going on.

'She probably was before. Maybe she will be again. At the moment she's what I told you – shattered.'

'Daddy says she was potty about her husband. He also said she was inclined to promiscuity.'

'That's a bit pompous.'

'Daddy is a bit pompous about sex,' she said. But her arms stayed round me. 'Couldn't she help you?'

'Mrs Benskin? She only married him ten years ago.'

'So you're baffled, O mighty one?'

'Never more so,' I said.

'Where's Dave?'

'Night off,' I said. In fact he'd gone to see Angela Rossie, but it was his own idea.

'So you're staying?'

'Yes please,' I said.

'Would you like to eat before or after?'

'So long as it's not during,' I said. So we went

to bed, and oblivion, and then got up and waited while the steaks defrosted in the microwave, and I tossed the salad and drank g. and t., and we stayed happy if not oblivious, at least for a time. Rosario her maid also had the night off and was spending it with her boyfriend in Ongar, and the whole place was ours, and the steaks were right and the claret was right, and yet–

'Did you see Joachim?' she asked.

'Well of course,' I said. 'That's why I went to Oxford.'

'How was he?'

'Not bad considering,' I said.

'Considering what?'

'You mean you didn't know he'd had a stroke?' I said.

She put down her fork, its wodge of red-brown meat untasted.

'A stroke?' she said. 'Joachim?'

'It must have been,' I said. 'He didn't seem to want to talk about it – but that's what it must have been. I mean he was paralysed down one side, and the way he sat in the wheelchair–'

'Joachim?' she said again, and then she began to cry. I got up and went to her and tried to hold her, but her body wouldn't bend to mine, not this time. These were private tears.

I went back to my chair, and my steak and claret, and waited for the tears to stop. It took a while, but at last she said, 'I'm sorry.'

'That's all right,' I said. 'It was tactless of me – breaking it to you like that. I hadn't realised you were that close.'

'Close?' she said. 'Not for years – but I always

liked him. He was an awfully good teacher.'

The last words somehow acquired a double meaning she hadn't intended, and she flushed so that the red stained and spoiled her good looks.

'He must have liked you too,' I said. 'He had your photograph on his wall.'

'Along with others, no doubt.'

'Just a few.'

'Are you by any chance being ironic or jealous or just generally unloving?'

'None of those,' I said. 'I suppose jealous comes nearest, but it's more regret really. That I didn't meet you sooner.'

'You think that Joachim and I were lovers?'

'Does it matter what I think?' I said. 'Either you were or you weren't.'

'And I used to think that I was the realist,' she said. 'Pass the wine.'

So I passed it and she poured and drank, and that seemed to be the end of the conversation. So I left her to it and went off into the drawing-room and turned the telly on. It was the South East News and a girl with a terrible hair-do was saying that there had been a burst water-main in Fulham and the traffic in the region was appalling. I thought that made my day, but there was more.

'Reports are coming in of a murder in Oxford,' she said. 'Dr Joachim Kessler of Leicester College was found dead in his rooms this evening. Oxford police are anxious to interview two men who called on him earlier in the day.'

There was a gasp behind me, and the girl with the wrong hairdo was saying: 'And now sport. At close of play Middlesex–' I switched her off and turned to my own girl, if that's what she was.

'She said – Joachim was dead,' said Sabena. 'She said the police want to talk to you and Dave.'

'Sounds that way.'

'You didn't know – you couldn't have known–'

'Of course not,' I said. 'He was alive when we left. He was expecting a visitor.'

'What visitor?'

'A girl,' I said.

'What girl?'

'He didn't say,' I said, and then I almost added that I'd seen her and how pretty she'd been – but things were bad enough without that.

'Use your phone?' I said, and she nodded, not even surprised that I'd asked her, though we'd long since given up asking each other's permission for things like that.

I phoned Dave, but he was still in pursuit of his beloved, so I left a message on his machine, and told him to get himself round to my place on the jump, first chance he could, then turned back to Sabena.

'I'd better go,' I said.

'Yes,' she said. 'I think you better had.'

'Call me when you want to,' I said. 'I'll leave it to you.'

'Very well,' she said, and I left her. To kiss her would have been impossible, to shake her hand absurd.

I got a cab quick enough at that time of night, just across the road from the Brompton Oratory. I know the bus is cheaper, but a) Dave wasn't there to hold my hand, and b) I'd had about enough for one day. Only I hadn't allowed for the burst water-main. Just off Lillie Road it was and carrying on like it was the Trevi Fountain. Somebody had already put up a line of cones across the road, and my cabby eased to a stop and pushed back the sliding window.

'It'll have to be the back doubles, guv,' he said.

The trouble was everybody else had the same idea. The turn-off road was blocked solid, so I paid him off instead. I wasn't more than ten minutes from home, and I needed a ten-minute think.

What I had to think about was the lack of progress. Like the old song said, that's the only thing there's plenty of, baby. A superabundance, in fact. Pretty girls, sexy widows, corpses, missing aircraft, what you might call peripheral wealth in massive quantity, murky secrets from the past; this case had them all, but they didn't make a pattern. They did not, in Dave's word, cohere. And yet there was something, and I stepped up my walking pace to find it – walking fast's the only way I *can* think. And then a car went past me and braked and stopped, and it was all too sudden, too abrupt. So I looked behind me and another car was there already pulling up, then a man getting out: an elegant-looking man in a shirt that looked like silk, designer jeans, trainer shoes. I looked at the other car's occupants, but I knew what I was going to see. A pair of young lovers in lookalike clothes Bad. Distinctly bad. Poor old Ron Hogget with not a rozzer in sight, not even a witness, and inside the houses all the tellies turned up loud. I was in for a belting – if I was lucky.

The girl lover hung back, and her feller came for

131

me at the run. For the first time I realised just how big he was, and anyway he had the girl for back-up, so I thought I'd risk it with the elegant one instead, and turned and ran at him. Not to hit him: I'm just no good at hitting people; but from my junior-school days onwards there wasn't a lot of people who could match me when it came to dodging a belting... But I had forgotten the trainer shoes. The elegant geezer was faster than I was, and younger, and in much better nick. He cut me off and grabbed for me, just missing my coat, and I whirled and ran back the way I'd come, to where the big geezer waited, his girl-friend behind him looking as if she was in for a treat.

I whirled again, but the elegant one had already moved in closer, not racing; saving his strength to duff me, and when I whirled again the big one was waiting and his fist swung, low and dirty, and I went down on my knees as the two moved in. And then I went blind. At least that's what it seemed like with my eyes full of a silvery whiteness that took a frightening time to clear, and I *was* frightened, even when there were no more blows.

And then the brightness became car headlamps, and I found I was watching Dave. His car was broadside on in the street, lights blazing, and he was fighting the big bloke. The elegant one already looked a little less elegant, moaning in the gutter, silk shirt torn. I tried to get off my knees and I found I couldn't, then grabbed at an un-emptied dustbin and hauled myself up as the big geezer swung a fist at Dave and he ducked under-neath it and struck with three fingers, rigid, at the big feller's gut. He made a noise that sounded like 'woomph', but even so he backed up against a garden wall and tried a kick, but Dave knew that one and his hands were waiting, he grabbed and twisted, and the big man yelled and went round the way a top spins, and screamed as he did it.

And that, I thought, is that. But it wasn't. Because the bird gave up being a spectator and came at him using the sort of language she shouldn't, but she didn't come at him like a bird, all teeth and fingernails. Oh no. She held one hand like a fist, the other extended flat like an axe-blade: what Dave told me was the true karate stance. And, as she came on, Dave backed off, and I can't say I blame him. You see, he wasn't frightened, I knew that, but he's always been very chivalrous about women has Dave. He can't help it.

Anyway he backed off and she threw a fist strike and he swayed away from it smooth and graceful. When he's fighting he moves like a dancer – but then she threw another one and he didn't sway quite fast enough and I heard him gasp as he took it on his shoulder. It wasn't what she'd been aiming for, but it must have hurt, the noise he made. All the same he backed off again and she moved in for another try.

'Please, love,' he said. 'Don't make me–'

But she wasn't even hearing him. This time it was the other hand, the axe-blade, and she swung it hard to where he had been a split second before but was no longer. So she missed, and of all the hundred and one things Dave could have done to her, he pushed her away.

'Knock it off,' he said.

But she tried a kick instead, low and hard and

dirty, and Dave saw it coming and stuck his leg out, her shin smashed against his calf, and she screamed, piercing, shrill. Dave went to her.

'Are you all right?' he said.

She spat in his face and swung another fist-strike, but Dave's hand moved faster and she fell like he'd pulled a rug from under her. Then he knelt beside her.

'I'm sorry,' he said. 'You made me–'

And as he spoke the elegant one got fed up with lying in the gutter, found a knife from inside his shirt and moved up behind Dave. I found a bottle from the dustbin – Harvey's Amontillado, nice neighbourhood – and threw it hard and straight. It hit him on the back of the neck, and he went down. Dave whipped round fast, even before the bottle hit the roadway, and we both looked at the young geezer. He kept getting to his feet and trying to walk, then finding he couldn't and falling down again.

'Hallo, Dave,' I said. 'Thanks for your help.'

'Not at all,' he said. 'Thanks for yours.'

I moved forward, and found I was better at it than the young geezer. 'We'd better go over this lot,' I said.

'Yeah,' said Dave. 'Nice and quiet.'

He went over to the big one and knocked him down again. This time he didn't get up.

'And quick,' I said.

We got to work, the quickest and crudest way there was. Just lift everything and go through it later. Then we got in Dave's mini-cab, the Vaux-hall with appalling springs – and drove away from the carnage. As we left a man's voice behind us

134

called, 'What's going on out there?' He didn't sound as if he wanted to know all that much.

Dave said, 'I heard on the radio – about Kessler. So I rang you at Sabena's. She said you'd gone home. So I set off to join you and found that water-main doing tricks.'

'Just as well you did.'

'Your lucky night,' said Dave.

'Yes.'

I can't have sounded all that convincing, because Dave said, 'You and Sabena had a row?'

'Sort of.'

Dave found his way back to Lillie Road.

'Your place or mine?' he said.

'Yours.' Sutton might still have left a rozzer outside my house; one that was good at being nosey.

So we went to Dave's place and Dave made me a gin and tonic and poured himself a lager, then lit a cigarette.

'I'm sorry, Ron,' he said, 'but it's been a bit of a day.'

'Too true,' I said. 'Shall we see what we got first?'

Dave emptied the haul out of a Sainsbury's carrier from the car and on to the table. They were the most anonymous looking bunch I'd ever met, apart from about six hundred quid in notes and change. Four hundred of that was in fifty-pound notes, and one of them had been sliced in half then Sellotaped together. Otherwise all we had was fags and lighters, a couple of ballpoint pens and a lipstick. And two coshes and a hunting knife. Not a diary, not a letter, not even a driving licence. Of course there could have been stuff in their cars, but my guess was that those cars were hired what with their passion for security. What stuff they had they'd kept with them. There had to be something. I looked in the girl's handbag again, every compartment. Zilch.

'I hated duffing that bird,' said Dave.

'You had to,' I said.

'Yes, but even so—' He dragged on his cigarette and I tried not to breathe in. 'Another thing – I thought I'd seen her before.'

'You have,' I said. 'This afternoon. At Oxford.'

'The girl student?'

'That's right.'

'She had her back to us reading a notice.'

'All the same I'm right,' I said.

'You are,' he said. 'At least I think you are. Do you reckon she croaked poor old Kessler?'

'It wouldn't be all that difficult.'

'No, poor old sod,' said Dave. 'It wouldn't be difficult at all.'

I began to rip the handbag to bits. Some of the lining was torn, which made it easy, but where it was obstinate I used the hunting knife on it. While I was at it, Dave looked at the coshes. No more than bits of hosepipe really, with a lump of lead sealed in one end, and short enough to fit a pocket – or a handbag, which was where they'd come from.

'Home-made stuff,' said Dave. 'Crude—' he tapped his palm with one and winced '–but effective.'

I'd reached the last refuge of the handbag; the space between the lining and the leather, and sure enough there were things there. Like a new penny, and a paper-clip, and a pill that looked

136

like an amphetamine. And if they were clues I was in the wrong business.

Dave said, 'Let's see the knife', and I passed it over. He took his time with it. 'Nice,' he said at last. 'Very nice. Hunting knife. You could cut a deer's throat with that knife no trouble at all.'

'Or a middle-aged ex-RAF pilot's,' I said.

'Jesus,' said Dave, and looked again at the knife.

'I don't know all that much about these things,' he said. 'With guns they tell me it's different – an expert can tell when they've been fired even if you clean them as soon as you've pulled the trigger. But with a knife... I don't know. There might be tiny bloodstains – you know, minute–'

'Yeah,' I said. 'There might at that.'

He looked at it again. 'There's the maker's name on one side, as I said, and another name on the other. It says "Fayolle".' He spelled it. 'Then Châlon-S.C. d'O.' He spelled that too. 'Châlon-sur-Saône, that must be. Côte d'Or. France. Burgundy to be precise.'

'You reckon he was a Frog?'

'Could have been,' said Dave. 'But the bird wasn't.'

'Too true,' I said. 'Not with that accent.'

'Not that it makes any difference,' said Dave. 'We've still got a problem. That knife could be evidence. Vital evidence.'

Then he stubbed out his cigarette and I began to feel better.

'Very true,' I said, 'but we can't just hand it over to Sutton and say "Have this tested in the forensic lab", now can we?'

'Why not?'

'Because we were in Oxford this afternoon, that's why not. You fancy explaining that to Sutton?'

'So was she.'

'You know it and I know it, but it's two men the police are looking for.'

'Yeah,' said Dave. 'I remember.' Then he looked at his watch, got up and switched on the radio again, and twiddled till he found a news broadcast. We heard all about a plane crash in Bulgaria and a space-launch in Russia and a car bomb in Newry, County Down, and at last they got to Dr Kessler. The police were still anxious to interview two men who had called on him shortly before the murder. The college porter had described both men, but what it amounted to was nondescript appearance, with no particular accents or characteristics. All the same, if anyone could assist in their enquiries...

'What else could he say?' I said. 'He never even looked at us.'

'Sport,' the news-reader said. 'At close of play, Middlesex were–'

Dave switched the radio off.

'All the same we'll have to turn in the knife,' he said, and I knew he was right.

'Soon,' I said. 'Word of honour. I'm just not up to it tonight.'

By the look of relief on his face Dave wasn't up to it either.

'Now tell us about your girl-friend,' I said.

'Less of your sauce,' Dave said. 'My cause isn't exactly hopeless, you know.'

'Isn't it?'

'No it bloody isn't.' Swearing, I thought. He must be keen. 'I went over to see her, just like we agreed. Brave Dave Baxter, the fearless private eye.'

For the first time I realised he was wearing his best outfit; pale grey double-breasted suit, white shirt, Paratroop tie, almost-Gucci loafers. I hoped he hadn't damaged any of it. It would be on my bill.

'She likes private eyes?'

'Watches them all the time on the telly. The debonair, witty ones. So I was debonair and witty.'

'What did you tell her?'

'We'd been working for her old chum Benskin – she called him Uncle Bertie – till he was killed. And now – vengeance has been sworn.'

'So it has,' I said.

'Fair enough.' He took out a packet of cigarettes, looked at them and put them back. Heavy work, vengeance.

'She wished me – us – luck.'

'Finding Bertie's killer?'

'Yes.' His gaze went to the knife, then away. 'And the Dakota.'

'You told her about the Dak?'

'Of course not.' He was indignant, and quite right, too. 'She knew.'

'Who'd told her? Uncle Bertie?'

'Yeah,' said Dave. 'And, speaking of Benskin, don't you think you should phone the widow?'

'Why?'

'She knows we went to Oxford.'

'So she does,' I said. 'And she'll either tell the rozzers or she won't. If she hasn't she'll keep. If

139

she has they'll have left my place by now to come screaming over here. So go on about your Ange.'

'She asked me how much money there was in finding an old Dakota.'

'Did she act like she knew what was in it when it disappeared?'

'My guess is not – but I didn't want to press too hard. So I told her you handle the business end, but you'd see me right.'

'You need money, do you?'

'I said I'd take her to Stringfellow's,' said Dave.

'You need money. What else did you get?'

'The flat's nice. Just two rooms, but nice things. Especially one of the rugs. You'd have liked it. We had a drink. Lager for me. She had a Diet Pepsi.'

I let him go on. It's the only way he can tell things. Saves time in the long run.

'Then the phone rang. She took the call in the bedroom. I listened – but the door was too good a fit. So I took a look round instead.'

'And?'

'Lots of cards on the mantelpiece. Invitations, you know. What the Sloane Rangers call "stiffies".'

Don't ask me how he knows what the Sloane Rangers call things. He's a good-looking lad.

'All to parties and things. Nobody we knew. But under a paperweight – one of those glass-ball snowstorm things – there was a pile of postcards. There must have been dozens. The kind you send on holidays. You know – "Wish you were here" sort of thing.'

'No fat ladies?'

'Views,' he said. 'Views of places I want to go to. Like Arles and Florence and Sardinia and Klosters. And one of Venice. Or quite near, anyway.'

'How near's that?'

'You tell me,' he said. 'It was a picture of the Villa Malcontenta on the Brenta Canal.'

'Did you nick it?'

He looked shocked. 'Of course not.'

With Dave, love will always be a problem.

'Just as well,' I said. 'We don't want you blown. Not yet. Was there a message?'

Dave screwed up his eyes. He was concentrating. 'All well. Missing you. Home soon. Bobsy.'

'Popsy?'

'Bobsy. B-O-B-S-Y. Man's writing, I think.'

'Postmark?'

'Venice. Date May 23rd.'

The day I'd had a visitor at Abano Terme: a visitor with a gun and four thousand nine hundred and fifty quid.

'And then?'

'She came back in. Said she had to go and see George Watkins.'

'And so?'

'I drove her there.'

'I'm listening.'

'Nothing fancy. As you say, it's Notting Hill,' Dave said. 'All the same he's loaded.'

'How d'you know?'

'Drives a new Porsche. His watch is a Cartier – and I'd like the name of his tailor for when I make my first million. Also he'd bought her a necklace.'

'How d'you know?'

'I saw it,' he said. 'She took me in with her. Never saw such a place. Wall to wall computers... The necklace was diamonds and rubies – just

141

right for her colour. Must have cost thousands.'

'How did she explain you?'

'Said she'd hired me as a minder, on account of the necklace.'

'Did he believe her?'

'Too true,' said Dave. 'He has to believe her whatever she says... He's scared of her.'

'She's got something on him?'

'I don't think so,' said Dave. 'I reckon it's just her. He enjoys being scared of her. He's the doormat type. He's doing a job for her.'

'What sort of job?'

'He started to tell her. "About that job you gave me," he said. Only she shut him up. Curt, you might say. Very curt. "We mustn't bore Mr Baxter," she said. And he gave a sort of slavish look. The poor sod.'

'And then?'

'I drove her home,' Dave said. 'He didn't even get to kiss her.' By the look on his face I gathered Dave had.

'And then?'

'I saw her safe inside and left.'

'Pity,' I said. 'I could have done with a bit more about the job he's doing for her.'

'I wouldn't have got it from her,' said Dave. 'And anyway – it was just as well I didn't dawdle. I came straight round to you.'

I looked at the knife, the coshes, the jumble of money. 'Don't think I'm not grateful,' I said. 'Now about tomorrow–'

'Where are we going?'

'The Hebrides,' I said.

9

There'd been no police watching the house, or if there were they'd been coy. So all I had for company was my nightmares about being belted, and the even worse ones about withholding evidence. From the cops – and from Michael Copland. There'd been a message from him on my tape. Very upset he was. After all he'd done for me – then not a word. Curt wasn't in it...

Dave came and picked me up just as I was finishing breakfast. He wore the suit again, just like I told him. His other gear was in the car. I had stuff to take as well. Only with me it was a bit of a problem. Like I said, my place could still be watched in a coy sort of way. So in the end what we did was carry out my biggest suitcase with the little one inside it – give them something worthwhile to worry about – and made a big deal out of putting it in the car boot and locking and checking. Then off we went like we hadn't a care in the world and Dave kept checking his mirror and he drove around looking businesslike and I kept looking at street maps. The nearest we got to the Hebrides was Mendelssohn on Radio 3.

We had two cars for company, an ageing but immaculate Jaguar and a Ford Sierra that had a few engine modifications that gave it the take-off speed of a missile. Either one could have eaten Dave's Vauxhall for breakfast, and I wished, not for the first time, that we were rich like George Watkins and owned a Porsche. Only we didn't need it, not with Dave driving. After a bit I looked at my watch when the Jag could see me and Dave made for the West End. The Jag and the Sierra settled down to follow: Cromwell Road and Brompton Road and the underpass, and us off up West and not a care in the world.

We turned off by the Mayfair Hotel and Dave got lucky. On our way through Shepherd Market a furniture van pulled in behind us and sealed off the road like a cork in a bottle. Dave set off back down Park Lane and into the underground car-park. Two minutes to get my little case out of the big one, then a number 73 bus, upstairs, because Dave wanted a smoke, and anyway you get a better view from there – like an unmarked police Jaguar with a driver and his mate looking into every taxi, and scared what Sutton might say. That made twice we'd ditched a police tail in three days. No wonder they looked worried.

At Kensington High Street we got off and walked round the corner where the hotels are and got a taxi to Heathrow and Terminal One and the Glasgow shuttle.

On the way north, Dave said, 'I've never been to Scotland.'

'Me neither,' I said. It was daft. I'd been all over Europe, to the States and Hong Kong and Australia, but the furthest north I'd ever been in my own country was Cambridge.

'Ah well,' Dave said, 'it can't be any worse than Northern Ireland.'

That was not the attitude, and I told him so:

but then what was the attitude?

We'd come to look for criminals on a scale so vast they made Capone seem like a sneak thief. We were going to seek evidence perhaps of murder, betrayal, certainly violent death. And the chance of wealth, too. More than a chance: the proceeds of brutal routine: removal of wedding rings, watches, even gold fillings. Not even Northern Ireland could be worse than that.

Dave said, 'What are we going to do if we find anything?'

'You mean like tell the rozzers,' I said.

'Like we did with that hunting-knife.'

'All I'm asking is a little time,' I said.

'It's just – I saw him,' said Dave. 'I've seen plenty, I know that. And some of them looked a damn sight worse than he did – but that was a war. You expect it. But with him–'

'That was a war too,' I said. 'It should have been over more than forty years ago, but for him it wasn't...'

Choppers Ltd sent their entire board of directors to meet us: two hard young men who looked very like Air-Vice Marshal Cattell, which wasn't surprising. They were his nephews. Nephew Nigel had a piece of white card with my name on it. He took my luggage and headed off through arrivals to the lounge. Nephew Martin took Dave's case and followed to a neat little Japanese truck marked Choppers Ltd, and we drove away from the glitz and glamour of Glasgow Airport to the harsh world of commerce, the charter area for ageing jets and turbo-prop transports – there was even a converted Comet 4B that the young men found

145

embarrassing, as if it were a fading beauty refusing to acknowledge the onset of age – and then at last the pride and joy of Choppers Ltd, the flagship and maybe the only ship, a French Gazelle that gleamed as if it were polished every day of its life. Having seen its owners, my guess is it probably was.

They'd worked out a flight plan and I passed it to Dave to okay it, because this time he was as vulnerable as me – you can't use kung fu on a helicopter...Then we went aboard, Martin tested the straps, Nigel took the controls and the engine fired and I suppose the rotors spun. I was much too afraid to find out.

I hate helicopters. Maybe it's the noise, which is shattering, or their closeness to the ground, or maybe it's just that *flimsy* look they have no matter how big they are – not that this one was big – but, whatever it is, it scares me. It was different for Dave: in Ulster he spent half his life in the rotten things; but I was scared. We had a way to go, too: more than a hundred and twenty miles over Oban and the Sound of Mull, then on to South Uist, land that was all grey heather, and sea that was all grey water. And then the sun came out, and the sea gleamed green, and the heather when it came was blue and pink and grey all at once. Beyond North Uist then, and the chopper began to dance its way down: journey's end until we had to do it all again in reverse and go back to Glasgow.

We landed on Culm, first having made a tour of Moyra, which must have taken all of seven minutes. Moyra was awful: a shapeless mass that

146

rose straight out of the sea: grey stone outcrops for the most part, covered here and there by grey lichen. Not a bird, not a flower, not a blade of grass, not even a weed. The only sign of humanity – though it was humanity long departed – was a series of notice-boards that had been erected here and there on clifftops and headlands, facing out to sea. What they had once said I had no idea, – I could guess: Danger. Keep Out. This Island Kills ... But now it looked like part of a corpse that had killed itself. It was a relief to land on Culm.

To begin with there were birds. They were messy, they were noisy, especially when the chopper landed, but at least they were alive. Then we landed on grass, and walked on wild flowers. There was even a committee of welcome, which shook me a bit. That hadn't been in my script. No way. But it was there: a man emerged from a clump of trees: in his forties, but fit with it, wearing about five hundred quid's worth of Tommy Nutter clothes, hand-lasted shoes, Omega watch and a shotgun that looked as if it would cost more than suit and watch together. Behind him was an old, stone-built house that looked as if it had survived the winters of four centuries and was ready for the next four, and, behind the house, grass that sloped down till it became a beach, and a stone mole that lay at angles to the beach, and riding at anchor by the mole a thirty-foot cruiser at say ten thousand pounds a foot.

The man made a gesture with the shotgun that could have been welcoming or equally easily have been a threat. Dave wasn't in any doubt. He hadn't any weapon handy so his whole body was a weapon. I took a quick look at Nigel and Martin. They had a kind of wary toughness about them that reminded me of their uncle. But it was our new chum who had the shotgun.

'Nice of you to drop in,' he said. 'I was just out to see if I could get a few rabbits.' This was so staggeringly obvious a lie that even Dave blinked. I gawped like a yokel at a freak show. Out after rabbits in those clothes, those shoes?

He was a well-built man, not so tall as Dave but thicker, hard-muscled, and somehow very Scots: red hair turning grey, eyes of a darker grey, hands that had worked hard in their time.

'My name's Finlayson,' he said.

The Scots accent was held back, but it was there. Something else was there too: he was drunk, which explained what Dave called the lie's ineptitude.

'Nice day for shooting,' I said.

I didn't know whether it was or not, but I had to say something or he might start blasting.

He giggled instead. 'It could be,' he said. I could see it was going to be one of those days.

'You live here?' I asked him.

'If you call it living,' he said. 'That's my place there.' He gestured at the farmhouse.

'Your boat as well?' said Dave.

'My boat as well,' said Finlayson. 'What's it to you, nosey?'

'Nothing,' said Dave. 'It looks like a nice boat, that's all.'

At once Finlayson was mollified.

'It is a nice boat,' he said. 'As a matter of fact it's a very nice boat indeed. You going to Moyra,

148

by any chance?'

'That's right,' I said. 'We're reporters. We think there may be a story there.'

'Oh, there is,' said Finlayson. 'Believe me. A very sad story... I'll let you get to it.'

He moved off, not showing his back to us, to where his very nice boat was waiting. When he'd got aboard we began to take the stuff from the chopper: the inflatable and cylinders from the box that Nigel and Martin had brought, and the wet-suit from my suitcase. Nigel and Martin watched. They were good at it, but all the same I made them help Dave and me down to the water's edge with the gear. Finlayson sat in a lounging chair and watched us sweat. From time to time he would lift a large glass of what looked like whisky and toast our endeavours, but the shotgun never strayed far from his hands.

At last we had done, and the boat was inflated, Dave had stepped the outboard engine while I stripped and put on the wet-suit. Dave changed into shirt and jeans. From the power-boat Finlayson applauded and I blew him a kiss, then I strapped on the cylinders.

Martin said, 'Will you be long?'

'It'll be light for hours yet,' I said.

'You're paying by the hour,' said Nigel.

Dave said, 'Then you've no worries, have you?' They looked at him and were silent, and we pushed off.

The engine fired at the third try, which saved us from humiliation at least. Dave said, 'Straight over?' and I nodded. He aimed us at the island, and we yelled opinions about Finlayson. Most of them were just routine insults, but I came up with one that had a bit more sense to it, so I kept it to myself. He worried me...

I'd brought a pair of Japanese binoculars with me; small but powerful, like the Japanese are, and as we got near I got busy with them, and it was just the way it had been from the air, bare as a skinhead's skull, and about as charming as a tumour. Here and there were small black cliffs like fungus, pierced now and again with caves. I made a waving motion with my arm and Dave took the inflatable round the island and it was all as we had first seen it: not one living thing. We reached a patch of shingle at last and Dave said 'This do you?' and I said 'Why not?' and he ran us aground and got out dry-shod and I followed, and we hauled the inflatable out of the water, then Dave took off for a recce round the caves, and I sat and worried about my idea.

When Dave came back he looked as worried as me.

'What's up?' I asked.

'This place,' he said. 'It gives me the willies. It's not just that it's dead. It's as if it had never lived.'

'I know what you mean,' I said.

'Then why did we come here?'

'Because it's all there is,' I said. 'There's nowhere else to go. If it isn't here–' But it has to be here, I thought. If it isn't we've had it.

Dave put on his long-suffering face, but we shoved off even so, and started looking for the dark water we would have to have. But the first time it was a shelf of rock, and the second time it was a sunken boat. Third time lucky, I thought,

150

and we went on looking, but there wasn't a third time, and I was too tired to dive any more.

Nigel and Martin stood waiting on the shore, looking happy because we were so obviously empty-handed, and suddenly I couldn't stand it.

'Go back,' I said.

'I thought you were tired,' Dave said.

'I've just had a rest,' I said, then Dave too saw the sad consoling smiles that Nigel and Martin were trying on for size, and put the inflatable about, or whatever it is you do.

We went back towards the shingle because we had to start somewhere, but this time we tried a bit farther out. My muscles ached and my bones ached and the cold was beginning to get to me, but on the other hand Dave was watching. So I checked I hadn't forgotten my torch, fell in the way they'd taught me, and went down for a look. Down, down, down, down to the depths of the sea, like in the poem I learned at school. Not that it was all that far down, not really. I mean I did use the torch because it was handy, but I could have managed without it if I'd had to. I mean there was plenty of light to see that I'd found an aeroplane with blokes in it. Third time lucky...

It was an old plane, more than forty years old, and sizeable – bigger than a fighter anyway – with what was left of two blokes up front, which was a good beginning. And behind them more blokes, five of them, sprawled all over the place. But no seats... Even better. If Palliser's theory about lifting out SS men was right, there'd been no time – or opportunity – to put in seats. They'd have had to sit on what they'd brought. And that was when

151

things started to go wrong. They hadn't brought anything – or rather there was nothing there except their bones and a few pieces of cloth and boot by the time I got down to them. And the reason for that was obvious. There was a dirty great hole in the aircraft's side where some other joker had got in before me and taken out whatever it was the deceased had been sitting on.

I did something nasty. I went in through the dirty great hole and examined the deceased one by one. I'd never seen a more deprived lot of corpses. Not a ring, not a wristwatch between them. I swam forward to the pilots' section and my light showed me what was left of the instrument panel. 'McDonnell Douglas', it said and 'DC3', so I'd got the right aircraft, or at least the right make. But that wasn't so important by then...

I did something nastier. I pushed the navigator's remains to one side and looked around. Nothing. I told him 'Sorry' and did the same to the pilot, who was slightly smaller, but jammed against the aircraft's side so that I had to use more pressure and I could feel the bones begin to separate. I eased off and tried again, pulling him away, and he sort of floated free, one arm drifted towards the navigator as if he was saying look what this bastard's doing to me. But he was sitting, as the saying goes, on a fortune. All it looked like was a neat box wrapped in canvas, but it was a fortune. It had to be. I told him sorry too and did what I could for his arm, then grabbed the box and swam free. It was either that or vomit.

The world had never looked sweeter, and the inflatable seemed like a heavenly chariot. Even

Dave – no, that's going too far. Not even that day did Dave look like an angel. For what was to come he looked better than that. He took the canvas-covered box from me, I flopped aboard and we were on our way. When I'd got the mask off Dave flicked a look at me and then his eyes went back to our course. One look was enough.

'Rough?' he said.

'I wish I still smoked,' I said.

'It must have been rough. I take it you found the Dakota?'

'I found *a* Dakota,' I said, then told him a lot more, in detail.

The main problem was what to do with the box when we got back to Culm. There was a plastic sheet we could cover it with, but then it would just look like a box covered by a plastic sheet. As it happened we got lucky. When we ran the inflatable back ashore Nigel and Martin were busy doing an overhaul on the helicopter. By the time they'd put back whatever had to be put back the box was in my suitcase and I was changing. Finlayson's cruiser had left the beach and was out to sea, but motionless, marking the point of a 'V' between the two islands. Nigel and Martin came over to join us as I pulled my pants on and tried not to think about how much I needed a drink.

'Everything okay?' said Nigel.

'Why not?' I said.

'I mean can we go back to Glasgow now?' said Nigel.

'Just as soon as we pack the inflatable,' said Dave, and they noticed his use of the word 'we' and sulked. All the same they helped. As a matter

153

of fact they did most of the work. They'd also noticed Dave.

When we'd loaded the chopper Martin said, 'Finlayson came back ashore and went to his house. Then he left a message for you.'

'What did he say?'

'He said, "Mi casa es su casa,"' said Martin. His face wore the half-embarrassed, half-resentful look of the true Brit forced to communicate in a foreign tongue.

My other language is Italian, on account of that's what my mother was, but I knew enough Spanish to cope with that, and anyway I'd once stayed in a hotel in Beverly Hills where it was written on every blank space.

'My house is yours,' I said.

'Pity he didn't say his boat,' said Dave.

'Let's look at the house.'

We set off, and Nigel and Martin followed. For all I knew, they'd been over the place a dozen times already, but there wasn't much I could do about it except turn Dave loose, and that was out. We needed Nigel and Martin to fly the chopper.

We reached the front door of the house but Dave somehow seemed to get ahead of me without meaning to. His hand reached out and pushed, and the door swung open. Dave eased in as easily as oil flowing, and after he said 'okay' I followed, and then Nigel and Martin. We were in a square, flagged hallway that might well have functioned as a living-room too, but there was no way of telling. The room was empty. Completely. Ahead of us was a flight of stairs, and on the floor, painted on the flagstones in red, the two words 'Al Bar' and an arrow pointing. To the bar. It began to look as if Finlayson had been to the Costa Brava.

Dave said, 'You want me to look upstairs?'

'Take it easy,' I said.

'Sure,' said Dave, then turned to Nigel and Martin. 'You too,' he said. 'Remember Mr Hogget's the boss.' His feet made no sound as he climbed the stairs.

'What are you up to, Mr Hogget?' Nigel said.

'Visiting,' I said. He sighed, and they said no more and we waited in silence till Dave came down again.

'Same as here,' he said. 'Not a damn thing.' It bothered him so much that he lit a cigarette, and Nigel and Martin looked shocked, and I suppose I did too.

'Let's look at the bar,' said Dave, and we followed the arrow to another door, another stone-flagged, empty room.

'Dining-room?' said Nigel.

'Probably,' said Martin. Both were looking at a door facing them, an old four-plank door like all the others, and painted white just as they were, but on this one the same red paint had written 'Bar' and underneath 'Libre'. Free bar... The end of the rainbow to my old man. His Holy Grail. Dave moved forward and depressed the old-fashioned latch and shoved. The door swung open.

We were looking at a refrigerator powered by bottled gas. Dave went in and I followed and froze. The room was the house's kitchen: and it was furnished – in a way. Sink and taps, and an antique stove that used the same bottled gas as the fridge – and an old deal table and five hard old chairs.

155

One was empty. On the others were four tailors' dummies. And three of them wore civilian suits, and wide-brimmed soft hats like the kind you see in old movies, and the fourth wore a flying jacket and padded pants and a helmet that made him look like Biggles's kid brother. Each of them had a glass within reach, and playing cards in their hands. Poker. 'Jesus,' said Martin, and I can't say I blame him. He'd had a shock.

I looked at the hands. All four had rubbish. The best was the pilot, and all he could manage was a pair of tens. But in front of the empty chair was an empty glass, and beside it another poker hand, four aces and a king.

Dave said 'Ron' and nodded at the fridge. More red lettering on the door, 'Bebidos Libres' – 'Free Drinks'. I took a deep breath and pulled it open, before Dave could move. It was my turn to take a risk. After all, Dave had said I was the boss, so I had to lead from in front. Now and again, any-way. In the fridge was a pack of clear plastic glasses and a bottle of champagne. Dom Pérignon, 1978. Nothing more.

I lifted it out and examined the bottle and the foil cap. Both were intact. All it was was a bottle of very expensive champers, so I took out the plastic glasses and removed four. Why not? It was Dom Pérignon and it was free. If Finlayson had bought it retail it was worth ten quid a glass. I poured.

'What is this?' said Nigel. Martin was still being upset by the dummies.

'The best champagne you'll get today,' said Dave. 'Cheers.'

Nigel gulped, and a few seconds later Martin did the same.

'What I mean is,' said Nigel, 'it looks fishy to me.'

'Define "fishy",' said Dave, and Nigel gawked. He hadn't thought the word 'define' belonged in Dave's mouth.

'Not right,' he said at last.

'Criminal?' I asked him.

'Well... Yes.'

'Where's the crime?' asked Dave.

'Finlayson had a gun,' said Nigel. 'And all this. Empty house... Red paint... Blood red... And these dummies. I mean look at them. They could be the work of a psychopath...'

'Psychopaths can't be criminals,' said Dave, 'on account of diminished responsibility.'

Again Nigel gawked. This time Martin joined him.

'I know what's bothering them,' I said, and topped up the glasses.

Dave was straight man at once.

'You do?' he said.

'They want more money.'

'But why?'

'Because they think they can get it.' I turned to Nigel. 'Don't you?'

'Well, you must admit it all looks jolly fishy,' he said. 'Maybe we ought to report it to the police. After all we have got licences to lose–'

'Report what?' Dave asked.

'This.' Nigel gestured at the poker game. 'Maybe psychopaths aren't criminals, but the police still like to know about them. Then there's your skin-

157

diving act.'

'What about it?'

Dave again. I don't know how he does it, but the way he said those three words frightened me, never mind Nigel.

Nigel floundered.

'It just seems odd, that's all. Diving off a deserted island. Getting us to hire your gear.'

'You said you'd get us a good price,' said Dave. 'It wasn't bad at that.'

'I still think the police should be told,' said Nigel, and looked at his brother. 'Right, Martin?'

'Oh, absolutely,' said Martin. The prospect of money acted on him like smelling salts.

'You were told,' said Dave, 'that we were doing research for a paper on Post-War Britain.' Nigel didn't quite sneer.

'We found some,' said Dave.

'So you say.'

I got the feeling Dave was about to get physical, so I shared what was left of the Dom Pérignon out and said, 'You chaps get on well with your uncle?' They didn't seem to know the answer to that.

'But then you have to, don't you? He's got a seventy per cent stake in Choppers Ltd.'

'How do you know?' Martin asked.

'He told me... Seventy per cent means he's the boss. He asked for your co-operation. And your discretion. And that's what I'm asking.' I turned to Dave. 'Give them another fifty quid.'

He looked surprised, but peeled off five tens. Actually it made sense. Fifty quid was a) a bribe I could tell the Air-Vice Marshal about, and hence a gag on Nigel and Martin, and b) it was Palliser's money, not mine. I finished my drink. 'Now take us home,' I said.

10

The helicopter took off and the clouds parted and the sun came through as we waltzed across the sky for one last lingering look at Moyra and Finlayson's still motionless cruiser, before levelling off for Glasgow. The racket seemed even louder on the way back, and I wished there'd been more champagne. I was petrified till the thing got down, and Dave went out on the jump the way they'd taught him in the Paras, and helped Nigel and Martin unload our cases. I was past helping anybody with anything. Those dead men in the Dak had finally caught up with me. I was shaking so much when I got out I nearly tripped over the chopper's skis – or whatever they call the things it lands on. Dave took one look at me, then led the way to the nearest bar, and bought me a large brandy and a lager for himself.

'Delayed reaction?' he asked, and I nodded, and tried not to spill the cognac.

'Nothing wrong with that,' said Dave. 'Take your time.' It took another large brandy, but I was rational at last: or as rational as I ever am.

'You want to talk now?' said Dave.

'I have to,' I said. 'It's not the dead men though–'

'It's that box,' he said, and I nodded. 'Like the knife,' he said.

'Could be,' I said.

'It must be,' said Dave. 'It's all there was.'

For a geezer with a good degree Dave can be slow sometimes.

'It's all there was when I went down,' I said. 'I reckon there was five cases missing.'

'Missing where?'

'The passengers didn't go empty-handed,' I said, 'and the pilot had a spare outfit somewhere – he must have had. It was on the dummy.'

'That's right,' said Dave. 'Those dummies were all dressed right – smart even. They didn't look as if the clothes had been in salt water.'

'Their cases must have all been water-proofed,' I said.

'Finlayson?' Dave asked.

'Who else?' I said. 'And it wouldn't just be clothes. Thirty-foot cruisers don't come cheap.'

'So what do you reckon's in that box?'

'The pay-off,' I said. 'Finlayson got the rest, but he missed that one.'

'Ron,' said Dave. 'I don't see how we can keep it quiet. It's as bad as the knife.'

'It could be a whole lot worse,' I said.

Dave lit a cigarette then, his fifth that day.

'So Benskin was wrong,' he said. 'About Day and Denville, I mean.'

I shrugged. 'Looks like it.' Then I yawned. More delayed reaction. 'I'm glad it's over.'

'Me too,' said Dave. He looked me over, assessing how much more I could take. Apparently the answer was quite a lot.

'We were shot at when we flew over Moyra,' he said.

'Finlayson?'

'Could be,' said Dave. 'But it would take something with a bit more range than that shotgun.'

'You'd better tell it,' I said.

'You remember the caves?'

'Of course.'

'There must have been dozens,' said Dave. 'Some just about big enough to hide that box in, some big enough to accommodate that poker game. I went over the lot.' He paused, then added: 'You believe that?'

'Of course,' I said. 'If you say so.'

'I'm saying so. And every one I went into was empty. Some I back-tracked on, but they were still empty the second time. Even the third.'

'So?'

'So there was somebody else in those caves.'

'You get a sign? A footprint or something?'

'I got zero,' said Dave. 'Zilch. All the same there was somebody there. Believe me, Ron, I know. I have to know. If I didn't know I'd be dead.'

'You're saying he's good?' I said, and Dave nodded.

'The best,' he said.

'What was he doing there do you suppose?' I asked him.

'Watching us,' said Dave. 'Seeing how we shaped up.'

'And now he knows,' I said. 'My God, Dave, why didn't you tell me before?'

'Before you'd dived, maybe?' Dave said. 'Or maybe after you'd dived? You had enough of your own stuff to worry about.'

'Tell me about the shot,' I said.

'It was when that Nigel took us over Moyra,' Dave said. 'I looked down to see if I could see him but of course I couldn't. He's far too good. But I did get a kind of flash that might have been metal. You remember how the sun came up just then?' I nodded. 'It must have been a rifle of some sort,' Dave continued. 'So, when we got down I took a walk round the chopper. There's a dent on the side of one of the skids.'

'We're lucky he missed,' I said.

'I don't think he did miss,' said Dave. 'I think he fired that shot as a warning. Watch our step, so to speak.'

'But supposing we hadn't seen him?' I said. 'After all you're the only one who did.'

'So far,' said Dave. 'But Nigel and Martin will spot it. That chopper's their whole life.'

'They mightn't tell us,' I said.

'They'll tell their uncle,' said Dave. 'Sooner or later it will get to us.'

I didn't want to believe him but I had no choice.

'It isn't over at all, is it, Ron?' Dave asked.

'No way,' I said.

I found a phone that took a British Telecom call card, and began making calls. There was a load of things still to be done, and because it wasn't over I had to start doing them... On the shuttle back to Heathrow we worked out our next moves. We would split, I said, and Dave would carry the luggage, take a taxi to the West End and pick up his car, if he wasn't being tailed, and if he was it would

162

be the third time in three days and he'd have to ad lib something. In the meantime I would take the Tube to South Kensington and do a little research in the Benskin library – if *I* wasn't being tailed. And if I was then I'd have to ad lib too.

Dave said, 'When you say I take the cases, do you mean the box as well?'

'Well of course,' I said. 'You don't suppose I want to lug it all the way to Jocasta Benskin's, do you?'

'You really must trust me,' said Dave.

'What choice have I got?' I asked him.

A bit later Dave said, 'Is it all right if I have a go at opening it up?'

'I doubt if I could stop you,' I said.

Then the plane touched down and there was nobody waiting for us, which wasn't all that surprising. Even a prodnose like Sutton would think it was a bit early for us to flee the country, and even if he had done he'd be watching departures, not arrivals.

Just before we split Dave said, 'I wonder where Finlayson's off to?'

'Somewhere where they speak Spanish,' I said.

And they'd never heard of extradition. Dave lifted the cases and set off for the taxi queue. 'See you, Ron.'

'Hasta la vista,' I said.

Outside the flat in South Ken I took my time but it didn't seem to me that the place was being watched. No loiterers, nobody looking for a phone booth, nobody sitting in a parked car, yawning. Time for Ron to go to work. So I went inside and told the porter I was expected, and the porter decided I looked solvent enough for him to risk a phone call.

She didn't like me. The chances were that she would never like me, not even if I learned to wiggle my ears. I didn't belong in the household of a lady – or at least in that of someone who'd been married to a gentleman poking and prodding and sticking my nose in. She didn't like my calling her Beverly either, but that was the only name I knew. I mean I could hardly call her Miss Brisk, now could I?

'You're to work in the study,' she said at last.

'That's right,' I said.

I got another one of her looks for that. When it came to what was right and what wasn't in that house, she was the one who decided.

'This way,' she said, and led off down the corridor. Her blonde hair was smooth and glowing, and she walked with a bit of a wiggle that must be built in, I thought. She couldn't be putting it on, not for me. Which brought me back to why she didn't like me. I mean I may not be the answer to every girl's prayers, I thought, but I'm not that bad. Ask Jocasta. And there was a slip of the Freudian kind. I should have been telling myself to ask Sabena. But, whoever I should have asked, Beverly's dislike was excessive, and it worried me.

We reached Benskin's study, and it was the same spectacular mess as the last time, except for some additions on the enormous desk: keys for cupboards and filing cabinets, a bottle of Gordon's gin, and another of Schweppes's tonic, and ice in a bucket and lemon ready sliced, and smoked salmon sandwiches and a bottle of white wine in a cooler, a Sud Tiroler Pinot Grigio.

'Mrs Benskin said I should tell you that she hoped you liked smoked salmon.' For her part, her voice implied, I could choke to death on the first mouthful.

'Love it,' I said.

'I'll leave you to it then.' She turned away.

'Where will you be?' I asked her. 'Just in case I need you.'

It was a fair question but she found her own way of answering.

'If I'm needed,' she said, 'just lift the phone and press the red button and we'll talk.'

She turned again and was gone, and I looked at what remained of Bertie Benskin's life. He'd gone well towards his three score and ten, and here was the evidence to prove it. I awarded myself one gin and tonic before I got down to work. Bertie's had been a rich, full life.

And he'd kept everything. There were perhaps a thousand books and at least nine hundred of them were about aeroplanes. One of them, the most recent, had a fifty-pound note in it, apparently serving as a bookmark. It was one of the most extraordinary examples I'd ever seen of what it must feel like to be really rich. I ploughed on.

There were theatre tickets and tax demands and the menus of squadron reunion dinners: there were wine-lists and old diaries and address books and an attempt – soon abandoned – at a Teach Yourself German course: there were golf scores and bank statements and share prospectuses and outdated season tickets. And letters from what seemed like a thousand girls. Photographs too. And every single one of them was pretty. Bertie had done all right, even before Jocasta. The letters ranged from the cloyingly sentimental to the frankly carnal, but none I looked at said anything about Dakotas. I went through the photographs: the earliest ones in uniform, WAAFS and ATS and WRNS, then others in tweeds or swimsuits or ballgowns: one in nothing at all. I tried them for names: lots of Bettys and Carolines and Helens – but not too many surnames. They hadn't been feeling all that formal when they sent him a letter with their picture enclosed.

Then I found one of Wendy Lawrence, now Palliser. And Denville. It had to be. They were seated at a table in what I guessed to be Hatchett's, sharing a bottle of champagne with Bertie and yet another bird. On the back she'd written: 'Dear Bertie, Frank asked me to send you this. It *was* a super night, wasn't it? Love. Wendy.'

Champagne and a posh club and New Look finery for the girls. Things must have been going well. Berlin Airlift, I thought, and continued to look for a reference, *any* reference, to Dakotas. There was none. None that I could find anyway. A 1957 diary – he'd won a packet at Goodwood that year; an appeal for the Cheshire Homes – he'd sent a hundred quid. It was written on the letter. A whole stack of business letters from Palliser, all telling him what to do, but no Dakotas.

I looked at my watch. It was nearly ten o'clock and for once I wished I enjoyed smoking, so I had a sandwich and a glass of wine instead. The sandwiches were delicious: brown bread buttered just right and cress and a squeeze of lemon on the salmon. Delicious. No wonder Jo Benskin clung on to Beverly... I just hoped she hadn't used ground glass as well as black pepper, and looked around the room, trying to imagine I was Bertie Benskin, flyer, hero, lover of women, all-round good egg – and a killer, too. They'd given him a medal for it. His weapon had been the plane he flew, and I tried to think of him up there, cold inside his heavy flying gear, watching while the searchlights probed the sky like blades, and the pretty little fireworks flashing down below were the bombs he'd dropped on them, the shells they'd fired at him. There was no evidence of that Bertie in all the stuff I'd looked at. And then I realised that there was. The room was full of it, on every wall. The pictures of planes. The Wellington and the Lancaster – the ones he'd fought from – and the Spitfires and the Hurricanes of chums Palliser and Day. Only Denville didn't get a mention, I thought. And then suddenly he did. On the wall above where the collection of *Flight* magazines was stacked. Denville had his place in the room too. There was a picture of a Dakota.

I was on my way to it, hands outstretched, as avid as a junkie for his fix, when the door opened and Miss Brisk came in. I carried on past the Dakota picture to the filing cabinet, and took out the household account file for 1978, and leafed through it trying to look absorbed.

'I was wondering if you'd finished your meal,' said Beverly Brisk.

'Thank you,' I said. 'It was delicious. If you wouldn't mind leaving the wine.'

167

She gave me a look that assured me that all her worst suspicions were confirmed and left me to it. I waited for a few minutes in case she sneaked back on me, then lifted down the photograph and began to take it to bits. I did this very carefully because when I'd done I had to put it all together again, and all the tools I had were a pocket screwdriver and a nail file, and Bertie's desk set.

At last I got there. The treasure was between the photograph and its grey cardboard backing, put in flat so you'd never know it was there. More photographs the treasure was, grainy and amateurish and old, but I was long past being choosy. I put the Dak photo back together and hung it up again, then got down to work. The first one was another picture of a Dak, but on the ground this time, with a group of blokes in flying gear. Bill Day I recognised at once – because I'd already seen a picture of him when he was young – then Denville for the same reason. The other two I knew had to be Palliser and Bertie, but it took some believing – especially of Bertie. In the photograph he looked like a good heavyweight in the middle of training. Next to Bertie, wearing overalls, was Kessler. Like the others he was grinning hard into the camera, as if life could not possibly be better.

The other photograph was of Palliser and Bertie and a couple of geezers I'd never seen before. They were at the bar of a nightclub, and one of the blokes was taller than Palliser, and the other one shorter, and as Palliser was average height they were a tall bloke and a short bloke. They were also flyers. I don't know how I knew they were, but they were. Bertie, who'd obviously had a few, was

168

pretending to shoot the short one, using his hand as a pistol the way kids do. Palliser looked as if he was adding up the bill in his head, and the tall stranger was looking at a couple of girls who weren't wearing very much who appeared to be singing. The nightclub was about as anonymous as a nightclub could be, but the girls, I was sure, were German, just as I was sure the strangers were airmen. One box Brownie masterpiece, and one nightclub flash souvenir. West Berlin, I thought. Tempelhof Airport and whatever version of the 'Blue Angel' those tenth-rate Marlene Dietrichs infested. Back to West Berlin and the airlift – and two more flyers to look for. On the back of the AA Airline snap was written 'Aunty Bessie. Palmerston Street'. Bertie Benskin's writing. Kessler had told us Bill Day had said that. Bertie had said, 'Messing about in boats.' I'd messed about in a boat and found a Dakota...

I realised I was nodding and sat up straight in my chair. Not even eleven o'clock yet, but I'd had a trying day. All the same, there was still work to be done. I took the Hurricane's picture apart and there was nothing. In the Lancaster there were two photographs: a girl dressed in the fashion of the 1940s, and Jocasta in the fashion of the 1980s. The first and the last, I thought, and how prophetic he was. I put the picture back and opened up the Spitfire. Three photographs, this time: Palliser, Bill Day, and the little fellow at the nightclub, all in flying suits, and all laughing. On the back of Palliser's picture just the words: 'He can't help it'; on Day's there was a question mark, heavily crossed out; on the little chap's three letters: RIP.

169

I added the happy snaps to my collection, hung up the photograph and stood up and yawned. There was nothing left to do now except think, and I was far too bushed for that. I lifted the phone and pressed the red button instead.

A voice said, 'Mm?'

'I've finished for tonight,' I said.

'Oh, no you haven't,' said Jocasta Benskin. 'You come in here at once.'

So I asked her where she was, and I knew it was a stupid question even as I asked it.

'In the bedroom,' she said. 'Where else?'

So I went there. It was either that or run away, and I might need to come back to finish my job.

It was a lovely room, which didn't surprise me. Bed was what she was for, and she'd make sure she'd got it right. The thing was it was tasteful too, just like her sitting-room, and maybe that was Bertie's influence or maybe she was a good learner. Whatever the reason, it was a nice room to be in, pink and cream for the most part, a double bed with a tented canopy, cream-painted furniture, pink curtains. Chinese silk rugs, I noticed, pink flecked with gold, and one picture, Giorgione's 'Sleeping Venus', body and spirit so perfectly blended it makes Titian's 'Venus With a Dog' look like a scrubber.

My Venus had put a few clothes on – not many: just a transparent silk nightgown and a translucent silk robe, but she was as much dressed for action as her late husband in his flying suit. This time she didn't look at my crotch. Even the way she lay back on the pillows, relaxed yet expectant, showed that she had all the time in the world. Her hair was loose around her shoulders, I remember, her eyes bigger than ever. I stood on a Chinese rug looking down at her, but there was never any doubt who was in charge.

'Alone at last,' she said, and chuckled. Nobody else I'd ever even heard of could make a chuckle sound as if she were taking your pants down. Then her gaze was on my face, her eyes blinked.

'Jesus,' she said. 'What happened to you? You look as if you'd seen a ghost.'

If I hadn't, I'd come close to it.

'It's been quite a day,' I said. 'Do I look that bad?'

'Take a look in the mirror.'

I did so, and found she hadn't lied. I looked appalling, and very, very old.

'Was it Kessler?' she asked.

'I liked him,' I said.

'Everybody did,' she said. 'Not just us girls. Is that why you–?'

'No,' I said. I couldn't lie to her. In the first place I was too tired, and in the second place I liked her too much.

'I'm sorry he's dead,' I said. 'I know who killed him and I'm going to see they pay for it. But it isn't just that. There's more.'

Seven dead men more, and your lovely Ron almost making it eight.

'You want to tell me?'

'I can't,' I said. 'Not yet... But thanks for letting me look around.'

'It was useful?'

'One step further,' I said. 'But I found something nice for you.'

171

'About Bertie?'

I showed her the two pictures; the thirties girl and her, and told her my theory about first and last love, and she began to cry. She did it beautifully, as always.

'Damn you,' she said. 'You've put me right off. But then you meant to – didn't you?'

'It's just–' I hesitated. These were not easy words to say. 'The more I find out about him the more I like him. Respect him, too.'

'He was a man,' she said. 'A real man. Just like you.'

Dave's the one who takes care of the masculinity, I thought, but I was too tired to argue, so I thanked her for the Pinot Grigio and turned to go.

'Just a minute,' she said, and reached up to take my hand, held it to her left breast, which was every bit as splendid as I'd thought it would be. Then she looked at my crotch.

'There's a good boy,' she said, then sat up and kissed me. Somehow I broke free and trudged to the door.

11

No police that I could see, not outside the house, but I had enough on tape to start a detective series. More in anger than in sorrow was Sutton. Miffed, as Michael Copland would say... Michael Copland. I still hadn't phoned him either... Then

Dave's voice came on. No name, no identification: just the message. Dave's no mug.

'I got home all right,' he said. 'Hope you do too. You come up with some good stuff sometimes. I'd like a word.'

That meant he'd opened the box, so I phoned him. He answered on the first ring.

'I just got in,' I said.

'Get anything?'

'Not much,' I said. 'Did you?'

'More than you,' said Dave. 'A lot more. Talk tomorrow?'

'I'll call you,' I said, and we hung up. No names and no goodbyes. I went up to my bedroom and looked at my bed the way a sultan would look at a harem, but I knew it wasn't on, so I packed my other suitcase and went to a hotel in Notting Hill where I knew I'd remain anonymous. The owner's a mate of mine. I once found his daughter for him. She was seventeen and pregnant and far gone on heroin when I found her, and now she's an SRN at a hospital in Dorking. He wouldn't give me away on the Day of Judgement, not even if the Archangel Gabriel was heading the enquiries. I slept ten hours then ate a breakfast the owner cooked himself, then I phoned Dave.

'You remember that girl who was on smack? I'm with her dad,' I said.

'Be right over.'

He was too, and I was in the lobby waiting. No bill, no money – my mate wouldn't hear of it – no evidence I'd ever been there. Just as well for both of us.

Dave wasn't driving the Vauxhall. He doesn't

always, not when he's not working. He's got a nice little VW Golf he keeps to impress his birds, and that was what he had that morning.

'So we're in disguise?' I asked him.

'We don't need company, Ron, believe me,' he said. 'Where can we go and talk?'

Too early for pubs, and in the car we might be spotted, so we drove off to Westminster and left the car in a car-park, and took one of those river cruises. Not too many people, and none of them that could hear us, not with the guide bawling statistics into his microphone. I saw Dave had brought a sports bag with him, and it didn't look empty...

'You fancy a thirty-foot yacht like Finlayson's?' said Dave. 'Or a Rolls-Royce Corniche or a castle in Spain?'

'Out of my half?' I asked. 'Or do we go shares?'

'Your half,' he said. 'And after you've bought what you fancy you could buy a suite on the *QE2* for a world cruise with what you've got left over.'

'You're exaggerating,' I said.

'Certainly,' said Dave. That's because I'm hysterical, and I'm hysterical because I have to be minder to what you – quite literally – came up with.'

'Jewels?'

'Mostly,' said Dave. 'Gold too. And some papers. You'll have to take a look, Ron. Can't we go back to that hotel?'

'Not during the day,' I said. 'We'll have to go up West.'

'Where up West? That Sutton'll be taking Fulham apart.'

'Not Fulham,' I said. 'Knightsbridge. Sabena's.'

'Blimey,' he said. 'You sure you can?'

'Well, of course I can,' I said. 'We're engaged, aren't we?'

'I was forgetting,' said Dave, which was bad enough, but then he made it worse. 'You sure Jocasta Benskin won't mind?' he asked.

When we got to Sabena's I was lucky; she was out and Rosario was in. She said Sabena had gone to a beauty salon and shouldn't be back for an hour, and I said we would wait and she said 'Of course', and went off to make the coffee. Dave sat and looked at the bag and I knew that no way would he open it before Rosario came and went with the coffee, any more than I would, which meant that I had first go. I showed him the pictures as we sat in that drawing-room that was as much a part of my life as my own house. No chic and not much style; just a lot of money and a lot of comfort. It was as if she and Jocasta had swapped roles. I forced my mind back to what Dave was saying.

'Two more flyers,' Dave said. 'Isn't four enough?'

'There's only one now,' I said and he looked up at me hard. 'For a certainty?'

'For a ninety per cent certainty.'

'The Dakota off Moyra?'

'The big bloke was navigator: the little one was pilot. That's why Benskin put RIP after his name. The big feller wasn't mentioned because Bertie wasn't absolutely sure. The little one had the box.'

'Then he died rich,' said Dave.

'But I doubt if he died happy,' I said. 'He hadn't

175

bought his Roller – or a suite on the *QE2*.'

'Maybe he didn't deserve to,' Dave said. 'Can you check this?'

'Cattell will tell me,' I said.

'You mean you trust that man?'

'Of course not,' I said. 'But he's in and he acts like he wants to stay in.'

'Anybody else?'

'Mrs Palliser,' I said.

'Palliser won't like it.'

'Then he'll have to bloody lump it.'

Dave blinked – I don't often swear – then he said, 'Yes, Ron. I reckon he will.'

Then Rosario came in with the coffee, and when she'd gone it was time to open the box.

There was a sort of Treasure Island feel to what we were doing: mysterious box scooped up from the sea, all those dead men and a dead man's chest so to speak. I don't know what I'd expected to be there: doubloons and pieces of eight and moidores, I suppose: as a matter of fact I did once find a moidore for a Hong Kong millionaire coin collector, and I know I'm digressing but that's because of what the box did in fact hold.

Dave had done a neat job on it: cut away the canvas wrapping, breaking the locks without too much damage, and now he opened the lid for me and what was inside was four more little boxes. These too had been wrapped in canvas, and he'd taken that off and tried the locks again, but this time he'd had to get physical. Those locks knew more about how to stay shut than he did about how to open them so, as he told me, it was hammer and chisel time, only careful, he didn't want to damage the contents. When he finally busted in he made his first discovery: each little box was waterproof. He handed me the first one, and it was a lot heavier than it looked and not just on account of what it was made of. It was full of gold rings, and gold weighs heavy, and there were hundreds of them one on top of the other, resting on a bed of padded velvet: black it was, so the rings glowed more bright, and some were signets and a few were just for decoration, but the mass of them was wedding rings, red gold and yellow gold and white gold, and I didn't like what I was looking at one bit.

'Any more of these?' I asked him, but Dave didn't answer: just handed me the next box and I opened it.

Jewellery. Earrings and necklaces and brooches on the top, including a pair of earrings by Cartier – or so it looked like to me – rubies and diamonds and emeralds, art-deco style – 1920s – and if they weren't by Cartier they were by Van Cleef and Arpels, and either way you could swop them for a Roller, or maybe even two by today's prices... I lifted off the top layer and underneath was what I'd expected, more rings: mostly engagement rings this time, and every one of them expensive...

The third box Dave passed over contained more jewellery, men's and women's: rings and dress studs and tie-pins, a couple of combs, even a powder compact resting on a thick manila envelope. I opened it to find what looked like page after page of notes, with here and there a name. It was all in German, a language neither Dave nor I could handle. Dave handed over the last box.

'You won't like this,' he said.

'I haven't liked any of it.'

'This is worse,' he said.

And it was. The box was filled with little pellets of gold, not much bigger than buckshot, hundreds of them. Handfuls, you might say. But I didn't touch them.

'You know what they are,' said Dave.

'I think so,' I said. 'Gold fillings. For teeth.'

'And that bastard in that bloody Dakota took them as part of his pay-off.'

It was my turn to stare. Dave doesn't swear any more than I do, but he had much better reasons than I had. Handfuls of them. I felt sick.

'What now?' Dave asked.

'We pack up and scarper. Get rid of that box.'

'Suits me,' said Dave, and loaded up the big box. All I kept back was the notes or whatever they were in German. Then I rang for Rosario and told her we had to go and we'd be in touch. She looked surprised. It was the first time I'd ever left that house without seeing Sabena.

I met her on the doorstep instead. She was going through her handbag looking for her keys as Dave and I came out.

'We happened to be passing so we popped in,' I said.

'Just to say hello,' said Dave. We've got this appointment you see.'

'Mustn't be late,' I said. We sounded terrible.

Her eyes stayed fixed on the sports bag. It seemed to fascinate her.

'Off for a game of rugger, Ronaldo?' she asked.

'Business,' I said. 'Just business.'

'Then I mustn't keep you,' she said. 'Dave, I hope you'll pop in again some time when it's over.'

She was into the house and slamming the door before I could answer.

'She's peeved,' said Dave.

'Who wouldn't be?' I said.

We went to Harrods and I bought a case big enough to hold the box, then on to a safe deposit place in Mayfair where I rent just about as much space as would contain the case. The safe deposit rental costs me more than my mortgage, but this year Palliser would pay. Of that I was absolutely certain.

From Mayfair I telephoned and got an appointment, and we drove to the City. 'La Belle Epoque' wine bar again. Cattell seemed to have a horror of entertaining people at his office. This time I took Dave with me. Dave's my way of signalling that I'm in the game for keeps. He doesn't have to pull faces or flex muscles or anything. All he has to do is be there. It almost always works: it did that day. Cattell led us to a table and waved at the bar, and the same beautiful young lady brought over a bottle of champagne and three glasses. Krug NV this time. Cattell watched and waited, smoothing down the wings of white hair until she had poured and smiled and left.

'Something's up,' he said. It wasn't a question. Not with Dave there. Cattell motioned at the glasses on the table, lifted one and said 'Cheers'. Dave and I said the same and we drank. Nectar, Krug NV. The wine for gods. But I was in such a state I didn't even taste it.

'Your nephews,' I said. 'They blackmailed me for fifty quid.'

'Seems a very small amount to risk a jail sentence for,' Cattell said.

'Depends how often you do it,' I said, and his hard red face got redder.

'Tell me about it.' I told him.

'So it's your word against theirs,' he said.

'Both our words. Dave's and mine. Anyway I'm not going to the police.'

'What are you going to do?'

'Up to you,' I said.

'Let's have it.'

'You're the main shareholder in Choppers Ltd. If word got around your nephews were on the take it wouldn't do you much good.'

'Will word get around?'

'Not if you do me a favour,' I said, and showed him two of Bertie's photographs, the short flyer and the tall one.

'Good Lord,' he said. 'It must be forty years.'

'You know them then?'

'Two flight lieutenants,' he said. 'In bombers. The big one's name is Myers. The little one's Todd.'

'You knew them well?'

Cattell sighed. 'I'll tell you,' he said. 'I've no doubt you'll find out anyway. We met because of the airlift. They were both in the same squadron. Halifaxes.'

'Any good?'

'Myers was a good average, I'd say. Todd rather more than that. No good asking how you connect these two with a Hebridean island?'

'None at all,' I said.

Cattell shrugged and poured more champagne.

'I got into this to oblige Sir Montague,' he said, 'because I owe him a favour. Quite a big one. But there are limits. Damn it, I'm entitled to be told something.'

'Believe me,' I said, 'the biggest favour I can do you is to tell you absolutely nothing.'

He looked at me hard. It was a survivor's look.

'You mean that, don't you?' I nodded. 'Would you say what I've done for you has been useful?'

'Extremely.'

'So I've done enough to square Sir Montague.' He didn't ask me: he told me – for the second time. 'Nigel told me about the man with the boat – but he'd forgotten his name.'

'Finlayson,' I said.

'There was a Finlayson in Palliser's squadron,' Cattell said. 'Sergeant Mechanic. I should chase him up if I were you.' He downed the rest of his glass and rose. 'Must rush,' he said. 'Busy day.'

'Thanks for the champagne,' said Dave. They were the only words he'd uttered, but then they were all that were needed. We waited till he'd gone, then:

'Funny bloke,' Dave said.

'Funny?'

Dave took his time about it. 'He thinks he's tough and maybe he is tough,' he said at last. 'But there's a soft streak somewhere – and that's what you have to watch out for. Where now?'

'Finish your drink,' I said. 'I've got to call Michael Copland.' After four tries and forty pence I got him. He was not happy.

'You promised me a story,' he said. Like a kid at bedtime.

'You'll get one,' I said. 'I told you... When the time's right.'

'And when will that be? Next Christmas?'

'Soon,' I said. 'That I promise you.'

'And in the meantime you would like a little something from me?'

'It'll be worth it.'

'Oh yes? Just what are you offering? Or is that a secret?'

'Murder, buried treasure, scandal in high places, financial double dealing, lust, blackmail and broken hearts,' I said.

'Jesus,' he said. 'Tell me what you want.'

I told him and he said it would be no problem. I never thought it would be, not after what I'd promised to deliver...

We went to West Sussex. The Golf is a nice eager little car that deserves an airing, and anyway I wasn't all that anxious to bump into Sutton, so we went to West Sussex instead to see Mrs Palliser, at the address I'd got from one of Bertie's six address books.

Outside of certain parts of London, the area Mrs Palliser had chosen must contain the most expensive real estate in England. Pop stars of the megastar kind live there, and serious money too. Banking money, brewing money, even inherited money if there was enough of it: enough still to support the Rolls, the Land-Rover and the Porsche, the gardens and woodland and the dinner parties for twenty. And when it all got to be too much you could do what Mrs Palliser did and live in Thornaby House, just down the road from Petworth, where anything upsetting was illegal.

Thornaby House stood in about five acres of trees, flowerbeds and lawns that looked as if they'd been cut by nail-scissors. Its gravel drive was raked, its front-door brasses gleamed. Nowhere could I see a sign that the place was a nursing home. Dave shifted uneasily.

'We should have phoned,' he said. 'I told you we should.'

And indeed he had, all the way from London, but I reckoned he was wrong. If we'd phoned and she'd said no we had no chance of ever seeing her, but this way at least we could get close. The rest was up to me. I looked at the large, expensive cars by the house.

'Just park your nice roller-skate,' I said, 'and show a little faith.'

He planted the Golf between a Volvo estate and a Ferrari, and I got a card out of my wallet and wrote a few lines on the back. On the lawn nearby, a lot of rich and idle persons sat in deck-chairs and watched me do it. I hoped they'd put the Golf down to eccentricity, and walked to the gleaming door trying to look like a man whose other car is a Porsche. Then I rang the doorbell.

The man who opened it wore black trousers, a gleaming white shirt, a black tie. His black shoes gleamed, and his dark, smooth face looked as if it had been shaved five minutes before. He looked leaner and fitter and younger than me, and I wished that I'd brought Dave along. I handed him the card.

'For Mrs Palliser,' I said. He didn't take it.

'It is usual to telephone,' he said.

'It's – urgent,' I said. 'There's a message on the back.' I tried to hand over the card again.

'I'm afraid not, sir,' he said.

He was handsome as well as athletic, with that soulful look on his face some Italians get just before they turn you down flat.

I took a chance and tried again in Italian, speaking the way my mother had taught me, like a real Veronese. 'The lady's husband has sent me,' I said. 'There has been a robbery at their home.'

'You are a policeman?' He spoke Italian too: like a Southerner.

'Private,' I said, and he relaxed a little. 'Private' might mean money.

'There is also the matter of the death of an old friend of hers. I have news of that, too.'

'Does she know her friend is dead?' said my mother's compatriot. 'I ask because the doctor would not want her to have a shock.'

She would read the papers: she would know.

'She knows,' I said. 'There are business affairs to be arranged–'

'Inheritance?' I nodded, yes, and he liked that too, sniffing money again.

'If you help me achieve this interview,' I said, 'I shall of course be under an obligation which I must honour.'

He looked out over my shoulder, squinting into the sunlight. 'You will not be too long?'

'You have my word,' I said, and he smiled, no doubt ironically, and took the card, found a tray from the hallway and moved out towards the lawn.

'Wait here,' he said.

'I'll be by the VW,' I said. 'I want a word with my partner about honouring my obligation. He'll do it when I talk to Mrs Palliser.'

He smiled again, with no irony at all. 'Bravo,' he said and walked off towards a woman sitting alone in a sun-lounger, with a table handy, and playing cards. I went over to Dave.

'Get twenty pounds ready,' I said. 'Give it to my chum if I talk to the lady.'

'Need me?' said Dave.

'I don't think so,' I said, and at once he was into the VW's glove compartment, and took out *À la Recherche du Temps Perdu*. I saw he'd got to Volume Five, and wondered where he'd found the time to do all that reading. Then my new mate turned away from the lady in the sun-lounger and I went to meet him.

'She will see you,' he said.

'Thank you,' I said. 'My partner will take care of you,' and walked on.

No question that once, nearly forty years ago, Wendy Palliser had been a very pretty girl. The evidence was still there, in the wide grey eyes, the thick short hair now more white than blonde, the admirable legs. What I hadn't allowed for was the intelligence in those cool, grey eyes. Mentally I began to prepare my excuses for Dave. What I got from this one wouldn't be up to me: it would be up to her.

'Mr Hogget,' she said. 'How nice of you to come and see me. Do bring up a chair.'

There was another lounger handy, and I grabbed it and sat.

'Carlo tells me you speak excellent Italian,' she

185

said. She had a game of patience going, and kept on playing as we talked.

'My mother was from Verona.'

'I went to the open-air opera there once,' she said. 'In the amphitheatre. *Aida*.'

'It very often is,' I said.

She laughed. 'Acoustically dubious,' she said. 'But rather fun. Like a circus with cultural ambitions. But you haven't come to talk about culture.'

'Mr Palliser,' I said.

'You've come to talk about the circus,' said Mrs Palliser. 'Oh I say, what fun.'

It was going to be difficult: I could feel it.

'I put it on the back of the card,' I said. 'Your husband – and Mr Benskin.'

'The *flying* circus,' she said, then almost at once looked sad. 'Poor Bertie – I was very fond of him, you know.'

'So was I,' I said.

'You knew him when he was alive?... But weren't you the one who found the body?'

'I was,' I said. 'But I'd met him before. Just once.'

'He was an absolute darling,' she said, and her eyes grew misty. Another blonde ready to weep for him. Whatever it takes, Bertie had it in quantities.

Mrs Palliser scooped up the game of patience she'd been playing and made the cards into a pack. She was ready to listen, maybe even answer.

'Ask your questions, Mr Hogget,' she said.

'Before I do,' I said, 'might I ask – how fit are you? I mean the strain of discussing a friend's death–'

'My dear man,' she said, 'I haven't had a day's

186

illness since 1974, and that was Asian 'flu. I live here because I want to – and because I can afford it. Ask your questions.'

'Did you know about the Dakota?' I asked.

'Of course. It was half their personnel – and half their capital equipment. Of course I knew.'

'Did you know about the rumour? The SS men on the run?'

'There are always people who make sure you get to know about things like that,' she said. 'In every walk of life. Flying is no exception.'

'Excuse me, Mrs Palliser, but I must ask you this,' I said. 'Did you believe those rumours?'

Her eyes gleamed then, cold and grey as ice in the ocean. At last she said: 'Yes, I suppose you must ask it. From where you sit it's a fair question. The answer is that when I first heard I said no, not possibly; then after a while I began to wonder. But now it's back to no again.'

'May I ask why, please?'

'Because of the men involved,' she said. 'They just couldn't.' And there it was again.

'You were engaged to Frank Denville?' She nodded. 'You loved him then?'

'Love.' She said it as if it were a word she'd heard a long time ago, and was trying to remember what it meant; the way Sutton said 'Sleep.'

'He gave me great joy,' she said. 'I used to regret at one time that I'd never had a child, but now I think that perhaps I did.'

'Forgive me–' I said.

'Don't waste any more time apologising,' she said. 'Ask your questions.'

'From what you told me – was he a weak man?'

187

'He was in Transport Command,' she said. 'In his time he'd flown Hurricanes, Spitfires, Mustangs, Blenheims, Wimpeys, Halifaxes, Mosquitoes – a Flying Fortress even. Sometimes in atrocious conditions. He wasn't a weak man in a plane.'

'And out of one?'

'Weak as water,' she said, but at the same time she smiled.

'So when the two of them were together – Bill Day would be the leader?'

'Bill was always the leader.' Here we go again, I thought. 'But Bill would never do it – help the Gestapo, the SS, any of that scum – and that was another reason why Frank wouldn't either.'

'Were you in the Air Force too?'

'The Women's Auxiliary Air Force we called it in those days – WAAF. Nice blue uniform, the King's Commission, the pick of the nation's young manhood. What fun it was, you must think.'

'And was it?'

'No... So many of them died, you see.' She looked at her watch, then at the door.

Four o'clock, and Carlo emerging with a crystal jug and two glasses. Ice clinked in the jug as he put it down, then left.

'Would you like some of my lime squash?' she asked.

'Please,' I said.

She opened her handbag, took out a half-bottle of Gordon's gin and poured some into the jug, swirled it around, then poured two glasses' worth and handed one to me.

'Gin and lime,' she said. 'How this takes one

188

back to the dear dead days.' Bertie had said almost the same thing: 'It'll help me to remember.'

'Cheers.'

We sipped, and I longed for the sharpness of tonic water.

'Poor Frank,' she said, then looked at her glass. 'Now why did I say that?'

I made an inspired guess – or maybe it was just half-inspired.

'Maybe you know where he is,' I said.

'Maybe I do.' For a moment her eyes clouded. 'But if I – hid him away – isn't that what you're saying?'

I nodded.

'It would not have been because he was guilty. It would have been because he was innocent and didn't know how to cope – and that's enough about Frank. Ask me about something else.'

'Did you know a man called Finlayson?' I said, doing what I was told.

'Tony did,' she said, and sipped again.

'Your husband?'

'Not then,' she said. 'Then I was still engaged to Frank. I suppose you could say that they all knew Finlayson, but Tony did all the hiring and firing, even then.'

'Finlayson worked for you?'

'For the airline. He was their chief mechanic. He'd been in Tony's squadron.'

'He was good?'

'Technically excellent.'

'And morally?'

'I had my doubts about him, but they're still unresolved.'

'Why so, Mrs Palliser?'

'Because he disappeared, Mr Hogget, quite soon after the Dakota disappeared, and I find it difficult to equate my assumption of his guilt with my certainty of Bill's and Frank's innocence.'

It must be the gin, I thought. With some it's singing: with her it's big words.

'Where did he work?' I asked her. 'Berlin?'

'There or Heathrow,' she said. 'It had only just opened when we moved in.'

'We?'

'I worked there too,' she said, and smiled. This time it wasn't the gin: it was remembered happiness.

'I was on the pay-roll as company secretary,' she said, 'but I did just about everything. Costing, payloads, wages, contracts, flight-plans even. The boys trusted me, you see.'

'It doesn't surprise me,' I said.

'Why thank you, Mr Hogget,' she said. 'Have another drink.' Then she topped us both up before I could stop her. From a tree nearby some sort of bird began to sing in a respectful sort of way, so as not to disturb the clientele.

'Blackbird,' Mrs Palliser said. 'Frank taught me how to recognise them. He knew a great deal about ornithology.'

I knew nothing, but I liked what I was hearing.

'Where did Finlayson live?' I asked.

'Scotland,' she said. 'At least I think so. He was a Scot, definitely. But not the kind of man one talked to about things other than the job in hand.'

'How old would he have been?'

'Then? Early thirties, I suppose.'

190

Early seventies now. Not my chum with the shotgun and the thirty-foot boat. Not by twenty-five years at least.

'How did he get on with your husband?'

'He obeyed instructions. Most people do when Tony issues them, don't you find?'

'He and I had a dust-up.'

'Indeed?' She reached for the jug and I picked up my glass. 'What about?'

'My original brief was to find the Dakota. He said it was vital, so I got to work. It isn't easy following a trail forty years old.'

'I suppose not,' she said.

'Anyway I made a start – learned a few things. Doing my job. Then Mr Benskin was murdered and your husband told the police I had a taped message from Mr Benskin. He also knew it would make trouble for me with the police.'

'Then why? – I mean if you were working for him–'

'Because he was afraid they'd find out something I couldn't if they started to dig.'

'And could they?'

'Of course,' I said. 'They've got a small army to investigate, and hardware and software and forensic labs – of course.'

'But you're still working for Tony.'

'He offered me more money,' I said. 'It may not be the most fragrant reason, but I'm saving up to get married.'

'I hope she's nice,' said Mrs Palliser.

'So do I,' I said. 'She always has been so far. Did you know Joachim Kessler?'

'I liked the way you did that,' she said. 'Chang-

191

ing the subject before I was ready.'

'It's standard technique,' I said. 'Did you?'

'Not when he worked for the firm,' she said. 'I met him later. When he came to Oxford. Wittgenstein and all that.'

'Did you like him?'

'Yes,' she said. 'I did. Not to sleep with. I'd rather gone off all that by the time I met him, but the mind was really remarkable.'

'So they tell me,' I said. 'How about Bonny Bessie's house in Palmerston Street?'

She was drinking gin and lime when I said it and she went on drinking it, before putting down the glass to say, 'You're trying that trick again.'

'Sort of,' I said.

'Who is Bonny Bessie?' she asked. 'And why does she live in Palmerston Street?'

'I was hoping you'd tell me,' I said. 'Kessler told me he'd heard Bill Day say it to Mr Benskin. And Mr Benskin said something about messing about in boats.'

'That's from *The Wind in the Willows*,' she said. 'By Kenneth Grahame. Ratty says it to Mole.'

'Quite right,' I said. 'Lovely stuff. Mr Benskin then added: "What a shame. What a bloody shame."'

I waited, but all she said was, 'But that doesn't make sense.'

I sighed a real Sutton-type sigh. It was what I feared she would say.

'Is it important?' she asked.

'I doubt it,' I said. 'Not to me anyway. If it had been important Kessler wouldn't have told me.'

I stood up. Time to go. 'I thank you for your

help,' I said.

'You shouldn't,' she said. 'I doubt if I gave you any. But I can still try... Did my husband lose anything when he was burgled?'

'He said not.'

'He had a gun, you know. I expect he needs it. His has been an adventurous life. Did he mention it at all?'

'No.'

'I suppose not,' she said. 'Guns are such very private things, Mr Hogget. Rather like illicit love affairs.'

'What kind of gun is it?'

'A Smith and Wesson .38 Chief's Special with a checkered walnut stock and square butt,' she said.

'You remember it well,' I said.

'It's not the sort of thing one easily forgets,' she said, and held out her hand. 'Goodbye, Mr Hogget. Do come and see me again – if you should judge another visit to be appropriate. I am sure you will know whether it is or not.'

I left her to the sound of tinkling ice-cubes, and liquid pouring into a glass.

Dave said, 'She has the wrong name.'

'My sentiments exactly,' I said. Either it was catching or she had a special kind of gin.

'Wendys should be sweet and wholesome and good at hockey and kind to animals,' said Dave. 'Tuck you up when you've got a fever and not too much upstairs. The J. M. Barrie syndrome.'

'It takes all sorts,' I said. 'At least we know Palliser's got a gun.'

'The right sort of gun,' said Dave. 'Want to go and look at it?'

That's my boy, I thought. No can we's or should we's. Just – let's go.

'All in good time,' I said.

'How about dropping in on Sutton then, before he drops in on us?'

'To talk about that knife and the bird outside Kessler's room?' He nodded. 'If we do,' I said, 'I'll never find out who killed Bertie.'

'You found the Dakota,' said Dave.

'It isn't enough,' I said. 'I want to know who killed Bertie.'

'You think you owe it to Jocasta?'

'I owe it to him,' I said, and wished Dave could have read his letters.

'You reckon you can get whoever did it then?'

'I reckon I have to,' I said.

12

We went back to London and I got Dave to drop me off at a research library I know near Regent's Park. As soon as I got out he was off like the Golf was a Ferrari, and I guessed he was going to see Angela. But I couldn't keep him on a chain – how could I? And anyway he might learn something, like I might in the library.

The place always seemed inhabited by blokes – women too – who looked like solicitors hoping to find some geezer whose rich uncle in Australia has died and left them a fortune, and I joined the merry throng. Nice little library. Comfortable, and all the right books. Their charge is a bit steep, but nobody rushes you, and they honour a request for anonymity to the point where there's even a few private rooms for the shy type like me. First off I looked up Palliser in the Registry of Companies and discovered that his wife was also a director and shareholder, which didn't surprise me. She'd acted from the first as if she had her own money.

Next was Palmerston Street. I decided to assume it was in London, for no better reason than that you've got to start somewhere, and London has more places than anywhere else. I got a Palmerston Crescent, two Groves and five Roads, but in the end I got a Street as well. Just one. But maybe one was all I needed. The Palmerston Street was in Putney, which is by the river, and I remembered what Bertie had said, according to Kessler: 'Messing about in boats.'

So I took the directories back and swapped them for the oldest A-Z I could find, and handled it with care, just as the librarian had told me to. A lot of solicitors had handled it before me... And there it was: along Upper Richmond Road and across Putney Bridge and turn right along Ranelagh Gardens for Hurlingham Park. Round the Park and keep going right and there was Palmerston Street, nice and handy for Hurlingham Dock and Trinidad Dock, and all the boats you could mess about in just one life-time. So, for a few minutes, I felt pretty good, and then I got back to reality. Palmerston Street was one thing, Bonny Bessie quite another.

To begin with Bonny Bessie, also known as Aunty Bessie, had been an aunty forty years ago, which meant there was a chance she might be dead – or ga-ga. And in London, more than most places, people move on and move out. All the time. And I didn't know a living soul in Putney. Then I started to show some sense again. I didn't live there, but I knew *somebody* who did: my sister; Anna Maria Muspratt née Hogget.

Very Italian, my sister. She's married to a bloke called Sydney Muspratt. He's an assistant bank manager on his way up and as English as fish and chips, and their kids are as English as he is, but my sister was born Italian and she'll die Italian: which means she's an expert at making her husband happy, and not just with pasta – and at gossip. Church and neighbours and the Parent-Teachers' Association and the WVS – if anybody could find an Aunt Bessie in Putney it was Anna Maria Muspratt.

But it was no good ringing up my sister to explain anything as complicated as this. As I say, she's Italian. If you're going to tell her anything complicated she wants to see you do it. I went out and squandered some more of Palliser's money on a taxi and paid it off at Hurlingham Park. After that I walked, brisk and confident like a man who knows where he's going. A man who keeps looking about him all the time is a man people remember. Anyway I knew exactly how to get to Palmerston Street...

It was like an awful lot of London since the war. At one time it had been all terrace houses, with a

196

little bit of garden front and back, and a lot of those still survived, and a fair number of them had been spruced up: good paint, prettier doors and windows, barbecue at the back. Money was moving in. Still a few survived as they'd always been, the homes of clerks and what they called superior artisans. They too were clean, the gardens neat.

But the war hadn't neglected Palmerston Street. It had its bomb, like so many others, and a big one it must have been too, to judge by the number of houses missing. They hadn't rebuilt the little houses: they'd tried a block of flats instead. Not the nasty great high-rises you see in some parts: just seven storeys and car-park and scraggy lawn and wilting trees, but alongside its neighbours it looked about as appropriate as a nudist climbing Everest. Kids in abundance, and scooters and prams. It didn't look like Aunt Bessie country, but the little houses might be. She'd be seventy at least and probably more, but the National Health Service knows its stuff...

I walked the length of the street and kept on going, working my way back around the park to where my sister lives. Not all that different from Palmerston Street really: a bit bigger, a bit more garden at the back. Nice garden too: roses and carnations and gladioli: Sydney's very keen. But there's herbs too: marjoram and basil and rosemary: onions and garlic too. My sister sees to that...

I went round to the back door because that's where the kitchen is, and sure enough she was there, and opened the door in a flash – moves like greased lightning my sister.

'Tommaso,' she said, and flung her arms around me and kissed me like I'd just got back from a shipwreck. In fact Sabena and me had been over to her for dinner just a few weeks ago.

'How are you, sis?' I said.

'Tommaso – *per che non mi hai telefonato?*' she said, and dragged me into her kitchen.

I was christened Thomas Ronald Hogget, but of all the family she's the only one who calls me by my first name because it sounds better in Italian.

When I could get a word in I suggested we should speak English and she shrugged and said 'Okay' as if she was humouring one of her kids. To her it doesn't make *sense* for anyone to speak English when they can speak Italian.

'How's Sydney?' I asked her.

Sydney was great, I was told. He'd just taken the kids off to Barnes for cricket practice. Cricket meant nothing to Anna Maria, but a father's duty – she knows all about that. She approved, and told me so in English better than mine. Then she took a bottle of Verdicchio from the fridge and poured two glasses. I took mine and sipped. White wine was not what I wanted, but it was better than trying to explain to my big sister why I'd spent the afternoon drinking gin and lime.

'How's Sabena?' she asked me.

'Okay,' I said.

She gave me a look that could have blistered paint.

'Tommaso,' she said, 'I don't understand you. I really do not. You've managed to get yourself engaged to a beautiful woman who is rich and talented as well – and God knows how you did it – I mean look at you – yet when I ask you how she is you tell me she's okay. What's the matter with you? Have you and Sabena had a row?'

'Not a row,' I said. 'No. It's just – I've been too busy to see much of her. I've got a job on.'

'I know,' she said.

'You've been talking to Sabena?'

'I didn't talk to anybody,' she said. 'They talked to me.'

'Who, sis?'

'The police. Inspector Sutton. Sergeant Cairns.' I should have known. 'They came here yesterday.'

'What did they want to know?'

'Where you were. They said you were not to leave the country.'

'I didn't leave the country.'

She ignored that. Where I went was not important. It was my social relationships that worried her. 'They don't like you, Tommaso.'

'It's mutual.'

'Can they – hurt you?'

'They can make life difficult,' I said, 'but not impossible. I'll manage.'

She gave me another one of her looks, one of the affectionate kind.

'Obstinate all the way through,' she said. 'Just like mamma.'

'You reckon she was obstinate?'

'She had to be,' my sister said, 'to stay married to father.' She had a point.

'You seen him?'

'Last week,' she said. 'He needed money.'

'Drunk?'

'Of course,' she said. 'He'd been looking for you. You were out. It made him angry.'

'He should have phoned,' I said, but I knew he wouldn't. His only hope of getting at me is to take me by surprise. He'd come and see me and make a nuisance of himself until I gave him money to go away. Dave called it Danegeld.

'What have you come for, Tommaso?' Anna Maria asked, and I told her just enough.

When I'd done she said, 'You don't want much, do you?... All those years ago.'

'I'm sorry,' I said, 'I shouldn't have asked.'

'Oh, don't be a fool,' she said, and poured more wine. Her eyes were gleaming. 'It's your sort of thing, isn't it? and you reckon I can do it?'

'If you do you must send me a bill.'

'You can bet on it,' my sister said, and then, being my sister, she added: 'It won't get anyone into trouble, will it?'

Well, of course it would but I didn't want to put her off.

'Not this time,' I said, and kissed her, then went to pay my next visit.

I've known Mr Kagan for the best part of ten years, ever since my second case, when he translated some documents for me from French into Hebrew, on account of I was delivering some stuff the Israeli government was collecting at the time. Dodgy it was, especially as Dave was still in the Paras, but I needed the capital... Leon Avramovich Kagan, Russian Jew, as old as the century. He'd twice been a refugee from his own country: once when his family was driven out by the Tsar's government, and once after they'd sneaked back just in time to be driven out by the Bolsheviks. So for a while they lived in Berlin, and then in Budapest, then Naples, and everywhere he went he learned a new language, so in the end he came to London and set up in business as a translator. As I say, I'd used him for years, and if he charged high he was worth it: fast, accurate and discreet.

By the time I'm talking about he'd retired, but not from me. We got along pretty well because once I'd found something for him: the grave of his sister, whom the Nazis had shot outside Lyons in 1943. It had been a great relief to Mr Kagan to know that she had died quickly, and he felt that he owed me for it. So naturally, when it came to having documents translated and no questions asked, Mr Kagan was the only one. Only there were complications; like his being Jewish, and the papers were all about Germans. At least they looked that way – some of them even had the Third Reich eagle seal stamped on them. He would do it, and he would promise me silence, but he was pushing ninety and he went a lot to gossip with other old Jews at what he called the Schul, which is the synagogue. On the other hand there wasn't anybody else.

I went to visit him at the little mews house in Knightsbridge his father had bought for five thousand quid. The last offer he'd had was three-quarters of a million but he hadn't sold. He was hanging on for seven figures, he said. That was the only incentive he had for living; that and the message from the Queen. He's a raving royalist, Mr Kagan. Came of being in the ARP during the war, he said. Before that he'd been a Menshevik-type

Red but, when the bombs started dropping in 1940 and the King and Queen refused to leave London, he became a royalist, and pretty handy for Buckingham Palace at that, the mews where he lives.

It's a nice little house, one of a terrace, and done up a treat. He'd done pretty well translating, but his father had done even better in furs. So I admired the gleaming red door and the glowing brasswork and knocked just the once. His hearing's remarkable, and so's his eye-sight. In no time he was at the door, tall, incredibly skinny on account of his age, and yet tough with it. His eyes still gleamed, and his nose was like an eagle beak in the lined and sunken face. Blue suit like always, white shirt and an Old Etonian tie. That meant he still enjoyed a joke.

'Hallo, Mr Kagan,' I said.

'My dear Ron,' he said. 'Good to see you,' and grabbed my hand. He could still grip. 'Come in. Come in.'

I went inside, past the mezuzah on the door-post (very devout is Mr Kagan) and into the living-room with the furniture he'd bought at the same time as the house, thirties art-deco in decline, but worth a mint now on its own. On a small table by Mr Kagan's chair a chess problem was set out. By Mr Kagan's chair there is always a chess problem.

'Vodka or wine?' he asked me.

'Wine,' I said. Definitely not vodka, not on top of what I'd had, and especially not Mr Kagan's vodka, which he procured by devious means from the Polish Embassy.

'You young men,' he said. 'No stamina,' and

poured me a glass of Alsace Riesling. He had vodka.

'You have come to make me work,' he said. 'I am clairvoyant. I sense it.'

He could also see the envelope I carried.

'I've come to ask you to work,' I said. 'No one can make you do anything.'

He shrugged. 'So ask,' he said. I told him what I needed, and he listened. When I'd done, he said, 'You think this will be painful to me?'

'Almost certainly,' I said.

'But it won't help these Germans you speak of?'

'That I can swear to,' I said.

'Then you have no problem,' he said, and held out his hand. 'Let me see.'

'When I've gone,' I said. I didn't want to watch him read what I'd brought.

'Don't be in too big a hurry to leave an old man,' he said.

So we sat and talked, or rather he did, about Russia now and Russia then, Sputniks and Cossacks, the Princess Anastasia and Raisa Gorbachev. And then it was Pushkin, then chess, then the sister who died and how beautifully she had played the piano, there in St. Petersburg while the snow fluttered down outside. For him in St. Petersburg it was always winter, but he loved it even so.

And then it was time to go; one more night with my mate in Notting Hill; a double room this time, sharing with Dave, but that was all right too. Dave had helped me find my mate's daughter... Dave was late. I was worried sick by the time he got back, and we sat down to steaks and a bottle of

Gigondas '78 that I knew I was going to regret next morning. Dave poured wine while I reminded him how I worried.

'Yeah,' he said. 'Sorry. Only there was something I had to get. This.' His hand went into his pocket, and came out holding a gun. That's what I call the lot of them, regardless of shape or size, but Dave called this one a Colt Bulldog .357 Magnum revolver with the blue finish and the bulldog grip. 'I think we've been going around naked long enough, Ron,' he said.

I sighed, because I thought so too.

'Did you see Angela?' I asked him.

'Oh boy,' said Dave. But he didn't sound all that happy.

'She turn you down?'

'In a way,' he said, and then: 'She doesn't.'

'Doesn't what?'

'Do it.'

'Oh,' I said.

'It was all going very nicely,' he said. 'I mean I'd taken some champagne around, only I didn't even have to open it. Or I thought I didn't. You know what I mean.'

I knew all right, and what I didn't know Jocasta Benskin was determined to teach me. 'One thing was leading to another – at least I thought it was – then all of a sudden she sits up straight, then moves away. "I'm awfully sorry," she says. "I think perhaps I've misled you." So I sat and waited for enlightenment. I got it. "I'm a virgin," she says. "I intend to stay that way till my honeymoon."'

'That's too bad,' I said to Dave. 'Unless you're thinking of getting married.'

'Do me a favour,' said Dave. 'Her with a boy-friend that buys diamond and sapphire necklaces and drives a Porsche.'

'You mean she doesn't do it with him, either?'

'Of course not,' said Dave. 'I told you. She's a virgin... And anyway – how can I get married on what I earn?'

'You mean you want to?'

Maybe it was rude to sound so incredulous, but I couldn't help it.

All Dave said was, 'You haven't held her', meaning that if I had I'd want to marry her too, no matter who else was after my body.

'She wants to see you,' said Dave.

'Angela?'

'Of course Angela. Who else have I been talking about?' A bit snappy, but I forgave him on account of unrequited love.

'She phoned you at your place – tried hundreds of times, she said. That means at least three. All she ever got was your answerphone. I told her you had a lot on but she wants to see you. Her place tomorrow. Two-thirty. She's got a modelling session in the morning, then a lunch date with a magazine editor.'

I reckoned if Dave needed extra money he could always get a job as Angela Rossie's secretary, but I didn't tell him that.

'What's it about?' I asked him.

'She wouldn't tell me,' Dave said. 'Will you go?'

'Why not?' I said. 'She might know something useful.' I kept my voice as matter-of-fact as I could make it. Dave was looking like a large and angry dog, a mastiff, say – being forced to give up his bone to a West Highland terrier.

'You going to phone her then?'

'I'd rather you did that, Dave,' I said, 'if you don't mind.'

He didn't mind at all.

Next morning I told Dave I had some checking to do, which was true in a way, and Dave took himself off with the other great love of his life, the Colt Magnum, to get in some practice at a place he knew. I went to do my checking. At Angela Rossie's flat.

Her place in Milbourne Court might call itself Chelsea, but it didn't have anything like the class of her boy-friend's place in Notting Hill. No porter for a start, just a row of buttons to press, and the hope that someone would answer. So I pressed the one marked Rossie, and I got what I hoped I would get. Nothing. So then all I had to do was get inside, which I did by pretending to talk into the microphone while easing back the lock with the aid of the card that takes you everywhere. And they call it security.

She was on the fourth floor, and the lift seemed to take a fortnight getting there, but what else can you do? Walk up and meet the milkman coming down and he remembers you, because walking up's eccentric... To pass the time I thought about Dave, and how he'd scuttled himself with his own technique, because what Dave usually does is let the bird of the month rabbit on and tell her how much he respects her views. But where's the future in that if her view is that a virgin she is and a virgin she'll stay?

206

Her flat had two locks: one that even the credit card found laughable, but not the other. The other tested all the resources of my Swiss Army knife, the one I'd had specially adapted by a bent locksmith, and opens more doors than a letter from the Queen. But I got in at last without scratching the woodwork, and took my time looking round. There had to be something there, I was sure of it, because my opinion of Angela Rossie was nothing like Dave's.

I started in the bedroom. Not like Jocasta Benskin's, but comfortable enough. Three-quarter bed – lot of room for one, just right for two friends. Chest of drawers, wardrobe, dressing-table with all the best, most expensive make-up. But she'd have to have that, after all. Beauty was her business. Nothing in the dressing-table drawers except more make-up, and nothing in the wardrobe except dresses and shoes, say five thousand quid's worth. The chest of drawers was locked, another problem my Swiss Army knife solved for me. In the top drawer was a jewel box with the famous sapphire and diamond necklace and very nice too: plus a lot of other stuff that you can't buy at Woolworth's. And stacked alongside it blouses and skirts and slips, and nothing more. The second drawer was more of the same, and nylons and pantie-hose and handkerchiefs, and a faint and pleasing smell of lavender. The last drawer held the kind of garments they call intimate: bras on the left, panties and cami-knickers on the right, and all expensive stuff, too: Janet Reger silks and satins. Wasted on a virgin. I turned them over, and underneath I found something that simply didn't belong: a

Smith and Wesson .38 Chief's Special with a checkered walnut stock and square butt. It lay among all those expensive knickers looking like a bad Salvador Dali pastiche. Underneath it was a fifty-pound note. I picked it up, cautious of fingerprints, and looked at it. Guns petrify me, but all the same I had to handle the beastly thing, as the Sloane Ranger said. It was fully loaded, but so far as I could see it hadn't been fired for some time. I put it back, and swathed it in underwear. Time to look further. Nothing in the tiny kitchen. The living-room was the best chance I had.

The first thing was to find the postcard Dave had seen – the one of La Malcontenta. It was there all right, assuring her that all was well and he was missing her and would soon be home, and it was signed Bobsy. Capital B. I took from my pocket the photo of the letter that Dave had taken; all that aching passion unfulfilled and, sure enough, there was another capital B, and very much as in Bobsy. I'm no calligrapher, but then I wasn't giving sworn evidence on the witness stand. So far as I was concerned it was good enough. Bobsy, for my money, had been to Venice, and that was near enough to Abano. But he hadn't managed to get himself killed on the Brenta Canal, not if he was sending off love-letters six weeks later. Not even Angela could bring them back from the dead. I wished he'd sent her a photograph.

And there was another thing, I thought. Birds collect photographs. They *like* having their picture taken, and Angela Rossie was a model. It happened to be her living. There *must* be photographs. I went over to the bookcase that was stacked full of paperbacks in haphazard piles, except for one neat row at the top: *The Decline and Fall of the Roman Empire* in brown calf, and not her kind of reading at all. Not anybody's. The spines of the books were all dummies. I pulled them back, and behind was what I was looking for – about fifty thousand photographs.

At least ninety per cent were her, which was fair enough. She'd begun her career with Soames-Poynter modelling clothes, with the regulation clothes-horse figure they have: lean and hungry, according to Dave, with that disdainful look they all get because they're starving. And then it seemed she started to put weight on, and the coats and dresses stopped, and the stockings and undies began, and the disdainful look disappeared. She was eating regular, though that might have been because George Watkins was feeding her. There were several pictures of him doing it at places like Annabel's... He wasn't the only one. There were lots of pictures of her with blokes, including one I'd already met in an informal sort of way. He had a camera round his neck and his sleeves rolled up. He was trying to roll them down but Angela had hold of his hand, stopping him. His left arm was needle marks from wrist to elbow, but somebody had helped him kick the habit with the aid of a .38 down by the Villa Malcontenta. Fashion photographer, I thought, by the look of the studio they were in, and wondered who had taken the happy snap. My guess was Bobsy.

There was a picture of him, too: at least I hoped it was him. He had a sort of hungry look, which suited me just fine. Then I found another one of him and her at what seemed to be a fancy-dress ball with masks: two blokes and two birds: Bobsy and Ange had taken their masks off but the other two hadn't, and that bothered me because I had the feeling that I knew those other two, so I hung on to the photograph for further study. It's against all my principles, but it was a retty grotty photo anyway, and to take a picture of it would have made it worse. So I bunged the rest of the happy snaps behind Edward Gibbon and took my leave. There was still a lot to do.

First I stopped at a telephone box and put in a reversed-charge call to a colleague in Edinburgh, H.H. Crawford. To reverse the charges is a terrible thing to do to a Scotsman, but it would be on my – or rather my client's – bill, and we both knew it. Besides, what I was asking H.H. Crawford to do was very light work indeed, and we both knew that, too. After that I took yet another cab to the Strand, and went through the gates of Somerset House to look at a will or two. It seemed to me that Day and Denville must have been deemed legally dead long ago and, if that was so, their wills would have been proved. But there weren't any wills, not that I could find, and the nice lady who was helping me supposed they must have died intestate, which made sense. A lot of young fit men do. So I looked up Betty Rossie instead. She'd left everything to her husband, Alexander, in trust for her daughter, Angela. Her executors were Anthony Palliser and Barclays Bank. I looked up Alexander Rossie. He'd left everything to his wife Elizabeth, in trust for his daughter Angela. And *his* executors were Wendy Palliser and Barclays Bank.

From what I could gather, everything meant a leasehold flat in Chelsea, some ICI shares and about fifteen thousand quid. Not a fortune, but not to be despised, not eighteen years ago. Angela's mother had added a codicil: five hundred pounds left outright to a Mrs Elizabeth Jowett, at present looking after her flat in Chelsea. Another Elizabeth.

I began to wonder about Kessler's Bonny Bessie, but Somerset House couldn't help me there. Not any more. For that I had to take a walk to Saint Catherine's House, in Kingsway. Marriages first, I thought, I don't know why, except that for some reason I had the feeling that Aunt Bessie – if Elizabeth Jowett was Aunt Bessie – was the type to get married.

She took a lot of finding. The indexes to the registers at Saint Catherine's House are on open shelves, and seem to weigh about a hundredweight apiece, and since I didn't have a date for a marriage I had to pull out the ones for the dates I fancied and just keep going. My best bet, when I found it, was an Elizabeth Jago who'd married a Herbert Jowett in Putney in 1935. She'd been twenty at the time, which put her in her seventies now, if she was still alive. I tried the deaths, and she wasn't there, so I tried the births instead. They'd had a son in 1943, Robert Lachlan Jowett. Then I finally got a bit of sense and went back to the deaths. Herbert Jowett had died in Singapore in 1946. Cause of death, malaria. In other words it was odds on he'd been a Jap POW, and astronomic odds against he was the father of their child. I tried for a Thomas Jowett in both the marriages and deaths registers. No joy. Then I looked at my watch. I had twenty minutes to get back to Chelsea and see Miss Rossie. All the same I made time to telephone H.H. Crawford again in Scotland. Lachlan is a Scottish name after all and, if it wasn't much of a chance, it was still the only chance I'd had.

13

She'd gone to a lot of trouble. Even I could see that, and I'm no magazine editor. She was beautiful of course, but then she always was. That wasn't it. What it was was grooming, like a dog at a show. Or a prize bitch. She wore a dress of the kind of blue that exactly suited her, the kind Dave was ransacking the dictionary to find the words for. Her shoes looked new and her nylons were like gossamer. No jewellery except a pair of diamond-stud earrings, and the kind of make-up that looks like no make-up at all. And with it all that rounded slimness, the hazel eyes, the black, smooth hair... I began to feel sorry for Dave, even if I did have troubles of my own. When she stood there in the doorway I gawked. Any man would.

'It was sweet of you to call,' she said. 'Do come in.'

Then she turned and I followed her, and that was nice too.

We went into the drawing-room and she told

me that I'd find the armchair was comfortable, and it was. She curled up on the sofa the way the model-school had taught her: a kind of sexy gracefulness.

'David wasn't sure you'd be able to see me,' she said.

'I've been pretty busy,' I said, and I had, too. In that very room.

'It was kind of you to spare the time,' she said. 'Can I get you anything? A cup of coffee?'

'No thanks,' I said.

'A glass of wine? I know.' Then she was up and off before I could refuse, then back in with a couple of glasses and a bottle of Roederer Cristal in a cooler. The last time I'd seen it had been in her fridge. I wondered how much Dave had paid for it. 'You open it,' she said. 'I'm sure you'll do it far better than I could.' She didn't say how big and strong I was, but she looked it. I opened the bottle. Was I being seduced? I asked myself. All the same I poured the wine. 'Cheers,' she said, and sipped, then went back to resume her pose on the sofa, and sipped again.

'There's nothing like champagne, is there?' she said. 'It's almost a sexual experience.' I waited.

'But first you'll want to know why I asked you here,' she said.

I liked her use of words. 'First' implied everything but promised nothing.

'Of course you're looking for the Dak,' she said. 'A for Arthur. I know that.'

'Who told you?'

'Uncle Bertie. He always told me things.'

'How about Uncle Tony?'

'Do you mean Tony Palliser? I don't call him uncle.'

'Why not?'

'I don't like him. He tried to seduce me once.' I waited. 'He didn't succeed. I mean I like older men but not that much older.' My age? I wondered. But she was too smart to say it.

'And of course he's rich, too,' she said. 'Filthy rich. But then there's Wendy.'

'Wendy?' I said.

'Don't tell me you don't know about Mrs Palliser,' she said. 'You're much too clever. But anyway Tony Palliser never talked about marriage. Only bed. He got quite nasty when I wouldn't.'

'You think I shouldn't be working for him?'

'I didn't say that.' She moved on the sofa, and a nyloned knee appeared. I was in for a busy afternoon, it seemed. 'We all have to live. Only–'

'Only what?'

'If you find it he'll claim it.'

'Why shouldn't he?' I said. 'It's his property.'

'Yes, but not what's in it,' she said. 'That's not his. Never was.'

'And what do you think's in it?'

'Some sort of a treasure,' she said. 'Uncle Bertie told me that, too. Don't try to tell me you don't know.'

'You think I should give it back to its rightful owners?'

Another wriggle. The other knee showed.

'Of course not,' she said. 'I think you should keep it for us.'

'We'd have to find it first,' I said.

'I think I could help you there,' she said.

214

'No kidding?'

'I never kid about money,' she said. 'Believe me.' I did.

'All right,' I said. 'You've got something I need. Is that it?'

'I like to think so,' she said.

'And you can cut that out for a start,' I said. 'Business first, remember?'

'Yes, of course. But the thing is – are you coming in with us? Half each?'

'Us?'

'My friend and I,' she said. 'We're partners. In this thing at any rate.'

'George Watkins?'

'Oh! You know about Georgie? But of course you do. David told you.' She laughed, and I have never heard prettier laughter. 'No. Not Georgie. He's much too nervous. Mind you, he can be useful if we need him. Electronics and all that. But you haven't even said if you're in or not.'

'In on robbing Tony Palliser?'

'Would it bother you?'

'Not a lot,' I said. 'But wouldn't we be robbing Mrs Benskin too?'

'Uncle Bertie wouldn't even have looked at that money,' Angela said, 'and I doubt if Jocasta would either. Anyway she's rich enough already.'

'That must be nice,' I said. 'Being rich enough.'

'Yes it must be,' she said. 'But I'm not.'

'But you will be if you get a half of what's missing?'

'It'll be a start,' she said. 'Well?'

'It all depends on what you've got.'

'So it does,' she said. 'What I've got is the name

215

of the man who knows where A for Arthur is. All you have to do is get him to tell you where it is.'

'And how would I do that?'

'You and David would think of something.'

I found it hard to believe what I was hearing. Go and lift another one of her boyfriends and torture him was what it amounted to. 'I'll have to think about it,' I said.

'Of course.' She smiled; one of her best ones. 'But don't take too long. Now come and give me a nice kiss.'

'After I've thought about it,' I said, and she looked relieved. Lust didn't seem to be her best sin. What she was good at was avarice. I drank what was left in my glass and scarpered before she could make me change my mind. But at least I'd cleared up one problem. It wasn't my body she was after. So far as she was concerned Jocasta could have it.

I went back to Putney – more of Palliser's money for cabs – and told a lot of lies to a Municipal Employee. This time I was a solicitor from the firm of Ringwood, Bellman and True or whatever it was. I was their Mr Mould and I handed over my card to prove it. Useful things cards. I have them printed specially. There was a missing heir, and a recently dead relative in Canada who had bequeathed what I called a substantial sum. The Municipal Employee loved it, and went to an awful lot of trouble on my behalf, which was very nice of him. After all there was nothing in it for him... A Miss Elizabeth Jago, I told him, who had become a Mrs Elizabeth Jowett. That was when the slog began – going through the electoral roll. We found Mrs Jowett in Palmerston Street from 1938 to 1950, but then she disappeared and a Mr and Mrs Toogood moved in. Mrs Jowett didn't show anywhere else in Putney, which didn't surprise me. Not really. Mrs Toogood had now moved to a Putney Old People's Home, and her first name was Elizabeth. Bonny Bessie had married again – I'd bet my life on it. Moreover it looked as though she'd been widowed again too.

So that was my next call. I took a bus – not because I felt sorry for Palliser: I just couldn't find a taxi. At the Old People's Home my luck ran out. It looked nice, clean and airy and comfortable, with a couple of trees and some grass. Worth perhaps a twentieth of Wendy Palliser's little home from home, but nice. I rang the bell and got to see the matron who ran the place and told some more lies. I was still Mr Mould of Ringwood, Bellman and True, but I was a lot less specific about why. After all I had to meet the lady. But I hinted about money in a vague way, and the matron was delighted. Nursing people who had the disease called old age, which is incurable, had given her a toughness like armour, but for Mrs Toogood she was delighted.

'Oh, how marvellous,' she said.

'You realise that these are very early days–' I began.

'Yes, but even so. And Mrs Toogood of all people.'

You'd have thought I was the man from the Pools.

'It's a pity she's away,' the matron said.

'On holiday?'

'Oh, no. Just for the day. Seaside outing to Brighton. She loves it there.'

'Do you have a picture of her by any chance?' I asked her.

She did, too. Hanging up on her office wall. Some telly star or other had come round to hand out presents at Christmas and so naturally PR had taken a photograph, and matron had it up on her wall. She took it down and showed me. Mrs Toogood was the sort the camera goes for, even at her age, which must have been nearer eighty than seventy. Plump and jolly and good-natured; she must have been a good-looker in her day, of a type you don't see all that much now. The names drifted back from the old movies I'd seen on television: Alice Faye and Joan Blondell and Betty Grable. Mrs Toogood would have been right in there with them. No wonder she was fond of Brighton: it could have been built for her. One day, I thought, Jocasta Benskin will look like that.

'Perhaps I could see her tomorrow?' I said.

'Certainly. I'm afraid she'll be far too tired tonight. But it'll keep for one more day.'

Then the phone rang and she said 'Excuse me' and picked it up.

'Matron,' she said, and that was all she said for two minutes at least. I couldn't make out the words of the voice at the other end, but it was excited and shrill. The matron sat like a stone. Stunned with shock, the cliché says, but like a lot of clichés it's true. Then suddenly the tears welled up and flowed, and she made no move to dry her eyes, just sat and let me watch her weep.

At last she said, 'Get them home as quick as you can. I'm sorry, I–' Then she hung up in mid-sentence and found her handkerchief at last, and I sat and waited, but I already knew.

'I'm sorry,' she said at last. 'I'm behaving very badly.'

'Not at all,' I said. 'You've obviously had bad news.'

'We both have,' the matron said. 'That was one of my nurses. She was in charge of the Brighton trip. Mrs Toogood's dead.'

'How did it happen?'

'Outside a pub,' the matron said. 'Near the Lanes. There was a room with a piano. Bessie – Mrs Toogood – enjoyed a sing-song. They all did, but Bessie – how can I explain it?'

'She was the one who got them going,' I said.

'Yes,' the matron said. 'She was... She had more money than most of them, and she always bought more than her share. But that wasn't it.' For a moment I thought that she would weep again, but she fought it back. 'Bessie Toogood was life itself,' she said. 'In here, I mean. And now it's over.'

'Do they know who did it?' I asked.

By no means the question I should have asked, but she was still in shock and answered at once.

'A young man and woman. Really quite young. The woman hit her with some sort of cosh I'd suppose you'd call it – while the man grabbed her handbag. Then they ran to a car – quite a big car apparently – and drove off.'

'Who drove?' I asked. 'The man or the woman?'

'Neither. There was a man already there,' said the matron. 'It's grotesque.'

'In what way?'

'Bessie read the papers. She knew how often old people were attacked and robbed. So she never carried more than fifty pounds at the most... I mean three of them. For perhaps seventeen pounds apiece...' She covered her face.

'I hope she died without too much pain,' I said. Her hands dropped, and she looked at me hard. There were no tears left.

'I hope so too,' she said. 'That bitch smashed her skull to pulp.'

It was time to visit my sister.

Anna Maria was pleased to see me. She said so, and anyway the wine she opened said so too: champagne, or very nearly. Spumante anyway.

'You look happy,' I said.

'That's because you owe me money.'

'You found her?'

'Mrs Elizabeth Toogood,' said my sister. 'Formerly of 23, Palmerston Street – now in the Elm Park Old People's Home.'

'That was quick,' I said.

She grinned. 'I had a lot of help,' she said.

I sipped my wine. Roederer Cristal it wasn't. 'Let's hear it,' I said.

'My generation are all too young,' Anna Maria said. 'So I got on to the ones whose mothers were still alive. The ones who'd always lived in Putney. Half a dozen of them remembered her. Two gave her address. And now I've given it to you.' She held out her hand. 'Pay me.'

'In a minute,' I said. 'Tell me about her first.'

'They all liked her,' she said. 'Every single one. I know it sounds incredible – six women with

220

nothing but good things to say about a seventh. But it's true.'

'What was she *like?*' I said.

'Not "was". Is,' said Anna Maria. 'I told you. She's in the Old People's Home. You don't *listen.*'

'Sorry,' I said.

'She's cheerful, makes you laugh, they all said. Active for her age, which seems to be about seventy-eight. Very pretty when she was young – and probably no better than she should be.'

'Promiscuous, you mean?'

'That's a very hurtful way to put it,' said Anna Maria. 'The old girls were much kinder.'

'Why were they?' I said. 'It's the sort of thing you'd expect them to enjoy getting their claws into.'

She looked up ready to snap, but then she didn't. She's a shrewd one, Anna Maria. She knew I was right.

'I think it was the war,' she said. 'Quite a lot of women were that way then, the way they told it. I don't mean promiscuous necessarily. But they were lonely and their men were away, and there was the blitz and the buzz bombs. They all needed someone... So they didn't blame Mrs Toogood. Only she wasn't Mrs Toogood then. She was Mrs Jowett. Her husband was a POW of the Japs in Singapore. More than three years on her own.'

'Not quite,' I said. 'Not the way you're telling it.'

'She may have had a baby,' Anna Maria said.

'What do you mean, may?'

'She went to her sister's place in Nottingham for six months only my most reliable source doesn't think it was a sister. It was a midwife.'

221

'And still nobody disapproved?'

'Nobody.'

'She must have–' I checked and started again. 'She must be a remarkable woman. Anything known about the child?'

'No,' Anna Maria said. 'She lived alone until she got word her husband was dead. Then she married Walter Toogood. No more children. From then on she was Aunty Bessie to everyone.'

'Bonny Bessie was what I heard.'

'That would be the blokes,' my sister said. 'To my girlfriends she was Aunty. Always.'

'Did you ask why?'

'I know why,' she said. 'It was because of the way she was – like the aunt you always wanted – to her women friends, I mean.'

'And her boyfriends? During the war?'

'You don't want much, do you?'

'I want all I can get,' I said. 'Please, sis.'

'All right,' she said. 'But there isn't much. A lot of them liked the Yanks, what with being so friendly and outgoing and fond of a good time, but Mrs Jowett was an RAF girl. Right till the end of the war.'

'Any names?'

'Have a heart,' my sister said, and that was fair enough: I reckoned I knew a couple anyway. I took out my emergency money and gave her five twenties.

'But that's far too much,' she said.

'Going rate,' I told her. 'Go on, take it. The client's paying.' So she took it.

'Why are you looking for her?' she asked me. 'Or can't you tell?'

'She's got a bit of money coming,' I said. 'A lawyer asked me to find her.'

'And paid you so much you can give me a hundred pounds for just gossiping? I don't believe you, Tommaso.'

'Nevertheless,' I said, 'when your friends get around to asking, that's what you tell them.' I got to my feet. 'I have to go,' I said. 'Got a lot to do.'

'Have you seen Sabena yet?'

'I will,' I said. 'I promise you.' But not yet.

'I worry about you,' my sister said.

'Why?'

'Why should I tell you? Your head's big enough as it is.'

Then she kissed me and let me go.

Maybe my sister's questions had caused Bessie Toogood's death, and if that was the case then the responsibility was mine and mine alone. Or maybe it was just me anyway, running around being nosey, seeking old secrets. Or maybe it was neither of us, and I hoped to God that was the answer. I really had liked the sound of that woman. Time to stop thinking about whose fault it was and call on Mr Kagan.

When I got there the South East local news was showing on TV, and Mr Kagan shushed me as soon as I tried to say something. He looked terrible. 'The Brighton murder,' the announcer said, and I doubt if Mr Kagan would have heard me if I'd fired a shotgun. His whole being was concentrated on the screen. Out it all came: the female mugger, the male back-up, the driver waiting in the getaway car that might have been a

223

Ford Granada or maybe a big Datsun... And if anybody could help the police in the pursuit of their enquiries... That was the bit that hurt most. Because there was someone. There was me. I waited until the TV announcer's voice, hitting all the wrong emphases the way they do, was over, and Mr Kagan switched off the set. 'Terrible,' he said. 'Terrible.' Then he walked out of the room and I sat and worried about whether the documents I'd given him could possibly put him on to Mrs Toogood.

He came back with a bottle of vodka and two glasses, and this time I didn't argue, just took mine and knocked it back the way he did his. Ice-cold it was, but with a glow like a log fire in winter.

'Always the old,' Mr Kagan said, and I began to feel better and ashamed of myself for it. To Mr Kagan it was personal.

'Always the old,' he said again. 'And yet we are harmless. Why do they treat us so when we are harmless?'

'Because you're easy as well,' I said.

'Of course,' he said. 'I am a fool to ask such a question. Any Jew would be a fool to ask such a question.' He sighed. 'You knew of this case?'

'I've heard about it,' I said, glad to be telling the truth for once.

'An old woman. Happy with her friends. Glad to go out for a day at the seaside.' He poured more vodka, and this time I sipped.

'Not like the people whose dossiers you brought me,' he said. 'They were neither harmless nor easy. Not easy at all.' His piercing eyes grew pleading. 'It would be too much to ask if they are at liberty?'

224

'If they're who I think they are – they're dead,' I told him.

'Aah.' His sigh was pure satisfaction. 'Then they didn't live to spend it all.'

'All what?'

'The things they stole from Jews in the death camps... There were communists too, of course, and gypsies and partisans. But mostly it was the Jews who had the rich things.'

'They didn't live to spend any of it,' I said.

'Aah' once more, and then a look almost of shame.

'It is not very nice to be happy that men have died,' said Mr Kagan, 'even bad men. But these committed such wickedness–'

'They were SS,' I said.

He didn't even hear me.

'They stole from the dying and the dead they had themselves killed,' he said. 'It was a very successful way to make money. When the war ended they were very rich.'

'Do you know how rich?' I asked.

He shrugged. 'They kept records, of course.'

'*What?*'

'They were Germans,' said Mr Kagan. 'German Party members. Of course they kept records. So far as I can discover, the poorest of them, by the reckoning of 1945, had at least a hundred thousand pounds.'

'So five of them–'

'Half a million,' said Mr Kagan, 'plus another hundred thousand for the plane.'

'That's there too? The plane?'

'Patience,' Mr Kagan said. 'All in good time.'

225

This might well be the last big set-piece of his life. He wasn't going to rush it.

'Sorry,' I said. 'Take your time.'

'Everything was weighed, measured, recorded,' Mr Kagan said, 'so that wherever they finished up they would know precisely how much they were worth. Not such fools, eh, Ron? Not even when they handed over such dangerous knowledge to the pilots of the Dakota.'

'How could you possibly know that?' I asked him.

'Because they told me, these Reichsstandarten and Obersturmbahnführern – these important officers of the SS. They had made a bargain with the pilots–'

'A hundred thousand pounds,' I said. 'Fifty thousand each.'

'Just so. They made it because they had no choice. They had nothing to sell to the Americans or the British, and they were too late to turn their coats and join the KGB. And they had not been considered quite important enough to be taken by U-boat to South America. So they hid – and waited for an angel to help them – an angel with wings.'

'Have you any idea how much a hundred thousand pounds would be now?' I asked.

'I tried to find out,' Mr Kagan said. 'I know I should not – but the need to know was overwhelming. I'm sorry.'

I let it lie. I needed to know too.

'I have a friend who is a jeweller. I asked while we gossiped. Maybe he was fooled. But if not – he has no reason to talk.'

'How much?' I said.

'In the form in which it was – gold, jewels – maybe a million. Maybe a little more.'

'So we're talking about six million pounds in all?'

Six million it would be impossible to keep quiet, but it was all going to come out soon anyway.

'Rather more,' Mr Kagan said. 'There is another fifty thousand pounds which they call their *Eventualitätfonds* – Contingency Fund you would say. That was for the people who arranged their escape. It is all there. Written down.'

Another half million. 'Why did the pilots have all this?'

'Because they did not trust their passengers. They insisted on holding the documents till they reached their destination.'

'But how do you know?'

'Because the passengers wrote it down,' Mr Kagan said. 'They added an extra page.' He pushed a neatly typed sheet of paper at me. 'There is a copy. Beneath is my translation. There is also this.' He added four more sheets of paper. 'This I don't want to talk about, not even to you. The rest will take several days.'

'I may not need the rest,' I said.

'I should be happy if you did not. This hurts me. You would think old men would grow used to pain. But I cannot. Not this kind.'

I took out my wallet, but Mr Kagan shook his head. 'No,' he said.

'Give it away,' I said.

'No,' he said. 'I give you this as a gift. May God forgive me.' He pushed the stack of papers towards me, and I put them back in their envelope.

'I made some notes,' he said. 'But I burned them. So far as I am concerned I have never seen those papers.'

'What papers?' I asked him, and he smiled.

'You are a nice boy, Ron,' he said. 'Too nice for the business you are in.'

When I got back to our room I opened the envelope at once. If its contents were too hot for Mr Kagan, maybe they were too hot for Dave, too, but all I could see was a couple of pages in German followed by Mr Kagan's translation: a list of names, and sums of money beside them, and the reasons why it had been paid. One of the names was Joachim Kessler. He'd been paid five thousand quid for what they'd called 'removal of extraneous personnel' – Denville and Day. It seemed that forty years ago in Berlin gratitude only went so far – even if you were a philosopher. The second page related to the two pilots. Their names were there too, in the old-fashioned Gothic script that's impossible to read it you don't know how, which is why the Germans had used it... All that meticulous paperwork, those careful precautions against blackmail, and still they'd drowned like rats. For once there had been justice.

And that was about it – except for the loose ends, and God knows there were enough of them; the loosest of them all in a manner of speaking being Sabena. But she would still have to wait, I decided. She ought to have got used to that by now.

First there was the problem of Dave to be settled: Dave with a 357 Colt Magnum revolver. Needed a lot of thinking about, that did. A lot of thinking. Like I say, Dave's my best mate and always has been, but when a bird comes along he can get a bit huffy, and physical with it – never mind the gun. And the trouble with guns is that if there's one handy, sooner or later it'll go off, which is why I never use one; that and being a coward. And being a coward wasn't going to help me talk to Dave about his little Angie, either. I thought about having a drink, but on top of Mr Kagan's vodka I'd have ended up legless... He came in looking pleased with himself.

14

'I've been driving Angela around,' he said.

'I thought you were going to test that gun,' I said.

'That was this morning.'

'How was it?'

'All right,' he said. 'I phoned her and she was free for lunch, only she had a few calls to make after. So I drove her around.'

Usually he hates mini-cabbing but he spoke like it was driving the Queen in the State Coach to open Parliament. 'We had a lovely time,' he said.

'Smashing,' I said.

Dave took a good look at me, then he lit a cigarette and didn't even bother to apologise. 'All right,' he said. 'Let's have it.'

'It's a bit tricky,' I said.

'It's Angela,' he said.

How he knew I still have no idea except, like I say, we've been mates a long time.

'She's up to a bit of no good, Dave,' I said.

'You better be sure,' he said.

'Let me tell it and judge for yourself.'

'Do I have to?' Suddenly he slapped the table with his hand, hard. 'Listen to me,' he said. 'Talking like a wimp. Go ahead and tell me – only I hope to God you're convincing, for both our sakes.'

'Why on earth should I make it up?' I said. 'Do you think I'm enjoying this?

'I don't know what I think,' he said. 'All I know is I worship that girl.'

'Course you do,' I said. 'She's beautiful. Clever too. And ambitious. She likes the good life.'

'Who doesn't?' said Dave.

'Hear me out,' I said. 'She used to be a top model–'

'She still is,' Dave said.

'Not for clothes,' I said. 'Not any more. Clothes is where the money is, only she put a bit of weight on so now it's knickers and stockings and bras. There's a living in it – but it isn't a rich living.'

Then I hurried on before he asked me how I knew. He wasn't ready for that, not then. 'So she's got a problem,' I said.

'It hurts me to say this,' Dave said, 'but she's also got a rich boy-friend – and I don't mean me.'

'George Watkins the computer king,' I said. 'Okay. But she doesn't want to be a girl-friend.

Not his or anybody else's. She likes to be her own boss.'

'Maybe that's why she's a virgin,' Dave said.

The going was getting rougher every minute.

'I don't think she's the kind who needs love,' I said. 'What she's after is power. And for her that means money.'

Dave got to his feet then. 'Now you be careful,' he said.

'I'm not after a belting,' I said. 'Least of all from you. But people have been killed. *Nice* people. Sit down and listen and grow up.'

And he sat without a word. Then he took an enormous drag at his cigarette just to show me he had a little freedom of choice yet, and I loved him like the brother I never had.

'People like her,' I said. 'You, George Watkins, all kinds of people. Including Bertie Benskin.' He opened his mouth, then showed his class by shutting it again and waiting.

'I don't mean that Benskin necessarily wanted to go to bed with her,' I said. 'I should think his wife would have been all the women he needed for one life-time. But she's young and pretty and sweet when she wants to be – and Bertie would have appreciated that. And she used it. Uncle Bertie she called him. Always good for a loan.'

'How do you know?'

'I found a fifty-pound note in his study. As a matter of fact he was using it as a book-mark.'

Dave shouted his laughter. 'I wish to God I'd met him,' he said.

'Angela has one too,' I said.

'So do a lot of people.'

'Hers has the next number from his.'

Dave mashed out his cigarette. 'Fifty pounds?'

That's right,' I said.

'A whole note – or two halves?'

'Intact,' I said, then wished I hadn't. We were back to virgins.

'It isn't enough,' said Dave.

'She has a gun, too,' I said. 'A Smith and Wesson .38 with the square butt and the chequered barrel.'

'Like the one you saw in Abano?' said Dave.

'Exactly like it,' I said. 'Like the one Mrs Palliser said her husband has an' all.'

'So what you're telling me is you turned her place over?'

'I'm sorry,' I said, 'but I had to know.'

'And now you do know... But you didn't tell me.'

'I'm telling you now,' I said.

'And I'm beginning to wonder why,' said Dave.

'We're coming to that,' I said, and reached into my pocket, took out the photo I'd nicked from behind the phoney books. Dave looked at it. 'That's Bobsy,' I said. 'Don't you think?'

'Could be,' Dave said. 'It's somebody else as well. It's the geezer who tried to belt you.'

'Except you belted him first.'

'Masked ball,' he said. 'Sounds like Venice.'

'No way,' I said. 'She wouldn't go near the place. Some Yuppie do in Chelsea, Belgravia or Knightsbridge perhaps.'

'What about the two with the masks on?'

'Maybe they tried to belt me too,' I said.

'You're saying Angela knew about it?'

'She had to,' I said. 'It's the only way it fits together.'

He nodded, but he still couldn't let go.

'But if you're right,' he said, 'why did she start being nice to me – to both of us? After all, she sent for you too. Why didn't she just have another go at us instead?'

'Because she found out we were getting close,' I said. 'It was a lot easier to proposition me.'

'She did that?'

'You know she did,' I said.

'Champers?' I nodded. 'Roederer Cristal 1982,' he said. 'I hope you enjoyed it.'

'Put it on the bill,' I said. 'Anyway I turned her down.'

'You what?'

'All we did was discuss a deal.'

'You turned down that?' He was yelling again. 'I don't believe you.'

'We never lie to each other,' I said, 'and I'm not starting now.'

'But why not?'

'Because I didn't fancy her.'

He looked at me again, and knew that what I had said was true. 'Who do you fancy, Ron?' he said. 'Sabena or Mrs Benskin?'

Now wasn't the proper time. There would never be a proper time.

'Leave it out,' I said. 'She offered a deal. She knows where to reach the guy who's got the money. She offered me half for us to go and lift him and find out what he knows.'

'And how are we supposed to do that?'

'Thumbscrews, needles under the nails, electric

233

shocks up the you-know-where.'

'She said that?'

'She didn't have to,' I said. 'What other way is there? Then when we got the information she'd have us knocked off by Bobsy and his pals.'

'She didn't tell you who this geezer is?'

'No,' I said. 'But I found out.'

'Or how much is involved?'

'I found that out too. But not from her.'

'How much then?'

'Six million pounds,' I said.

'*Six million?*'

'In today's money. Then there was another million for those two pilots – and a half-million or so that just disappeared.'

Dave just sat there – looking at me and shaking his head. 'You're telling me we've got a million quid in a safe deposit?'

'Somebody has,' I said.

'Yeah, I know,' said Dave. 'But a million. Half each – that would be reasonable, wouldn't it?'

'She doesn't want half a million,' I said. 'She wants six million.' Dave shook his head as if I'd thumped him.

'Sorry,' he said. 'It's just the way she gets me. Like I was drunk or something. Take no notice.'

'Of course not.'

'The one who knows where it is – you reckon you're on to him?'

'My guess is his name is Robert Lachlan Finlayson... You've met him.'

'Never in my life,' said Dave, then: 'Oh. Up in the Hebrides. The geezer with the boat?'

The old Dave was taking over again, but I

234

couldn't start to relax just yet.

'His old man was in the Air Force during the war,' I said. 'When it was over he worked for Ad Astra Airlines as a mechanic. Got to meet Todd and Myers at Heathrow. I suppose it had just opened up.'

'But how would Angela find that out?'

'Uncle Bertie,' I said.

'He must have had it bad,' said Dave.

'He loved to gossip,' I said, 'and she was good at listening.'

And that was all there was to it, I was almost sure – but not quite. You can never be quite sure about that kind of thing. Not that it mattered. He was a very nice man and he was dead. 'Are you saying she killed him?'

'Had him killed,' I said.

'But why?'

'Because he found out,' I said.

'About the six million?'

'Or the fact that she was after it. Or maybe she asked too many questions about Finlayson. Maybe that set off his suspicions... I'm sorry, Dave. There's no way I can wrap this up. It looks like she had Finlayson's mother killed, too.' I told him about Mrs Toogood, and this time he heard me out in silence. When I had done, he said, 'As you so aptly put it, people have died. Nice people.'

'And one poor bastard on the Brenta Canal,' I said.

Dave said, 'It's up to you now, Ron.'

'Let me make a phone-call.' I dialled Jocasta Benskin's number, and she answered it herself.

'What happened to Miss Brisk?' I asked.

'Who?... Oh, Beverly. I don't know. She's disappeared. It's funny.'

'Why funny?'

'Angela's disappeared too. I phoned you about it but you weren't in.'

'I'm living somewhere else just now,' I said. 'How do you know she's disappeared?'

'I get so lonely,' she said. 'If you have to live out why don't you come here? God knows the bed's big enough.'

'Angela,' I said.

'She tells such lies,' said Jocasta Benskin. 'Told me she'd loaned poor Bertie a book and I let her in the study and she ransacked the place.'

Only a wife, I thought, could tell that study had been ransacked.

'How do you know she's disappeared?'

'I watched her go. In a car. A big one, not hers. Full of luggage. That was yesterday. I've been phoning ever since. Come to bed and you can tell me all about it later.'

'I can't,' I said.

'You will,' she said. 'You'll see.' Then she hung up. I told Dave what I'd learned.

'So what do we do now?' he asked.

'Ask questions.'

'I don't want to see her,' he said. 'Not yet.'

'Not her,' I said. 'George Watkins.'

'He's in it too?'

'She says so,' I said. 'Let's find out. He may take a bit of persuading.'

Dave's hand darted beneath his coat, came out holding the Magnum. 'I'll persuade him,' he said.

236

'Not with that,' I said. 'Dead men don't answer questions.'

But he wasn't listening.

'You know what, Ron,' he said. 'I don't believe she was a virgin at all.'

Kelham Mansions, Notting Hill, was a lot better than I thought it would be. I hadn't allowed for the fact that this part could be Yuppie country. Anyway Dave rang the bell marked 'Porter' and his mate appeared and opened the front door and I bunged him a tenner from Palliser and we went in.

Dave still had a head of steam up, and it didn't surprise me. For the first time since I'd known him he'd asked me to drive the car. On the way up in the lift I asked him again to take it easy and he said he'd try, then we got out and walked over to number 43 and I knocked because Dave looked like he might use the butt of the Magnum. From inside a voice said, 'Who is it?'

'Message from Miss Angela Rossie,' I said, and the door opened so fast he must have run to it.

Tallish, thinnish, starting to go bald far too early, with a mouth that looked weak and eyes that looked clever.

'Well?' he said.

'It's – sort of private,' I said. 'May we come in?'

'No,' he said. 'I know about you. You're Hogget.' He turned to Dave. 'And you're Baxter. I don't want you in my flat.'

So Dave scooped him up like he was some sort of untidy parcel and took him inside and I followed. It looked as if Dave had read the message of the mouth all right. I hoped he'd remem-

237

bered the eyes as well.

It wasn't a bad pad: not bad at all. I took a walk round it just to make sure Watkins didn't have any more visitors, while Dave held him and listened to his complaints. The bedroom was just a place to sleep, but comfortable. The three-quarter bed had made me realise how tired I was just by looking, and the rest of the furniture looked like money too, even if it didn't look much like taste. By the bedside were a couple of books: *Alice in Wonderland* and *Alice Through the Looking Glass*. We all have to relax sometimes – but these looked like first editions.

The bathroom and shower were brand-new and the best available, the kitchen just a place to use a microwave and a fridge-freezer. That left the living-room. Wall to wall computers, like Dave had said, but also a sofa and chairs with the same characterless, expensive look as the stuff in the bedroom. And Dave and George Watkins, of course. Dave had let go of him, but they were both still standing.

'You've committed an offence,' Watkins told me.

'Not yet,' said Dave.

That wasn't the way: at least not yet.

'I apologise, Mr Watkins,' I said. 'But if you'll just let me explain–'

'Why should I?'

'Because if you do,' said Dave, 'you increase the chances of not having your arm broken.'

'Now, Dave,' I said.

'Don't you now Dave me. This idiot seems to think he's in charge here.'

'I am not an idiot,' said Watkins. 'My IQ is

238

rather unusually high as it happens.' His voice was trembling, but even so he went on. 'For example I know that you're using a standard interrogation technique. You–' he nodded at Dave '–adopting the role of bully, while you–' this time I got the nod '–pretend to be my friend.'

'You know that, do you?' said Dave.

'It's obvious.'

'Well, of course it is,' said Dave. 'But that doesn't matter a monkey's manoeuvre. What's important about this technique is that it works – whether the subject recognises it's being done to him or not. Maybe it even works better if the subject does realise it, because then he's already worried about what the bully's going to do to him.'

'Mr Watkins,' I said. 'It doesn't have to be like that.'

'You see?' he said. 'You're still doing it.'

He could hardly get the words out his voice was shaking so much, and yet he said them. I hoped I wasn't going to like him too much.

'We really do have a message,' I said. 'About Angela Rossie.'

'You said from her.'

'Look, mate,' Dave said. 'You're in no shape to start arguing about a preposition.'

The clever eyes flicked across at him, recording the fact that this was an educated bully.

'You've come to threaten me through her.'

'You could put it that way,' I said. 'Or you could say we're doing you both a favour.'

'What a liar you are,' he said, and Dave hit him. It was a slap, open-handed and almost con-temptuous, but it knocked Watkins sprawling

239

into an over-stuffed leather chair.

'Manners,' said Dave. 'I shan't tell you again.'

Watkins rubbed his cheek then examined his fingers as if the pain had rubbed off on them.

'She's in trouble,' I said. 'Big trouble. I think maybe you are too.' I waited, but he didn't answer: just stared at his fingers.

'She's mixed up in a murder.' Still no answer. 'I'm not boring you, am I?'

'You are a bit,' he said. 'Such silly lies.'

I reached out and grabbed Dave's arm before the punch could land.

'He means it,' I said. 'He really thinks we're lying. We have to show him we're not.'

'Go ahead,' said Dave. 'It'll hurt him more than a belting anyway.' Watkins's hand dropped, the clever eyes looked again at Dave, then away. I took out the photograph, showed it to Watkins.

'She went to a ball,' he said. 'So what? She often does.'

'She went to a masked ball,' I said. 'It shouldn't be hard to find out where. There aren't all that many.'

Michael Copland would tell me, I thought – if he ever told me anything again.

'Why bother?'

'The bloke with her is called Bobsy.'

'Sounds like a queer,' Watkins said.

'He assaulted me. He did kill Bertie Benskin – and he was involved in the death of Elizabeth Toogood.'

'Never heard of her.'

'Elizabeth Jowett as was,' I said, and waited.

At last he said, 'I hear what you say' – the

240

current variation on 'No comment'.

Two days ago,' I said, 'she went on a trip to Brighton and got coshed and robbed. Bobsy drove what the Yanks call the getaway car. These two–' I tapped the two masked figures in the photograph '–did the coshing and robbing. Only they got a bit too enthusiastic. Mrs Toogood – Mrs Jowett as was – died. She was murdered.'

'By friends of Angela's,' said Dave.

'So *you* say,' he said.

'She has a gun in her flat,' I said, 'a Smith and Wesson .38. A man held a gun like that on me at a place called Abano earlier this year.' No answer. 'Later on that same bloke was murdered. Shot. The Italian police got the bullet out of him. It was a .38.'

'There must be thousands of .38 revolvers,' said Watkins. 'Maybe even hundreds of thousands.'

This time Dave was too quick for me. He reached across and belted Watkins again, a harder one this time, and Watkins yelled.

'See sense, man,' I said. 'She knows who got the treasure from the Dakota. She wants Dave and me to lift him and make him hand it over. *Make him.* That means torture him – and it was her idea.'

'She couldn't have,' said Watkins.

'But she did,' said Dave. 'Just like she knew an old lady was going to die. And how come you didn't know about it anyway? Don't you ever read the papers – watch television?'

'Not when I'm working,' Watkins said. 'And I have been working rather hard lately.'

'Doing what?' said Dave. 'A few odd jobs for Angela?'

241

Watkins tried to look determined but his mouth wouldn't let him. 'It's none of your business,' he said.

Dave's hand disappeared beneath his coat, came out holding the Magnum.

'You want to prove you're tough,' he said. 'Okay. I'm here to help you.'

I wasn't going to grab Dave's hand again, not when it had a gun in it, but then Watkins got lucky. The phone rang.

Dave aimed the Magnum at a spot precisely between Watkins's eyes. 'Answer it,' he said, 'and be careful what you say. Ron, you listen.'

Watkins reached out and picked up the phone from a small table, and I stood close and listened.

A man's voice said, 'Bathurst Hotel?'

'I'm sorry,' said Watkins. 'You have the wrong number.'

Then he hung up.

Dave looked at me. 'It's okay,' I said, and Dave lowered the gun.

'I was going to give you what we in the trade call a pistol-whipping,' he said, 'but let me ask you a question first. Do you believe what we told you about Mrs Toogood?'

'No,' said Watkins. 'I don't think I do.'

'Okay,' said Dave, and looked at his watch. 'There'll be news on ITV in a few minutes. If it says there she was murdered – will you call them liars too?'

'I don't want to know,' said Watkins.

'You're going to know,' said Dave, and at that Watkins took off, just like that, making a dash for the door. Dave stretched out one leg and hooked

Watkins's feet from under him, bringing him down, then reached down left-handed and pulled him back up on his feet, pushed him into a chair.

'Don't be silly,' he said. 'You've got to face the truth – you know you have. So just you sit still and behave.'

I switched on the set. Mrs Toogood's murder was the seventh item. The journalist reported on it from Brighton with a kind of gloomy relish that if anything increased its horror. There was no doubt that Watkins thought so too. By the look of him he was absolutely appalled.

At last he said, 'But she couldn't have.' I switched off the set.

'But she did,' I said.

'But why?' he asked. 'I make a lot of money. She doesn't have to do *that*.' He gestured at the TV set.

'She doesn't want *your* money,' I said. 'She wants her own. Money she can control.'

'Money she set up murders for,' said Dave. 'She's one of the ones who wants power, can't you see that? With her looks you'd think she'd get it through sex – but sex isn't what she cares about. For her the best weapon is money.'

Watkins was listening, not liking what he heard.

'I bet you she told you she's a virgin,' said Dave.

'But she is,' said Watkins.

'Because she said so? She fooled you. A couple of days ago she offered herself to my mate here.' The words were brutal, hurtful and meaning to hurt, but his voice was gentle, even kind.

Watkins turned to look at me. 'Angela?' he said. 'With *you?*'

243

That was neither kind nor gentle, but I let it lie. I'd been surprised too.

'I could get her what she wanted,' I said, 'and she thought she had something I wanted. Not her body that was just a bonus to sweeten the deal. Money was the big incentive. Always will be to her.'

'You're talking about the Dakota treasure,' he said.

'Right. I'm talking about torturing the man who's got it.'

'I thought you turned her down.'

'I did,' I said. 'On behalf of Dave and me. So she's gone back to Bobsy and her two friends.'

'Why didn't she just stay with them? Why go to you?'

'You keep telling us you've got brains,' I said. 'Why don't you use them?'

'Oh,' he said. 'Of course. Because there's three of them and only two of you. A bigger split.'

'Go to the top of the class,' I said, 'only tell us what you were working on first.'

He sighed. It was the sound of defeat.

'She said she had some gold to sell,' he said. 'I was finding out where she'd ... get a good price.'

'And no questions asked?' said Dave. Watkins nodded.

'You can make a computer do that?'

'All kinds of people have lists of gold-dealers,' Watkins said. 'Even the police. It's just a matter of hacking into the right memory bank.'

'You did it for her once before,' I said. 'You found the name of the man with the treasure.'

'Old RAF lists,' he said. 'A lot of that was old-

244

fashioned stuff in books.' He made it sound like clay tablets. 'But the computer helped too.'

'Why did you do it?' I asked him.

He looked puzzled. 'Why? She asked me to.'

'What Ron means,' said Dave, in that same gentle voice, 'is didn't it occur to you she might go and play virgins with the other bloke too?'

Watkins shuddered. He really was in pain. 'It occurred to me,' he said, then turned to me. 'Did you find out his name?'

'Same way you did,' I said, 'except I don't have a computer. He's Robert Lachlan Jowett.'

'Or Finlayson,' said Watkins. For some reason he seemed happier that I knew. 'What will you do now?'

'To her? Nothing,' I said. 'She's out of my class now.'

'The police?'

'Who else?' I said. 'Three people at least are dead because of her.'

'Three?'

'The young man outside the Villa Malcontenta. He wasn't awfully good but he did his best. Killing him was a bit severe, surely?'

'I think,' he said, 'I can't be sure, but I *think* he was a photographer. Rather keen on Angela – I mean he wasn't queer, so why not? – but fond of the odd jab in the arm. Angela worried about that.'

'Now she doesn't have to,' I said, and he shuddered again. 'Please go,' he said. 'I know I can't insist, but there's nothing else I can tell you. Please.'

Dave turned to me, raising his eyebrows slightly, and I nodded. His hand moved, the hard edge slamming into Watkins's neck, just below the jaw-line. He twitched once and lay still.

'Poor feller,' said Dave. 'What now?'

'Home,' I said.

'Your home?'

'You don't have to go,' I said. 'In fact I'd rather you didn't.'

'The police will get you.'

'I have to talk to them anyway,' I said. 'I'd just as soon look at my correspondence first.'

So he drove me home to Fulham in the Golf, and dropped me at Lillie Road and I walked it from there. Bit of a disappointment really. There weren't any rozzers, just a stack of mail inside the door and a lot of messages on the answer machine that were mostly Sutton or Cairns, except for the one from Jocasta Benskin. I still blush when I remember what she said. At the very end there was one from Palliser. Very sarcastic he was. All about how he would be glad of a progress report if I could possibly spare the time. Nothing from Sabena, which was sad, but then I hadn't phoned her, either. The mail was all junk except a reply from H.H. Crawford. It seemed he'd earned Palliser's money.

I phoned Michael Copland. I had six numbers for him, and the third one got him. It was his home, but then it was only eight o'clock. Far too early for his night shift.

'Oh, it's you,' he said, but I forgave him. I wanted something.

'Some things take time,' I said. 'Be patient. It'll be worth waiting for.'

'Newspapers can't wait,' he said. 'It's not what they're for. I need something now.'

246

'And you shall have something,' I said. 'Angela Rossie's disappeared.'

I waited for him to ask who the hell Angela Rossie was, but he didn't have to. She'd put in too much time at Stringfellow's and Annabel's.

'You mean she's eloped?' he said. 'Who with?'

'I mean,' I said, 'that she used to have a male friend – though probably not a boyfriend – who was a photographer and took heroin till he got himself murdered.'

'That's better than eloping,' he said, 'unless it was with a royal. Where was he murdered?'

'Just outside Venice,' I said, and told him all about it.

'Death in Venice,' he said.

That's been done,' I said. 'I saw the movie.'

'Everything's been done,' he said. 'It's the way you tell it – Venice helps it too. Not like West Hartlepool. What's the photographer's name?'

'That's for you to find out,' I said. 'I wish you luck.'

I did, too. I needed to know. I told him about the masked ball as well. He said he'd check.

'You always do,' I said.

'Too true,' he said. 'But thanks anyway. You'll let me know when you've got the big one?'

I said I would and hung up and went through the junk mail again. It was still junk, so I played Jocasta Benskin's tape back again instead, and did some more blushing. All the same she described the driver of the car Angela had left in – and it had to be Bobsy. She'd spotted the car too. It was a Ford Granada. To the owner of a Jaguar XJS this was no big deal...

I wondered if I should make myself a sandwich, but I knew I was just putting off the inevitable, and anyway I wasn't hungry. So I left the house instead and decided to take a cab to New Scotland Yard, because where could I park while Sutton and Cairns got nasty? I walked down the garden path instead, and just as I bent to open the gate some bastard shot me.

15

It was a feeling as if some great weight – a baulk of timber say, or a swinging church bell – had hit me on the side of the head: no pain, not then: just a sensation of numbing and overwhelming force. I folded up like a badly made toy, first to my knees, then flat on my face. As I pitched forward I thought I heard a car drive away. I'll never know for certain.

When I came to I was in a hospital bed and wearing hospital pyjamas. There was a big fat dressing on the side of my head, which ached as if I had the hangover of the century, and Dave was looking at me.

'How you doing, Tiger?' he said.

'Bathurst Hotel,' I said.

'You still delirious?' Dave asked.

'When the phone rang at Watkins's place, that's what the bloke said. Bathurst Hotel. And Watkins said, "I'm sorry. You have the wrong number." Oh my God, my head hurts.'

'Watkins didn't say that,' said Dave.

'Of course he didn't,' I said. 'I'm saying it. And you'll pardon the cliché I'm sure, but where am I?'

'Fulham General,' said Dave. 'Private room so you can be on your own.'

It didn't bother me. Palliser would pay.

'There's a policeman outside,' said Dave. 'I'm supposed to tell him when you're conscious. *And* the doctor.'

'In a minute,' I said. 'Who found me?'

'Me,' said Dave. 'I got to thinking. It didn't seem right you having to cope with those two rozzers on your own. So I came over to drive you down.' Parking never worries Dave. 'Only I heard this shot just as I was getting close–' Another bloke could have thought it was a backfire, but not Dave. Not after three tours of Northern Ireland.

'Then this Ford Granada came past me,' he said. 'Going like the clappers. A bird was driving. Bloke beside her in the passenger seat. Old chums of yours. They tried to give you a belting once. This time they were after something a bit more final.'

'You didn't follow them?'

'Of course not,' he said. 'I knew it was you they were after. When I saw you I thought you were dead. Then I wished I *had* followed them.'

'What did they do?'

'They tried to put one between your eyes,' Dave said. 'Only they were a couple of inches out. The bullet just creased the side of your head. Made a little groove then kept on going.'

'It hurts,' I said.

'Of course it does,' said Dave. 'You lost a bit of blood an' all. And you've had five stitches. You're

249

a regular hero, Ron.'

'If that bloke had practised as much as you I'd be a dead hero,' I said. 'That copper outside – did you tell him about Sutton and Cairns?'

'Of course not,' he said,

'Do it now,' I told him. 'Tell him I want to see them.'

'In your state?' Dave said. 'You're not fit.'

'Let's hope the doctor agrees with you,' I said. 'But I'll be showing goodwill, won't I?'

I winked at him, and even that hurt.

'Oh, and Dave,' I said, 'see if you can find a Bathurst Hotel in the phone book.'

'Sounds like it should be in Earls Court,' said Dave, and left me alone with my headache.

But not for long. Three minutes later I met the doctor. Five foot eight, I thought, while my head still banged like the big drum in a Salvation Army band, nearer ten stone than nine and with the kind of bossy certainty a lot of doctors who work in casualty wards develop. After all, they're the ones who hand out the painkillers – and the pain.

'I'm Dr Fine,' she said, and reached out to take my pulse. A nice voice, but with rather more volume than I needed just then. 'Head aching?'

'Yes,' I said.

'I'll give you something... You know you were shot?'

'Yes,' I said.

'Any idea why? None of my damn business, I suppose you're thinking, but we'll have the police here soon. Think you're up to talking to them?'

'I want to try,' I said.

She let go of my hand and I wished she hadn't.

Nothing to do with sex: it was just that I hadn't felt so safe since my big sister used to take me by the hand and haul me off to infants' school. Dr Fine was big, you might even say she was burly, but every solid ounce of her was female, feminine even. And Dave thought so too. I could tell as soon as he came in and got a look at her. And quite right too. The sooner he started getting over Angela Rossie the better.

'Oh, sorry,' he said, and Dr Fine glared at him.

'Get out,' she said. 'We're busy.'

Then the glare died.

'Haven't we met?' she said.

'The South Fulham Literary and Philosophical Society,' said Dave. 'The lecture on Politics and the Lyric Poet. You asked the speaker to define commitment and he couldn't.'

They both had a hearty laugh at the memory, and my head ached worse than ever.

'I just came to leave a message for Ron here,' he said.

'Get on with it then,' said Dr Fine, but her voice was indulgent.

'There's no such hotel,' he said. 'Our friend should have known that.'

'He did,' I said. 'If I were you I should go and have a chat with him.'

'Be a pleasure,' said Dave, and then to Dr Fine: 'All right if I look back later – just to see how Ron is?'

'I'll leave word at the desk,' she said.

'Because I was thinking I could maybe give you a lift home.'

She looked up at him then, a quick lifting of the

chin that was, and was meant to be, aggressive, and yet was vulnerable too. Brown hair she had, and eyes of a darker brown, that glowed against her clear pale skin. Good old Dave, I thought. He's not just resilient: he always picks a winner.

'Don't be too late,' she said.

'How could I?' said Dave, and left us to it.

'Friend of yours?' said Dr Fine.

'The best one I've got,' I said.

'Strange man,' she said. 'He doesn't look like an expert on Auden and Spender, now does he? Yet he asked far more devastating questions than I did. What does he do?'

'Drives a mini-cab,' I said.

'And what do you do?'

'I'm a private detective,' I said. 'But this is the first time I've been shot.'

'Don't make a habit of it,' she said, and then Sutton and Cairns arrived and I introduced them.

'Don't keep Mr Hogget chatting too long,' she said. 'He isn't well.' Then she left, leaving me feeling like a new boy watching his mum leave and the school bullies take over.

'Been in the wars, have we, sir?' said Sutton. He looked a lot more relaxed than the last time I'd seen him, but so he might. This time I was a sitting duck.

'Wars is right,' I said. 'I was shot.'

'Who by?'

I didn't shrug because I'd already discovered that shrugging was one of the fifty thousand things that made my head ache.

'I couldn't see,' I said. 'It was dark.'

'You must have some idea,' said Cairns, and

252

Sutton looked disgusted.

'What my colleague means,' he said, 'is that someone must dislike you.' He looked briefly at Cairns, and said, 'It is possible, you know, sir, for one person to dislike another. Intensely sometimes. Even to the point of attempted murder.' He gave a sort of shudder, then grew calmer. 'There's another thing,' he said.

'Oh yes?'

'The area around your house seems to attract violence. It was only the other day that someone actually *was* murdered there. I've been rather cherishing the hope that you and I might have a chat about that. At your convenience, of course.'

'Of course,' I said, and then a nurse came in with a couple of pills for my headache. Just as well, really. It gave me a bit of time to think, what with all that swallowing and sipping.

When she'd gone I said, 'I wasn't working for Mr Benskin, you know. It was Mr Palliser who hired me.'

'What sort of progress have you made?' Sutton asked.

'It's a very cold trail,' I said, 'but I did turn up a couple of people who might help.'

Instantly Cairns took out his notebook.

'A Dr Kessler, and a Mrs Elizabeth Toogood.'

'How do you spell Kessler?' Cairns asked, and Sutton got the disgusted look again.

'You don't,' he said. 'They're both dead.' Then he turned to me. 'You spread disaster wherever you go, it seems like.'

'Not me,' I said. 'I got shot too.'

'But you're still alive,' said Cairns. He didn't

seem exactly overjoyed.

'Sex and money,' said Sutton. 'That's what people get killed for. Except sometimes it's both. This one's money, I take it.'

I told them about the treasure. Sutton whistled.

'And all untraceable,' he said. 'Enough to kill for.'

'Three times,' I said. 'Nearly four.'

'So you don't think this pilot Day and the other one – Denville – got away with it?'

Again I remembered not to shrug, only just in time. 'Benskin and Palliser didn't believe they'd even done it.'

'But somebody did. Why not them?'

'Too pure in heart?' said Cairns, and how could I say, that's it exactly? All Cairns would think was that sort of purity was forty years out of date. On my bad days I'd have agreed with him. I have a lot of bad days. So I let it pass.

Sutton saved me the trouble. 'They were all good friends,' he said. 'All the same, Day and Denville were the ones who disappeared.'

'There's somebody else who's disappeared,' I said. 'A girl called Angela Rossie.'

Again Cairns's notebook came out, and this time Sutton let him use it as I told them about Angela, and her playmates. 'You're telling me she's a murderer,' said Sutton.

'No, I'm not,' I said. 'I'm telling you what I saw and heard. What you deduce from that is your business.'

'Fair enough,' he said, and rose. 'You've been very helpful.' He sounded surprised.

'I've also been shot,' I said. 'The two facts may

254

not be unconnected.'

He actually grinned then. 'Now now, sir,' he said. 'Don't spoil it.' They left me to it.

But I waited for a minute or two in case they sneaked back in to see what I was up to. When they didn't I picked up the private room phone Palliser was paying for and dialled his number.

'Good Lord,' he said. 'Are you still alive?' Polished irony: very droll.

'Only just,' I said, and that got to him. From there on in I had an audience. First off I told him he could expect the coppers quite soon, and he started to get peeved – until I told him why.

'*Angela?*' he said.

'And a bloke called Bobsy and a couple more I haven't been introduced to. They do try to kill me from time to time – but it's quite informal.'

'I want to see you.'

'You will,' I said. 'But not tonight.'

'Why not?'

'I've been shot,' I said, and of course he wanted details and I gave them.

'It's – well – incredible,' he said. 'Angela of all people.'

'Do you ever watch television?' I asked him.

'As little as possible,' he said. 'Why?'

'Or you could have seen it all in the papers... Surely you saw them in *The Times?*'

'Saw *what?*'

'Dr Kessler's obituary? Elizabeth Toogood's murder?'

'Of course I saw them.'

'But you said nothing.'

'The time to speak was forty years ago,' he said.

'Now it's in your hands. Have you found my plane yet?'

'I'll tell you when I see you,' I said. 'And if I were you I'd make sure I hadn't lost a .38 revolver as well.' Then I hung up before he could ask me where I was. Next I phoned my sister because she's all the family I have unless you count my father, and who in their right minds would do that? And then it was Sabena's turn.

She was out, and so was Rosario. All I could do was leave a message on the machine that wouldn't frighten her out of her socks.

'It's only me,' I said. 'I've had a bit of an accident, but it's nothing serious. I'm okay, honestly. I'll phone you soon.'

Then I hung up and Dave came in.

'You were right,' he said. 'The bastard shopped you. That was what you were on to, wasn't it? The Bathurst Hotel was a code. The way he answered said he had visitors they should take a look at.'

'They being Angie and her pals?' He nodded. 'After what we'd told him about her an' all. I thought he believed us.'

'Certainly he believed us,' said Dave. 'The poor sod just couldn't help himself.'

'Did you duff him?'

'A bit.'

'I thought you said he couldn't help himself.'

'He should have thought of that before you got shot,' said Dave. A bit cryptic, but I was grateful for the thought.

'What's he going to do now?' I asked.

'Stay out of sight if he's got any sense,' said Dave. 'He doesn't look very nice.'

'You didn't bash him too much, I hope?'

'No,' Dave said. 'No more than he deserved... I told him you were in hospital. I also told him that made him an accessory to attempted murder. He's got brains enough to know I could be right, so I reckon he'll keep his mouth shut. What now?'

'I've talked to the rozzers,' I said, and told him how much I'd told.

'So that just leaves the plane,' he said. 'What do we do about that?'

'We think about it,' I said. 'Tomorrow. I'm knackered, Dave.'

'Yeah,' said Dave. 'I could see how you would be.'

And anyway we had to stop because my sister arrived then, followed by a nurse she appeared to be dragging in, though in fact the nurse was trying to keep her out, and tagging along behind them was a porter with a cardboard box.

'You bloody fool,' said Anna Maria by way of a sisterly greeting, 'what did you have to do that for? And you–' she turned on Dave '–why can't you look after him properly?'

The nurse began to tell her I must have quiet and Dave began to explain he wasn't even there and I started on about how being shot wasn't my idea and the porter wanted to know where she wanted the box. Pandemonium in three seconds. Very Italian, my sister. We were still yelling when Dr Fine came in and called for order.

'Dr Fine,' I said, 'this is my sister – Anna Maria Muspratt. She's a bit worried about me.'

'So I gathered,' Dr Fine said.

257

Anna Maria took her box from the porter and gave him a quid and he scarpered, and Dr Fine said the nurse could go, and stood and watched as Anna Maria took out from the box two vacuum flasks, and a cold chicken in foil, and salad in a plastic box, and followed it up with some fruit and a couple of bottles of the Barolo Uncle Pietro in Verona sent us last Christmas.

'You giving a party?' she asked.

'He has to eat,' Anna Maria said, 'and we all know what hospital food's like.'

'A whole chicken?' said Dr Fine. '*Two* bottles of wine?'

'Red wine's good for you. He can drink the other one tomorrow, and anyway I brought some for Dave. Not that he deserves it.'

She switched to Italian then, which was maybe just as well. 'Why don't you stay and have some too?' I said to Dr Fine.

She looked at her watch. 'Why not?' she said. 'I finished five minutes ago.'

'Glasses and plates,' my sister said. 'Cups too. I brought soup and coffee.'

'You don't deserve such a sister,' Dr Fine said.

'Nobody does,' I said, and Dr Fine rose to look for crockery, and Dave went to help her.

'So you're in trouble,' Anna Maria said.

'Nothing I can't handle,' I said.

'Dave's the hero, not you,' she said. 'You're in trouble.'

'Yeah... Okay,' I said. 'But I'm not lying to you. I am in trouble, but I can handle it – I think.'

'If I can help you I will,' she said. 'So will Sydney.' Sydney was her husband. 'It's ridiculous –

Sydney *likes* you – and you're not even a blood relative.'

'I like him too,' I said.

'You should,' she said. 'He doesn't get into trouble.' She took a corkscrew from the box and opened a bottle of Uncle Pietro's Barolo. 'There's nothing we can do for you, is there?'

'We'll do it alone,' I said. 'Dave and me. After that – maybe I could come and stay with you for a while – if you wouldn't mind.'

'Of course I wouldn't mind,' she said. 'It's about time you had some proper food anyway.'

Then Dr Fine and Dave came back, and we ate and drank and talked about Verdi, and it was a very nice evening except that Dr Fine – whose first name I discovered was Myra – would only allow me one glass of Barolo. After Anna Maria left I asked Dave to pick me up next morning, and at first Myra Fine looked doubtful, but I knew my rights. She offered me a sleeping tablet too, but I didn't take it. Headaches were just part of the affliction, but a thick head would have got in the way of my thinking and I had a lot of that to do.

Only I fell asleep almost at once, and with the sleep came the dreams. I was in that Dakota with the Germans, and they didn't trust me because I'd never killed any Jews and I hadn't got a box full of treasure. Also I'd still got flesh on my bones, and they were skeletons. They were very worried that I was going to live. Death, they kept saying. Death. Death this day. Then the pilot left the controls and sat with us. 'Happy to oblige,' he said. He was a skeleton too. Then I woke up. It was three in the morning and far too late for a pill, so I did some thinking instead.

Dave came round for me at nine, by which time I'd had my bandage changed for something neater. We went back to his place and I used his razor while he made me some scrambled eggs. After I'd eaten I didn't feel quite so tired.

'What did you make of her?'

'Who?'

'Myra, you berk.' Then he saved me the trouble of answering. 'She's really something isn't she?'

'She really is,' I said.

'You going to go and see any of yours?'

'Now that's quite enough of that,' I said. 'We've got work to do.'

'Where?'

'Châlon-sur-Saône,' I said.

'Rough work?'

'Could be,' I said. 'I'm sick of this business. I want to get it over with.'

'How do we go there?' Dave said.

'Fly to Dijon,' I said. 'Hire a car from there. See if you can get us a flight for this afternoon, will you, Dave?'

'This afternoon? You're sure you're up to it?'

'My state of health isn't the point,' I said. 'We've got to finish this before they knock off anybody else.'

Dave reached for the phone. We got the last two seats on an Air France flight to Dijon and I went to get the passports. Not Dave's and mine, not the real ones, that is, just a couple I'd had made by a bloke who owed me a favour a couple of years back for when we were feeling shy. Cost me two hundred and fifty apiece, and worth every penny.

16

Châlon-sur-Saône is the sort of little town that makes you wish you'd been born a Burgundian. Neat but not finicky, with an old quarter full of charm but devoid of cuteness, and the river broad and deep enough to float your sixty-foot yacht. And, if you didn't want to sail, there was an airport for light planes nice and handy. A lot of sunshine too, to plump up the Pinot Noir grapes for your red wine and the Chardonnay grapes for your white. Add to that a standard of cooking that even other Frenchmen respect and you can understand why the villains go there. Honest men can't afford to. Dave and I were on expenses after all.

At Dijon we hired the best car they could manage, a Peugeot 605, which is a very good car indeed. We both wore our best suits, and Dave wore the Colt .357 Magnum in a webbing harness as well. No aggro at the airports; we'd bunged it into a suitcase. We didn't expect trouble on the flight, and we didn't get any. To the rest of the passengers we were just two more Euro-hustlers sniffing out a deal. My bandage only served to prove how tricky I was.

Same at the hotel we stayed at: the St. Georges, in the rue Jean Jaurès, where they approved of the car and the gold credit card I'd had made to go with the passports. Nice room, nice plumbing, nice beds. Dave sat up to read more Proust, but I lay on top of mine and kipped until it was time to change into something less formal and go to work.

First we had to find Fayolle's, the place the knife came from. No problem. Sports shop it called itself. Lot of stuffed animals and pictures of *la chasse*, and lethal weapons to fill in the gaps: Franchi shotguns, Remington hunting rifles, axes and knives. Nearly enough for a war in Black Africa.

We went inside and I let Dave do the talking. His French is streets ahead of mine – all I can manage is Italian on account of my mum. Dave got on well with Fayolle. Like a lot of Burgundians he enjoyed a good gossip. Also he was mad on hunting and he could see at once Dave knew how to shoot by the way he talked. Then Dave did something that surprised me. He bought a Franchi automatic shotgun and some cartridges, and that definitely wasn't in the script. And only when the shotgun was in its case and the case was wrapped in paper did he ask to see the knife. Fayolle handed him one.

'German,' said Dave, and Fayolle shrugged.

'They're good at knives,' he said. Dave touched the cutting edge.

'Could be sharper,' he said.

'That's what the other foreigner said.'

Dave played it very very cool.

'I don't think I follow you,' he said.

'This young man – he came in here with his fiancée to buy a knife. Not a good start to an engagement, one would think, but it was business after all. He said the same thing. Not very sharp.

I told him it was sharp enough to be in my shop. What he did with it was his own affair.'

'Another Englishman?' Dave asked.

'No.' Fayolle was quite certain. 'His fiancée was English, but he was Italian, I think – or possibly Spanish.'

'He didn't buy a gun?'

'Also no,' said Fayolle, and I could understand his regret. Guns cost so much more than knives. 'The knife seemed to be all he needed. Strange.'

'How strange?'

'He seemed to be very much a big-city type. Not like a hunter at all.'

Oh, but he is, M Fayolle. I'm here to tell you he is.

Dave paid in cash – I was a bit coy about having a shotgun entered on my phoney credit card account – then we drove off to the airport and I asked him why we'd just added another two thousand francs to Palliser's bill.

'You've been shot at once,' said Dave. 'Next time you'll at least be able to fire back.'

'I don't even know how to load it,' I said.

'I'll do that for you,' said Dave. 'All you have to do is shut your eyes and pull the trigger.'

'Shut my eyes?'

Dave chuckled. 'With that thing you'll be up so close it won't make any difference. Anyway it looks so nasty it might even *scare* them off.'

'It scares me off,' I said.

No luck at the airport, not at first, and we saw all there was to see. After all, it wasn't Heathrow, nor anything like it. Just a runway, a few huts and the odd fuel bowser, and maybe a dozen light aircraft scattered about: a fairly even split between jet and

263

piston. It was the piston craft we sussed out hardest, using the little pair of Jap binoculars I'd brought with me from London, because propellers had been, quite literally, a matter of life and death to Bill Day. But the oldest man at the airport couldn't have been more than forty.

And then we got lucky, if you can call it that. A Cessna put down, one of the bigger ones, and four people got out, two men, two women, in jeans and boots and anoraks, with neat canvas bags just big enough to hold a gun. Four hunters tooled up and ready to go, and Dave and me might be the quarry. They walked over to the Citroën that was waiting for them. Angela Rossie was the one who was laughing. And, even though I had warned Sutton, what could he do, even supposing he'd found them?

It was time to move on, but not far, as it happened. This time we had some real luck.

Dave turned the car and I looked round me at the small, neat hills and the vineyards beyond. I took the binoculars from Dave, but it was him all right: neat, even elegant, in dark blue slacks and a white shirt, flying a model aircraft with the sort of remote-control apparatus that fathers buy for their sons so that they themselves can play with them. I looked at the aircraft: it was a Spitfire, and Bill Day flew it as if he was going to meet a squadron of Messerschmitts head on. White-haired he was, and very tanned, the face old and lined even beyond his years, but the little Spitfire obeyed him the way a collie dog obeys a shepherd. I passed the glasses to Dave.

'Yeah,' Dave said. 'It's him all right,' and then as

264

the Spitfire banked then climbed for the sun: 'It's like watching a ghost.'

I knew what he meant. We could have been in a field in Kent, the thick end of fifty years ago, the alarm bells bonging, the voice on the loud-hailer shouting 'Scramble, scramble', and young men, no longer laughing, climbing into their cockpits to find out whether they would live till the evening.

Then a Mercedes appeared, a horn hooted, and we were back to the present. Day brought his little plane back to earth, and he and the Merc's driver loaded it into the Merc's boot. It was a toy again. This time Dave handed me the glasses.

'I think we're still in luck,' he said, and I thought so too. The Merc's driver was Robert Lachlan Jowett or Finlayson...

The Merc moved off and Dave followed, discreetly, keeping his distance, back through the elegant little town and on to the river, to a sort of mini-marina with moorings, and shops and a café bar nearby. The Merc pulled up near a big twin-diesel job that looked familiar, but Dave kept on going round a couple of bends, then stopped.

'What you reckon?' he said.

'Day didn't look scared,' I said.

'Maybe he should have,' said Dave. 'I'd hate to think he got croaked while we were so nice and handy.' Then he added, almost below his breath, 'DSO and bar. There won't be too many of them about, not any more.'

'We'll go and take a look,' I said. 'Only we'll be careful – just in case our nautical chum's got a few friends.'

'Suits me,' said Dave, and took the shotgun

from its coverings, gave it to me.

'Must I?' I said.

'You're the one who said he might have friends,' said Dave. His hand disappeared behind his back, came out holding the Magnum. He checked it and put it back in his belt, pulled down his denim jacket to cover it, then turned the car.

'Let's go to work,' he said.

We parked the Peugeot as close as we could, then set off for the boat, me trying to look as if I'd bagged four and a half brace of whatever was in season and given them to the poor.

'I'll go first,' said Dave, 'only for God's sake watch where you're pointing that thing.'

He moved off down the gangway and I followed, down into the cockpit. He had the door open and was into the main cabin before I had even got down the little companionway.

As he'd crossed the threshold Dave must have drawn the Magnum, because there it was in his fist, not yet seeking a target, just aimed at a point between the two men in the cabin, but closer to Jowett than Day. Jowett had the look on his face I'd expected, a sort of blend of outrage and fear, but Day sat, easy, relaxed even, as if he'd just come to the exciting part of a movie that hadn't been all that hot up to then.

'You're supposed to say "Who the hell are you?"' said Dave.

'Do you think I've forgotten?' Jowett said. His eyes moved from the Magnum to my shotgun, and I can't say I blame him. 'Up to the wall,' Dave said. 'Spread your arms.'

'Not wall,' said Jowett. 'Bulkhead. Don't you

266

know anything?' He was handling the situation better than Watkins had.

'Just do it,' Dave said. 'Take a look around, Ron.'

I went into the other cabin, and poked around the storage space and engine space. There was nobody. I went back again.

Dave was sitting now, the Magnum by his side, and Jowett had joined Day on a sort of divan. Day still had the alert, interested look of a man enjoying a film.

'Jowett's clean,' he said. 'I didn't bother Mr Day.'

'You don't have to,' said Jowett. 'He won't hurt you. And he isn't Mr Day. He's Wing Commander.'

Dave shrugged, but I didn't. It was too soon.

'Who's Beverly?' I said.

Jowett was silent, then Dave cocked the Magnum. In the stillness, the tiny sound was deafening.

'You wouldn't,' said Jowett.

'There's only one way to find out,' Dave said, and lifted the gun, aimed it two-handed.

'Beverly's my wife,' said Jowett. 'Now point that thing somewhere else.'

Day smiled in pleasure then, and Dave continued to hold the gun on Jowett.

'You too poor to keep her?' I said. 'Or is she just a bad sailor?'

'I didn't want her with me,' Jowett said. 'Too risky. Anyway – she was keeping an eye on Bertie Benskin until–' his voice faltered: he looked away from Day.

'Why?' I asked.

'Because he and Palliser were still friends, and we had to know what Palliser was up to.'

Day's smile vanished, but he gave no sign that he knew the names.

'What did you think Palliser might be up to?' Dave lowered the gun.

'Treasure-hunting.'

'What made you think he was up to anything?'

'I got word he was trying to trace my mother,' Jowett said.

'After all those years?' I said.

'He didn't need it,' said Jowett. 'I suppose you knew that?'

'I've been told by somebody who should know that he's rich.'

'It's true enough,' said Jowett. 'And he had good reason to want to leave things as they were.'

'Full fathom five,' said Dave.

'Your friend should know how deep it was,' said Jowett. 'He was down there.'

'So it *was* you,' said Dave. 'In the caves. Watching us. You took a shot at us an' all. Hit the chopper.' The Magnum came up again.

'Just warning you off,' Jowett said. 'Can you blame me?'

'Never mind that,' I said. 'If he didn't need it – why bother?'

'Bertie,' Jowett said. 'Bertie liked the odd tincture now and again. Liked chatting to the occasional popsy too.'

For a moment, his voice became a parody of Bertie Benskin's, and Day watched more intently than ever, but whether it was because of the voice or the dated RAF slang I had no idea.

'The popsy in question being Angela Rossie,' I said.

'Yeah,' Jowett said. 'She's a good listener, our Angie. From something Bertie told her she went to call on a man called Kessler as well – and listened to him.'

'He's dead,' I said.

'I read the papers,' Jowett said. 'Did she kill him?'

'She had him killed,' I said.

'That's our Angie,' said Jowett. 'Why keep a dog and bark yourself?'

'How close is she?'

'To what?'

'To you,' I said.

'She knows I exist,' said Jowett. 'And doubtless she knows my old man's dead.'

'Flight Sergeant Finlayson?'

'You have been busy,' Jowett said.

Dave said, 'Never mind the polished irony. Just answer the questions.'

Day looked so pleased I thought he might applaud.

'Sorry,' Jowett said. 'If it's any excuse – I meant it.'

'She tried to have me killed too,' I said. 'That's why I'm wearing this.' I tapped my bandage: soon Dave would have to change it again.

'She's a sweetheart all right,' Jowett said.

'It depends what turns you on,' I said. 'She made us a proposition, too.'

'Her idea was we should kidnap you,' said Dave, 'and torture you till you told us where the treasure was.'

269

For the last couple of minutes Jowett had started to relax. Now he went tense again.

'You wouldn't–' he began.

Dave talked right through him. 'It isn't such a bad idea,' he said.

'After what she did to your mate?'

'Who needs her?' said Dave. The words I longed to hear.

I said to Jowett, 'Tell us your side, then we'll see.'

Jowett said, 'Can I smoke?' Dave made a face: he wanted one too.

'Mind how you do it,' he said. Jowett lit up.

'You know about the Berlin Airlift?' he said. 'And Todd and Myers and Kessler?'

'And your father.'

'How did you get on to him?'

'I helped a bloke in Edinburgh make a few bob,' I said.

'So you already knew he was dead?'

'1978,' I said. 'Lung cancer.' Jowett looked at his cigarette.

'Poor old dad,' he said. 'He never saw any of the money, you know. Just worked out where it was.'

'And how did he do that?'

'He was a bloke with a lot of pals,' Jowett said. 'People like to tell him things. So–'

'You're skipping,' said Dave, and Jowett sighed.

'Okay,' he said. 'Palliser sent him to Berlin. He got his cut for servicing the Dak for a special flight. Five thousand quid in the hand. A bloody fortune in 1947. There were all kinds of things going on in Berlin then. You can't blame him.'

'I don't intend to,' I said. 'I can think of a few

270

people who might. Get on with it.'

'So he took the money and stayed quiet,' said Jowett. 'Then the word got out that Todd and Myers had disappeared. And he got to thinking. That plane had to have come down somewhere... That's where his pals came in – Air Ministry pals.'

'He heard about the crash off the island of Moyra.'

'He did more than that,' Jowett said. 'He bought Culm.' There was no disguising the pride in his voice.

'Then what took him so long?'

'The Ministry of Defence had it,' said Jowett. 'Kept a few technicians there to monitor the soil on Moyra. They didn't shift till a couple of years ago. He was dead by then.'

'So you took over?'

'It had become like a family business,' Jowett said.

'So your mum was in it as well?' said Dave.

'Ma?' This time Jowett's voice was incredulous. 'No way.'

'But she knew,' I said.

'Dad must have told her when he was drunk,' Jowett said. 'She hated it so much she chucked him out. That's why I call myself Finlayson sometimes, on account of dad. But I prefer Jowett. It's what I feel like.' Then he said, 'I didn't see much of her – not after dad and her split. I had to choose and I chose the old man, like to like I suppose, but that didn't mean I didn't love ma. I worshipped her.'

'You didn't stay with her.'

'I stayed with dad,' he said, 'and when Toogood came along we didn't want to spoil her chances. Just as well. He was good to her till the day he died.'

'But she knew about the Dak,' I said. 'And Angela knew she knew – and if that treasure ever got lifted your mum might see it in the papers and start to talk.'

'So she killed your mum,' said Dave.

Jowett put his cigarette in an ashtray, then covered his face with his hands.

'You're not kidding us,' said Dave, and Jowett put his hands down. His eyes were wet. 'You still went after the treasure,' said Dave.

Jowett started to get up then, but Dave held the Magnum on him and he sat. I noticed, to my surprise, that I was holding the shotgun on him too.

'I said my dad's five thousand quid was a fortune,' he said, 'and so it was. To him. But what I brought up – it was Aladdin's cave down there.' He took a last drag on his cigarette and stubbed it out. 'Even with three of us sharing – it's unbelievable.'

Then Bill Day came back among us: that is to say he looked less like a bloke in a cinema and more like a senior officer visiting other ranks. For a moment I thought about Kessler, and the five K. *he'd* got for putting the Wingco out of the way: five K. that finally turned into a fellowship at Leicester College, Oxford.

Bill Day said, 'I'm not at all clear what's going on.'

His voice was strong, unfaltering, confident –

and yet it was a voice out of history: the middle-class voice of the war years still heard on old movies. Dave and I gawked at him.

Jowett said, 'It's all right, Wing Commander.'

'How the devil can it be all right?' said Day. 'Frank Denville's dead.'

'That answers my next question,' I said, and Day glowered at me.

'You seem pretty good at asking questions,' he said. 'What I need is a few answers.'

Dave said, 'About what, sir?'

'Ah,' said Day, 'you rather have me there. My memory hasn't been all that good just lately. All the same – why the guns? Bloody silly things, guns – unless you want to shoot something.'

I passed Dave the shotgun and he gave Jowett one hard look before he took out the shells, put the Magnum back under his belt.

'Another thing,' said Day. 'I could do with a drink. Daresay we all could.'

Jowett got up, and at once Dave was up, too, watching as Jowett opened up a neat mahogany fitment that turned out to be a bar. He made us all drinks. Day stretched out at ease, sipped his scotch and soda and said, 'Get on with it, whatever it is.'

'It's about Frank Denville, sir,' I said.

'One of the best pilots I ever knew. As good as Bertie Benskin even. But he bought it – when was it?' He looked at Jowett. 'Two weeks ago, did you say?'

'About that,' said Jowett. 'Seventeen days.' He turned to Dave and me. 'I came over to have a word with him. He had a little house by the

273

airport – but when I got there he was dead. Shot.'

'I saw a lot of chaps shot up,' Day said. 'English, Americans, Germans – up in the air – cannon fire and machine guns. On the ground, too. That was rockets, mostly. From a kite called a Typhoon. Buggers to fly – but they cost Jerry a lot of tanks – trains, too.' He realised he was wandering, and came back to the point. It wasn't easy. 'What I'm trying to say is – getting shot's a young man's business. Frank was old. He should have died in his bed. Why didn't he?'

'He was murdered, sir,' Jowett said. 'I told you that.'

'Daresay you did,' said Day. 'But I forget things. I told *you* that.'

'How did you know Denville was here?' I said to Jowett.

'Beverly,' Jowett said.

'You mean Bertie knew?'

'He used to send him money.'

'And the Wing Commander here?'

'I've been mad,' said Day. 'Mad as a hatter. Ever since some bastard clouted me over the head in '49.' He glared at Jowett.

'It wasn't my father,' Jowett said. 'Honestly.'

'Of course not,' said Day. 'It was a bloody Jerry. I remember. His name was Kessler.' He looked round in triumph. 'I often wondered what happened to him.'

'Sir,' said Dave, 'I thought we told you. He was killed. Murdered.'

'Most likely you did tell me,' said Day. 'That damn bang on the head. Half the time nothing makes any sense... Murdered, you say? Not sur-

274

prising. Not really... You said something about a lot of money?'

'A fortune, sir,' said Dave.

'I used to fly Daks,' Day said. 'Frank Denville and Bertie Benskin and I, and a chap called Palliser. He wanted to make a fortune, too... I say, you chaps, I'm most awfully sleepy. Would you mind if I nodded off for a while?'

He was asleep almost as he finished speaking. Dave got up and took his glass from his hand.

'Why didn't Rossie's lot get to him too?' he asked.

'He's in and out of hospital,' said Jowett. 'He was in when they came calling.'

'Do you know what's wrong?' I asked.

'After Kessler bashed him it was amnesia,' said Jowett. 'Not only did he not know who he was – nobody else did either.'

'But he was a pilot,' I said. 'In the airlift. Somebody must have known.'

'He was supposed to be dead from what I hear,' Jowett said. 'But chaps like him aren't easy to kill. All Kessler destroyed was his memory. But Day was found in the Eastern zone. They kept him for over fifteen years.'

'But why?'

Jowett shrugged. 'Maybe they genuinely didn't know who he was. Maybe they thought he could tell them a few things about the RAF – once he got his memory back. Only he didn't get his memory back.'

'So what did they do?'

'Put him on a train to West Berlin. He wandered up and down the Kurfürstendamm for a

275

bit – then a rozzer found him and he ended up in another nuthouse. He says he preferred the East Berlin one. You met more interesting people, he reckons. Anyway he got his memory back in West Berlin, and wrote to somebody.'

'Who?'

'He won't say,' said Jowett. 'But I think it was Bertie Benskin.'

I also thought it was Bertie Benskin, but I thought it was somebody else too. Somebody else who loved the memory of Victory Rolls and Player's cigarettes and gin and lime, and Vera Lynn on the wireless, as well as Bill Day.

'Anyway,' Jowett was saying, 'whoever it was came over to see him and told him about the Dakota. Day decided at once he couldn't go back to England.'

'Why ever not?'

'He says it's because he doesn't belong there any more. My guess is he thinks he'll be sent to prison. Anyway, whoever it was fixed him up with papers.'

'But he's innocent,' I said.

'He's also crazy,' said Jowett, 'and he may be dying. The doctors here keep talking about a brain tumour. All the same, he's happy here.'

'You've shown a lot of concern for him,' Dave said.

'My father liked him,' said Jowett. 'Very much. And so did my mother – though not in the way you may be thinking. I'm beginning to like him myself.'

'What happened to Denville?' I asked him. 'After he was shot?'

'Not a lot,' Jowett said. The gendar
he must have disturbed a burgla
found the Wingco was in the loony
'Was anything taken?'
'Not a thing,' said Jowett. 'You
slipped up there. Except the gendarmes i⊔
just goes to show how quick they got to the scene
of the crime.'
'She isn't my Miss Rossie,' Dave said.
'You can have her for me,' said Jowett.
A propos nothing at all, Dave said, 'You were in
the army.'
Jowett looked outraged. 'Do I look that daft?'
he said. 'I was a marine commando. Were you in
the army then?'
'Para,' said Dave.
'Oh well,' Jowett said broadmindedly. 'That's
different.'
'Did the divers' course, I suppose?' I said to
him, and he grinned.
'It came in handy,' he said. 'After all, you have
to look ahead.'
'We'll have to talk about that later on,' I said.
'Why not now?'
I nodded at the Wing Commander. 'He comes
first,' I said.
'You reckon the little raver'll croak him?'
'Him, you, Dave, me,' I said. We're all in the
way of her money.'
'It's not her money,' said Jowett.
'Try telling her that,' I said.
'How can she know he's here?'
'She knows,' said Dave. 'Didn't you say Denville
was alone when she and her mates dropped in?'

.t shuddered.

better get moving,' he said. Suddenly it was
, but I didn't mind if Dave didn't.

Where?' I asked.

'Out of Châlon,' he said. 'This is where she'll come looking. Bound to. Take the boat down to the Med maybe?'

It was the most sensible way by far. Take the boat and stay away from land until we ended up in Nice or Monte Carlo or St. Tropez along with hundreds of other yachts and thousands and thousands of people wrapped round us like armour... The only sensible thing to do really, so I vetoed it. I had no choice. We were here to put an end to the thing, and to do that we had to be shot at.

'Not just yet,' I said, and then I remembered something.

'Over on Culm,' I said, 'all that stuff with the dummies and the card game, all that – why did you do it?'

'Damned if I know,' he said, 'except it made them look a bit more human. Down there in the sea they looked like a horror movie. Didn't you find that?'

I did, but I wasn't saying.

'And all that writing in red paint in the farmhouse. Why was it in Spanish?'

'To put you off the scent,' he said. 'It didn't work very well, did it?'

17

Day woke up the way a cat does, neat and contained and ready to go.

'What year is it?' he said, and Jowett told him.

'I often ask that, don't I?' Day said. 'It's on my mind, you see. I've lost rather a lot of years. Did I tell you about that terrible kite – the Typhoon?'

'You did,' I said.

'The Spitfire was much better. In fact the Spitfire was perfect. For 1940 anyway. But that year maybe I was perfect too. Now I'm pretty well what you might call surplus to requirement.'

'May I ask you something?' I said.

'Possibly.'

'Did Palliser make a pass at a Mrs Elizabeth Jowett?'

'What an extraordinary question,' said Day. 'Why on earth should I tell you?'

I looked at Jowett. His face told me nothing, but he knew where I was headed all right.

'It's important, Wing Commander,' I said. 'Believe me.'

Day too looked at Jowett.

'Tony Palliser made a pass at anything in skirts,' he said, 'but Betty wasn't like that. She remained true to her flight sergeant.'

'So it wasn't such a bloody shame after all.'

'Bertie said that,' Day said, and smiled. 'Nice woman. One of the best.' He looked at me. 'You

279

taking your merry men off to fight?'

'What makes you think so?' I said.

'You have that look about you... When you've done it as often as I have you can just about smell it... I daresay I could manage the shotgun if you need an extra man.'

'Now just a minute–' said Jowett, but Day ignored him.

'Pilots practise with shotguns – or they did in my day. Helps the reflexes. I was rather good.'

Jowett said, 'Are we going off to fight?'

'We have to,' I said. 'Sooner or later. Best if we get it over with.'

Dave said to Jowett, 'Done it before?'

'A bit,' Jowett said. 'That doesn't bother me.'

'What does then?'

'I don't see why I have to,' Jowett said. 'I didn't sign on with your mob, did I? What's to stop the Wingco and me going on like I said? – Down to Cannes, say?'

'Nothing,' I said. 'Nothing at all. Of course we'd have to tell a lot of people about you.'

'Who for instance?'

'Scotland Yard,' I said, 'the Sûreté, probably Interpol, the Israeli Government, and the lot who track down war criminals – you know – the Simon Wiesenthal organisation.'

'I'm not a war criminal,' Jowett said. 'I was hardly born then.'

'Try telling them that in Tel Aviv,' said Dave, and handed me the shotgun. 'Let's go.'

'Just a minute,' Day said, and got to his feet. 'I'm coming too.'

'Don't be barmy,' Jowett said, then went instantly scarlet.

'Precisely,' said Day. 'I can't be any other way, can I? But some things do get through, you know. That bloody Dak, and a fortune, several fortunes – and Myers. And Todd. Did you know Tod in German means death?'

And of course I had known, subconsciously anyway. That's why I'd dreamed it. Tod this day. Not Bill Day ... Todd.

'I used to be terrified of dying,' Day said. 'In fact I still am – if it's the way fighter pilots die. Mostly they're on fire. I couldn't stand that. Even now. But being shot – that won't be so bad, not if one's dying anyway.' He held out his hand to Jowett. 'Goodbye, old chap. It was very kind of you to look me up like this.'

'*Please,*' Jowett said.

Day smiled. 'It's no good,' he said. 'Honestly. These two gentlemen–' he gestured at Dave and me '–are setting a mousetrap. And I'm the only piece of cheese they've got.' He came to stand between us.

'Oh, shit,' said Jowett. 'I might have known.'

'Does that mean you're coming?' said Dave, then took his silence for yes and asked, 'You got anything useful?'

'He's got a shotgun,' I said. 'You saw it. And a rifle. Shotgun's better.'

'Bloody know-all,' said Jowett. He didn't seem all that bothered. He turned to me. They killed my mum,' he said. 'Did you think I'd forgotten?'

We set off in the Peugeot, all four of us – Dave had the Magnum, I had the Franchi automatic shotgun, and Jowett and Day both had Win-

281

chester pump-action five-shots. Dave looked at the shells.

'Twenty gauge,' he said. 'What are you going to shoot? Dinosaurs?'

'Whatever I'm told,' said Jowett. 'You're in charge.' He looked at Day, who was loading his shotgun without any problems.

'I knew I was into something dodgy,' he said, 'so I bought these two. They shorten the odds a bit.'

'Why not a handgun?' Dave asked.

'Never had much practice,' Jowett said. 'Anyway, in the Marine Commandos we were always taught to get up close. Nothing like a shotgun when you're really close.'

'Except your hands,' said Dave.

Day said, 'Excuse me, but if we're going to poor old Frank's place, it's the second turning on the right.'

How he knew we were going to Denville's place I've no idea. He'd neither asked nor been told. Maybe the cheese always knows where the mousetrap is.

Dave took the turn nice and easy, and we moved back at once from the late twentieth century to the early nineteenth: dirt road, real woodland, and a quiet that frightened me more than the noisiest street. The Peugeot didn't like it, but it could cope, and we eased and bounced our way between and over the potholes (even Dave couldn't avoid them all), past haphazard clumps of oak and elm and poplar and chestnut. Birds sang as if they were auditioning for a TV wildlife programme, and on the ground I felt sure were rabbits and hares, wild boar and foxes. It should have been enchantment, but all it was the prelude to fear, because when all the pretty scenery was over people with guns would be waiting, and the fact that the whole thing was my own idea was no consolation.

Jowett said, 'What do you reckon they'll have? The opposition?'

'Who knows,' said Dave. 'Something nasty.'

'Like what?'

'Heckler and Kochs, Uzis, maybe even a Czechoslovak job... How would I know?'

'I only asked,' said Jowett. 'I mean you're telling me I'm maybe up against a machine pistol firing God knows how many rounds a second and all I've got is a shotgun. You can't really blame me for just *asking*.'

All the same I wished he hadn't. Then Day told us we were close.

The Peugeot bumped its way into the middle of a clearing surrounded by bushes and small trees – what Dave told me later is known as a coppice – and we all got out. Just another shooting party. Dave went off to take a look and, as soon as he'd gone, Jowett lit a cigarette in a shame-faced sort of way. When Dave came back he mashed it out against the sole of his shoe.

'Nice-looking house,' Dave said. 'Nice little garden all round. Mostly vegetables. That means they've got a field of fire whichever way we go in.'

'You think they're there then?' I said.

'Put it this way,' said Dave, 'the Citroën's there and the Rossie bird is in the garden and the geezer who most likely shot you's having a snooze in a hammock.'

283

'They're there,' I said. 'Is there a phone?'

'Yeah,' said Dave. 'I saw the wires. Anything else?'

I thought hard, but there wasn't a thing. The last door slammed shut behind me.

'Nothing else,' I said. 'Come on. Let's get it over with.'

We moved to the edge of the woodland and looked down at the house. With all those trees about I'd expected something out of the Brothers Grimm, but it wasn't like that at all. Stone-built but modern, with picture windows – the kind that film stars leap through with a merry laugh because they're made of clear toffee. But these ones weren't. We looked at the elegant man dozing in a hammock, still elegant, and Angela Rossie in a bikini.

Jowett said, 'What are we supposed to do? Kill them all? – I mean, you say two of them's birds.'

'We arrest them,' I said.

'And me too, I suppose,' said Jowett.

'You'll scarper,' I said. 'Take a cruise down the Med.'

'And what about my ill-gotten gains?'

Day said, 'He'll give them back. What other choice has he?' Then with hardly a pause he said, 'Now here's the plan.'

We looked at him. He looked about twice as sane and three times as intelligent as the rest of us put together.

'I go in,' he said, 'creating the illusion that I've taken a gun out after rabbits. After all I do live there and they've only just arrived. I keep them talking, and you come up and take them. Piece of cake. Why is that girl almost naked?'

'Local colour,' I said. 'Gives the impression she's sunbathing in her garden.'

'Reminds me of the Windmill,' he said. 'Only the girls there weren't allowed to move.'

He was back in 1940, and the theatre renowned for its nudes.

'Any questions?' he asked.

'One of us should go with you,' Dave said.

'Certainly not. One of you with me would constitute a threat. Alone I'm just a useless old fool who can't even hit a bloody rabbit. Let's get on with it.' He left the cover of the trees and plodded towards the house.

'Jesus,' said Jowett.

'You're telling me,' said Dave. 'Give us the glasses, Ron.' I handed them over. 'The other two are coming out,' he said, and I saw my two trendies, still fully clad, right down to the guns in their hands.

'Heckler and Koch machine pistols,' said Dave. 'I was right. Come on.'

He set off at a run and we followed, through the woodland, racing for the back of the house. Once I tripped on a root and fell, and mercifully the Franchi didn't go off. The others didn't even bother to look back and I scrambled up and limped on. We reached the edge of the trees and broke cover, across grass, over a stone wall, and into the kitchen garden, then Dave gestured, and Jowett moved to one side of the house, Dave and I took the other, slowly, seeking each foot fall, wary of twigs and stones, until we heard Day's voice.

'I'm a little confused,' Day was saying. 'Have

been for years as a matter of fact, so you'll have to forgive me if I'm wrong, but aren't I staying here?'

'Of course you are.' That was Angela Rossie's voice, soothing, but full of authority. 'You don't remember Flight Lieutenant Denville saying we were coming?'

'I thought Denville had died,' said Day. 'Didn't that young man tell me so?'

'What young man?'

A male voice also full of authority, but by no means soothing.

'The one with the boat,' Day said.

'What boat?' The male voice again, but Angela Rossie cut in at once, sweet and soothing as ever.

'Do sit down, Wing Commander,' she said. 'Put that gun down and rest yourself.'

'Your friends have guns,' said Day.

'Like you they're fond of hunting. Now – tell us about this young man with a boat.'

I sensed Dave leaving me, crawling on his belly for the shelter of a currant bush to see what was happening. Soon I saw it too. Day seated on one of those excruciatingly uncomfortable iron chairs the French use as garden furniture, his shotgun beside him on an iron table, and the four hovering around him, the two trendies in the background, pistols in their hands, Angela Rossie and the elegant man standing over him, each with a canvas holdall handy. They were trying hard to look concerned but they were quite pitiless, and as wary as weasels.

'Nice young chap,' said Day. 'Wizard boat. I should have thought it too big for one man, but he coped very well. Brought it all the way from Scotland, he tells me.'

'Scotland?' Angela Rossie again. Still trying to be kind, but the strain beginning to show.

'The Hebrides actually. Little island. A plane crashed there a long time ago. My kind of plane. A Dakota.'

'And you say he's here?'

'Oh yes,' said Day.

'Do you think you could take us to him?'

'Nothing easier,' said Day, 'if that's what you would like.'

'It's a business thing,' Angela Rossie said. 'If I could just go and put some clothes on–'

Dave made his move then, standing up, the Magnum in his fist. 'Stay still,' he said. 'Nobody's going anywhere.'

At once Angela Rossie moved up close to Day, pulling the machine pistol from her bag as she moved.

'Whatever happens,' she said, 'the old man goes first.'

My elegant assassin produced his pistol and smiled as if life was good, then Jowett appeared from the other side of the house.

'I thought it was me you were after,' he said.

And still I peered from behind the house, the automatic shotgun in my hands as much use as an umbrella, even when the trendy double act swung on Jowett. His shotgun banged, and then the girl's pistol made a noise like a huge piece of silk being ripped in two. Her boy-friend fell, and then Jowett went down too, and Dave didn't move because he couldn't, blocked off as he was by Angela Rossie and Day.

Vaguely I was aware of the elegant man moving, and far more aware of the trendy girl screaming in hate, moving in on Jowett. I wasn't aware at all of myself leaving the wall's cover, even loosing off my shotgun seemed to be the work of somebody else, and the sight of the trendy girl knocked sprawling was no more than the fall of a body in a dream. Then the elegant man moved again, and there was one more bang, and I was surprised not to feel pain until I looked round. Dave held Angela Rossie with a wrist twisted round her back, her pistol on the ground by their feet, and Day stood apart from them now, holding his shotgun, looking at the elegant man who would never look elegant again.

Dave said, 'Take a look at Jowett, Ron,' and I went over to him. He lay on the ground and tried and failed to prop himself up on his arms, because the right arm had a bullet hole in it, and so had his shoulder. He looked up at me.

'Talk about the OK Corral,' he said. 'I could do with a visit from Doc Holliday now, come to that.'

'He was a dentist,' I said, and propped him up against the side of the house. I knew I mustn't start to shake yet. There just wasn't time.

Day said, 'That young man I shot. Is he dead?' Dave took one look.

'Yes,' he said.

'I'm glad,' said Day. 'He killed my friend Bertie, you know.'

How *he* knew was more than I could ask.

Dave pushed Angela Rossie ahead of him to the

trendy pair, and looked down at the terrible things a shotgun can do when it's used close up, then pushed the girl away from him as if whatever she had was contagious.

'And then there was one,' he said.

She stood there, looking at him, demure, shy almost, with the shyness that means hard to get, her body the card she hated playing, but the only one she had left.

'We can work something out,' she said. 'I put you on to *him*' – she nodded at Jowett – 'Surely that's worth something?'

Jowett said, 'Jesus Christ Almighty.'

'You'll have it all,' she said to Dave. 'You and your partner. Surely you can spare me a few crumbs?' Still Dave said nothing. 'All right then. Just let me go. I'll disappear. I swear it. You'll never see me again.' But still none of us spoke. She turned to Day.

'He's going to kill me,' she said. 'I know it. But you mustn't let him. You can't. I'm your granddaughter.'

'You're Betty's girl?' he asked and she nodded. 'Put some clothes on, for God's sake,' he said. Dave looked at me.

'Okay,' I said. 'But go with her. See if you can find something for our wounded hero.'

'In the bathroom,' said Day. 'There's a first-aid kit.'

Jowett had wrapped a handkerchief round his arm. It was more red than white, but he looked at ease, even relaxed.

'I've got to give back what I found, haven't I?' he said.

'Either that or we shop you.'

He grinned. 'You're all heart – you know that?' Then the smile faded. 'I don't think I could give back the boat.'

'Call it a finder's fee,' I said. 'You earned it – diving on your own.'

'I used to get frightened,' he said. 'Then I'd think of the money and in I'd go. All the same – it was nice when I stopped. Nice when you and your mate came along, too.'

'Why?'

'I wanted that plane found. They were bastards, all of them. Passengers and crew. I wanted it made known – only I couldn't do it.'

'You were going to disappear?'

'Course I was. With Beverly. No use being rich in the Hebrides. We were going to get a bit of sun... I hope you enjoyed your champagne.'

'Very nice,' I said.

'It was the best,' he said. 'That's what rich men always buy... The best... I should know. I used to be one.'

Then Dave came back with Angela Rossie in a shirt and jeans, and got to work on him.

Day said, 'Where's your mother now?'

'She was killed,' Angela Rossie said. 'She and daddy. In the Lebanon.'

'Oh yes, of course,' said Day, and turned to me. 'I can't let you kill her, you know.'

'I've no intention of killing her,' I said.

'We killed all the others.'

'They were trying to kill us,' I said.

'That's the way I used to rationalise it, too,' he said, and then his mind took another swerve.

'Where am I going to go?'

'Let me make a phone call,' I said, 'and we'll see.'

I waited till Dave had finished with Jowett. He looked surprised. 'He's almost as lucky as you,' he said. That was a relief. I went inside, and direct dialled. Wendy Palliser wasted no time on questions.

'I'll come at once,' she said.

'Can you hire a plane?' I asked her.

'Of course.'

I thought if Jowett had needed coaching on how to be rich Wendy Palliser would have been the one to give him lessons, and went back to the others.

Dave said, 'What do we do with her?'

'She's not our problem,' I said.

'Then whose is she?'

'That's rather up to her grandfather,' I said. 'Let's tidy up here and I'll get the car.'

We did what we had to do, took Jowett back to his boat and carried him aboard, then went to the hotel and paid the bill and set off to the airport.

She didn't waste any time. The sun was still high when the plane landed, a neat little twin-engined propeller job. Whatever they used for customs and immigration moved in close, as Wendy Palliser and a pilot I thought I had seen before got out. It was Nigel Cattell. I wondered if his uncle was a pal of hers. Wendy Palliser talked long and vehemently to a man in Douane uniform who waved to a petrol bowser and it refuelled the plane, as Wendy Palliser and my friend Nigel walked over to the Peugeot. I got out and went over to her. She

291

looked as easy and relaxed as she had in Sussex, and yet I knew the tensions must be twanging inside her like harpstrings.

'He's here?' she said.

'In the car,' I told her. 'With his granddaughter.'

'Oh God,' she said, and I turned to my chum Nigel.

'Go over to the car,' I said. 'We don't want to bore you with our gossip.'

He left, hating me because he was being sent away from highly lucrative blackmail. Wendy Palliser chuckled.

'I don't think he likes you,' she said.

I shrugged, and this time my head forgave me.

'Just so long as he's scared of my partner,' I said.

'Quite so,' she said. I didn't have to draw any pictures. 'You implied that Angela's friends are dead?'

'Yes.'

'Who killed them?'

'Two men you don't know, and one man you do.' For a moment only she looked less than relaxed.

'*Bill?*'

'Yes,' I said.

'Oh Lord,' she said. 'There'll be an enquiry, won't there? They'll go after Bill...'

'They're not in the house,' I said. 'Not any more. We took them off into the forest. Miles away. Left them out in the open. If anybody looks it'll be a gangland killing. Massacre. Whatever you want to call it.'

I told her how we'd dumped their guns and

ours in the river on our way to meet her.

'You don't mess about, do you?' she said.

I risked another shrug.

'There's still Angela,' I said.

'There's always Angela,' said Wendy Palliser.

We went back to the Peugeot. Day was wearing Nigel's suede jacket and golf-cap. We drove them over to the aircraft, and Wendy Palliser got out of the car, went over to the officials and began to spray French money and language in all directions as Day and Angela scrambled aboard, then she came over to me and kissed me and said, 'Wish me bon voyage.'

'Oh, I do,' I said. 'But are you sure it will be?'

'This is Bill Day,' she said. 'Of course I'm sure.'

Then she too went aboard, and they waited for their clearance, and Bill Day took off as if the plane were a Spitfire at Biggin Hill, and the year was 1940. We watched it go up until it was out of sight.

'Let's go home,' said Dave.

18

But still there were things to do. We went home all right, first checking on Jowett's boat. Holes in his arm or not, it was gone and so was he, which was what I'd expected. Off to join Beverly, somewhere where the sun was shining. Then Nigel said he'd make his own way back, and that was fine by us. We drove back to Beaune, and the papers said nothing about a woodland massacre and immigration said nothing about our passports. When we put down Dave fetched the Golf from the carpark and I yawned as if I hadn't slept for a week. Some of it was exhaustion at that, but a lot more of it was reaction to fear. We drove to Number 9, Astley Gardens.

The PAAA club looked closed, which didn't surprise me. Bertie Benskin had been its driving force, and Bertie, as I knew only too well, was dead. So Dave performed a theme and variations on Palliser's doorbell, and at last he came down and let us in. If he was pleased to see us he hid it well, but at least he let us into the drawing-room with the Aubusson carpet and the Tibetan curtains.

'Well?' he said.

'We found out who stole your gun and turned your place over,' I said. 'It was Angela Rossie.'

'But why on earth would she–'

'She was looking for a man called Jowett,' I said. 'Quite a lot of people were at one time.'

'Jowett?'

'His father was Flight Sergeant Finlayson.'

'Finlayson?' He tried and failed to look bewildered. He'd no idea what being bewildered was.

'Come off it, cock,' I said. 'He used to work for you.'

'Oh *that* Finlayson.'

'The very same,' I said. 'He's dead.' This time Palliser looked relieved, a much more convincing performance.

'But I'm glad you remember Finlayson. Maybe you remember Todd and Myers. They worked for

294

you too.'

'The only Todd and Myers I knew had a Dak of their own.'

'But one night you let them use one of yours – because you knew none of your pilots would do what they did – not even for the money they would get.'

'I don't like your tone,' he said.

'Who does?' I said. 'But it's the only one I've got. You'll just have to put up with it.'

'No,' he said, and rose. 'I can have you put out and I will.' He moved to the phone, then Dave got up too.

'Sit down,' he said. Palliser sat.

'You were bribed,' I said. 'Kessler was the go-between. He represented that bunch of SS bastards and he came to *you*. Not Bertie Benskin or Day or Denville – because he knew they'd boot him up the backside. He also knew you wouldn't – not if the price was right.'

'You can't prove any of this,' Palliser said. 'Not one word.'

'Oh, but I can,' I said. 'To the press, the police, the Israelis. Anybody who wants to know. Of course I can prove it. The SS were the biggest bastards in history but, being German, they were methodical bastards. They liked things on paper.'

'You're bluffing,' he said. 'You must be. There isn't any such paper.'

I said, 'Payment to former Squadron Leader Anthony Palliser for arranging access to aircraft, procuring pilots and flight clearances, various items of jewellery, including a diamond and emerald ring, total approximate value thirty-five

295

thousand pounds.

'Payment to pilots Todd and Myers to fly to Iceland, Greenland, Canada, and the United States: each pilot to receive jewellery and gold to the value of fifty thousand pounds per pilot.'

'Hey,' said Dave. 'You weren't doing badly, were you? More than half as much as the blokes who did the work just for looking the other way.'

Palliser was silent.

'They never got to the States,' I said. They never even got to Iceland. They went off course early on. I don't know why. Maybe they had an engine fault. Anyway they ditched in the sea off the Hebrides.'

'You can't know that,' Palliser said. 'You can't.'

'I saw them,' I said. 'All of them. Todd and Myers and your SS pals. They're all down there. Still. Tell me something, Squadron Leader, you didn't have a scheme to knock them off, did you – you and Todd and Myers – and hold on to the lot for yourselves?'

'It certainly sounds like the Squadron Leader's way of doing business,' Dave said. 'He thinks big. I'll say that for him.'

'There was nothing like that,' Palliser said. 'Or if there was it would be Todd's idea. Not mine.'

'Not Kessler's either?'

'No,' Palliser said. 'In normal times Kessler would have been a – very correct sort of man. That was why he admired Bertie. Bertie was even more correct than he was.'

'And yet Kessler came to you with this offer?'

'These weren't normal times,' Palliser said. 'He'd been almost killed by the Russians, then he'd been starved and frozen till he almost died. Our ... little venture was his one excursion into dishonesty. His bid for survival.'

'Is that your excuse too?' I asked him.

'Of course not,' Palliser snapped at me. 'It was a chance to make money and I took it.'

'That's why you told the rozzers I had a tape,' I said. 'You had to know what Bertie Benskin had told me. Had to. Because you had an idea he suspected you of being mixed up in this stinking mess – and if that came out everyone would know how you built up your fortune – and keeping that quiet was the most important thing in the world.'

'And did Bertie know?' he asked.

'Certainly,' I said. 'He left all sorts of hints lying about. He'd hid them but he wanted them found. He wasn't stupid, you know.'

'Oh dear God,' said Palliser. It was the only time I'd seen him shaken. My respect for Bertie went up another couple of notches.

'He left word,' I said. 'I've got it.' Palliser opened his mouth.

'Forget it,' I said. 'The Germans who paid you left word too.'

'Nobody must know,' said Palliser.

'Money,' said Dave. 'Is that all you can think about? Money? After you got two old chums killed and a third one put away?'

'You're talking nonsense,' said Palliser. 'I don't do that to my friends.'

'Benskin and Denville,' I said. 'And Day could be dying.'

'That isn't my fault,' said Palliser.

'Angela Rossie had Benskin and Denville killed

297

because they knew too much about the wealth you helped to salt away,' I said. 'And Day was in hospital because of the beating Kessler gave him.'

'That's not to say he's dying,' Palliser said.

'He was in and out of hospital for years,' I said. 'He's got a tumour on the brain.'

'Bill?' Palliser said. 'In hospital? But who took care of him?'

'You more than anybody,' I said. 'In the sense that you paid the bills. Only you didn't know it, it was your wife who looked out for him. Her and Bertie.'

'But why should she?'

'Because she loves him,' I said, 'and hates you for what you did to him.'

'I did nothing to him,' Palliser said. 'It was all Kessler's idea. Bill was my friend... Where is he by the way?'

'If I knew I wouldn't tell you,' I said, 'But I don't know.' I yawned again. This time it was fear of what was to come. 'Until yesterday he was staying at Frank Denville's house,' I said.

'You're lying,' said Palliser. 'Denville's dead.'

'He is now,' I said, 'but somehow Kessler didn't catch up with him. He made a run for it and your wife helped him.'

'And then married me?'

Denville had been a kind of child to her, to be guarded and cherished, or so she'd told me, but that wasn't for Palliser.

'We all make mistakes,' I said, then: 'I found your Dakota. You'll be getting a full report on it in three or four days. I'll send my bill with the report. One more piece–'

298

'I'll pay you nothing,' he said. 'Why should I? Your only witness is dead.'

'For a tycoon you're pretty thick,' I said. *I can shop you.* And if you don't pay up I will.' I could tell by his face that he believed me.

'One more piece of advice,' I said. 'In a week or so some men will come to see you. They may be Israelis: they'll certainly be Jews. What they'll want from you is the current equivalent of thirty-five thousand pounds sterling in 1949. What'll that be? Half a million? My advice to you is to pay it. Only pay me first or I'll make it even worse for you.' I turned to Dave. 'Let's go,' I said. 'This place stinks even worse than usual.'

Palliser stood up but made no move to follow us out. The last I saw of him he was looking round the room at his Aubusson carpet, his Regency furniture and Tibetan curtains as if he'd never seen them before in his life.

We went to the Golf. 'Where now?' Dave asked.

'I think I'd better go to see my girl,' I said. 'And you?'

'I think I'd better go to see my doctor,' said Dave.

He drove me round to Carrick Street, and there they all were: Rosario let me in, and Sabena sat with her father in the drawing-room. All three looked about as pleased to see me as Palliser had, then Sabena told Rosario to go and asked if I wanted a drink and I said no. She winced then as if I'd hit her because I wanted a drink very much and she knew I did. She knew most things about me.

'I take it this isn't a social call,' she said.

299

'That's right.'

'You haven't made any social calls for some time now,' she said. 'But I've received your messages such as they were. Were you hurt very badly?'

'I was shot,' I said, and she gasped. 'On the side of the head. What I believe is called a flesh wound. It's getting better.'

'I'm glad,' she said.

'Thank you.'

She slammed her hand down on her chair.

'For Christ's sake,' she said, 'will you stop behaving as if I had leprosy?'

'You remember how all this started?' I said. 'When that weirdo caught me in the mud bath in Abano?'

'I remember.'

'He was killed,' I said. 'Murdered. I think because he wasn't very good at his job and took drugs and probably talked too much. He was killed by one of a gang of thugs led by a girl called Angela Rossie. She should have sent one of the others.'

'Why didn't she?'

'Because she wanted to keep them in the background for later. For when the rough work came like murdering Bertie Benskin and an Oxford don and a nice old lady – and trying to murder me.'

She made the gasping sound again. I was hurting her, but there was no other way.

'You're saying it all ties in with the Dakota?'

'Of course it does,' I said. 'The Dakota Palliser paid me to look for – the Dakota he'd hired out to a bunch of SS thugs so he could get a start in big business.'

Sir Montague spoke at last.

'If he'd done that – hired out to the SS, I mean – why did he put you to work? He must have known that you're good at your job, so why pay you to uncover evidence of his own crime?'

'Because Angela was already on to the fact that the Dakota existed and he knew it. If she found it the whole story might come out. He couldn't risk that.'

'How did she know?'

'Bertie Benskin told her,' I said. 'He was a very nice man but a right little chatterbox. It was the death of him. Once he'd told her, she couldn't risk him telling anybody else.'

'Just like your Abano friend,' said Sabena.

'Angela's not a one for sharing secrets,' I said. 'Any more than you are.'

'And what the hell does that mean?'

I looked at her father. 'Do you want me to go on with this?' I asked him.

'It might be as well,' he said, meaning he wanted to find out how much I knew.

'You blew it when you told me you'd known a man who'd lost a Dakota,' I said. 'It's a hell of a thing to lose, and the way you said it, it sort of intrigued me. Then your chum– Air-Vice Marshal Cattell. He intrigued me too.'

'May I ask why?'

'Because he looks like an ex-RAF type and you don't. And yet you were. I looked you up. It isn't difficult.'

'The Air Force List?'

'It was all I needed.'

'I joined as an AC2.' He turned to his daughter.

301

'That's Aircraftsman Second Class.' He turned back to me. 'And I finished with the rank of sergeant.'

'In 1949.'

'That is so.'

'And yet you could have been demobbed in 1948. You volunteered for an extra year.'

'I was asked to.'

'Indeed you were,' I said. 'You were involved in the Berlin Airlift.'

He gave me a look that should have frightened me even more than Angela Rossie's thugs, but I was beyond fear by then. I yawned instead.

'That information isn't in the Air Force List,' Sir Montague said.

'It's on other lists,' I said. 'Other people's memories for that matter. All you have to do is ask enough questions.'

'And you did that?' Sabena said. 'Spied on my father?'

'Dave did,' I said. 'But I told him to, so you could say it's down to me.'

'I want you out of here,' she said. 'Now.'

'No.' Sir Montague reached out and touched her hand. I had never seen him do that before. 'I'm sorry, Sab. We have to finish this.'

'You worked on records for the Berlin Airlift,' I said.

'My rank was that of sergeant, as I said, but I was really a glorified clerk. The amount of paperwork in that operation was enormous. Fuel lists, cargo lists, personnel, flight paths. I'm pretty good at paperwork,' said Sir Montague, 'so they asked me to stay on and I obliged them.'

'You obliged yourself too,' I said.

'*Will you stop that?*' This time Sabena was yelling.

'I can't,' I said. 'Your father took a bribe of five thousand pounds – payable in kind – to alter a Dakota manifest.'

'What makes you say that?' said Sir Montague.

'I've seen the documentation.'

Sir Montague sighed. 'It was a diamond pendant and a Cartier watch,' he said. 'I sold the pendant to an Arab in Rome. I still have the watch somewhere.' He turned again to Sabena. 'I had no capital, you see. Absolutely none. And without capital I couldn't begin. So I acquired some and went into business.'

'Just like Palliser,' I said. 'Only he got far more than you.'

'But then in the end I did rather better than Palliser. Considerably better. Flair, I suppose you'd call it... You think I was foolish to tell you what I did about the missing Dakota?'

'As I said – it intrigued me.'

'It was meant to. I had to get closer to you in order to find out what you might uncover. That was why I set Cattell on to you. And his nephews.'

'And Sabena,' I said.

He sighed. 'I was in an impossible situation,' he said. 'No doubt I still am. You do have documentation, you said.'

'Not any more,' I told him. 'The bit with your name on I destroyed.'

'Is there anything you want in return?' he asked.

'Nothing,' I said. 'Just don't come near me ever again.'

'Fair enough,' he said, and rose to his feet. 'I'll leave you two alone. No doubt you have things to say to each other.' He walked out.

Sabena said, 'Have we? Got things to say to each other?'

'Not any more,' I said. 'Too many people are dead.'

'The ones you told me about?'

'Others too. The bad guys. I sussed them out and now they're dead.'

'Dave?'

'Never mind,' I said. 'I told you I was the one who sussed them out. Why don't you listen? Like I say it's down to me.'

'They all knew about my father?'

'Could be,' I said.

'So is he safe now?'

I made a weird sort of noise, and realised I was laughing.

'What a question,' I said, and then: 'Nobody's ever that safe. There's one still loose. But if he wants rid of her your father will have to do it himself. I've had it.'

'You can be very cruel,' she said.

'We both can,' I said. 'But setting up people for death – it isn't something I'd do for myself.'

'You think I betrayed you?'

'I know you did,' I said.

'But what else could I do? He's my father.'

'And I was about to be your husband,' I said, 'and I told you – over and over I told you – never to discuss my cases.'

'But it all seemed so trivial,' she said.

'But it wasn't.'

'No,' she said. 'I know that now... I take it we're finished.'

'I'm afraid so,' I said.

'This is awful for me,' said Sabena. 'I mean really awful. I doubt if you've any idea. In fact I doubt if any man could. All the same – I can't say I made the wrong decision. I just don't know. He's been awfully good to me, Ronaldo – and being in love is rather a luxury. I shall miss you.'

'Me too,' I said, and got up to leave. She came to me then, and kissed me for the last time. 'Goodbye, O Mighty One,' she said.

'Goodbye,' I said, and left her. I never saw her cry: not then, not ever.

I took a taxi back to Fulham. I was far too knackered to face the Tube, and anyway I had my overnight bag to carry, and my duty-free gin. I rather fancied some gin. Only when I got home there were messages: Sutton and Cairns, of course, but they could wait. But there was Mr Kagan as well, and Michael Copland. They neither of them sounded like tomorrow would do. I tried Mr Kagan first. Old men don't sleep all that much, and he was no exception. He picked the phone up on the third ring.

'It's me,' I said.

'Come and drink vodka.'

'Not now,' I said. 'Maybe tomorrow.'

'Tomorrow I have friends here. From Israel.'

'It will be a pleasure to meet them,' I said.

'You are sure of this?'

'Absolutely,' I said. 'I have something for them.

Something that belongs to Israel if it belongs to anybody.'

'You have it all?'

'Nearly all,' I said. 'Ninety per cent or maybe more.'

Some in a safe deposit in Knightsbridge, and the rest on the island of Moyra, hidden in caves that only Jowett and I knew how to reach. Every treasure should be guarded by a dragon, and what fiercer dragon than anthrax?

'You're a good boy, Ron,' Mr Kagan said.

'I haven't the brains to be anything else,' I said.

Then I started after Michael Copland, and ran him to earth at last at Stringfellow's. He said he'd call me back and did, almost at once. I'd never had a clearer line.

'Where are you calling from?' I asked him.

'My car.' He sounded surprised I'd asked him. 'Look, Ron – about that photograph. It was taken at a bash called the Casanova Ball at Grosvenor House earlier this year. The two in masks we think – mind you, we can't prove it but we think – were an Italian and his English girl-friend trying to set up a delivery service to run crack into the country from a factory outside Mestre.'

'Why were they trying? Why didn't they just do it?'

'The story is that they were busy raising capital.'

Oh boy, were they.

'What about the other bloke?' I asked.

'You stay away from him,' Michael Copland said. 'He's worse than the other two.'

Not any more, I thought.

'Drugs?' I said.

'Anything,' said Michael, 'so long as there's a profit. Last big job was a load of furs in Manchester – according to our crime bloke. Nothing ever proved, but he killed a security guard.'

'Would you like to know where they all are now?'

'Avidly,' he said.

'Try the press agencies,' I told him. 'Reuters or AP most likely. Look out for a story from a place called Châlon-sur-Saône. In Burgundy. That's where they are.'

'You're sure?'

'Positive,' I said. 'They're in a wood about five miles west of the town.'

'In a wood?'

'That's right,' I said, and remembered a line of Shakespeare Dave's fond of. 'They will stay there till you come.'

It's what Hamlet says after he's killed Polonius and hidden the body.

'You mean they're dead?'

Educated lad is Michael.

'Why don't you go and find out,' I said, and yawned.

'Ron, we've got to talk.'

'Later,' I said. 'There'll be more, I promise you. But not now.'

I hung up and thought about Bobsy. He'd tried to kill me once, maybe twice, and I'd scarcely even heard his voice. Then I found myself wondering if Angela had ever let him – in Dave's words – you know, before he died. My guess was not.

Next I found I was looking at the gin bottle. It had a sort of beckoning look that worried me, so I called Jocasta Benskin instead.

'Look,' I said, 'I don't know if you want to see me but–'

'Of course I want to see you,' she said. 'All of you.'

'Thanks,' I said. 'I really do need to be with someone.'

'You need to be with *me*,' she said, and then: 'Have you been crying?'

'Not yet,' I said.

'My poor lamb,' she said. 'You get yourself over here at once and Jocasta will do something about it.'

Jocasta did everything about it, so much so that I ceased to think about the dead – at least for as long as she held me. You can never wipe out the fact that you once decided to play God – or at least a police inspector – nor cease from worrying about why you did it. I worried too about the fact that Angela Rossie had got away – until Jocasta told me she hadn't got away, not if Wendy Palliser had her...

And that's it, I suppose, except that a few weeks later I got an unsigned postcard from Sydney, Australia, saying whoever it was hoped everything was well with Moyra. It was, too. All the stuff was where Jowett had said it would be, and Jowett and I were off the hook, and Mr Kagan sent me a case of vodka I still haven't finished. I'm strictly a G and T man... Nothing from Wendy Palliser. Or maybe there was. Shortly before I got the postcard a letter came for me, the padded kind marked 'Books With Care'. But they weren't books. They were the halves of ninety-nine fifty-pound notes. Dave and I spent a very happy morning sticking them to their other halves with Sellotape. But that was all there was. No word of Angela Rossie, or Wendy Palliser, or Bill Day. No word at all. Nor has there been, from that day to this.

The publishers hope that this book has given you enjoyable reading. Large Print Books are especially designed to be as easy to see and hold as possible. If you wish a complete list of our books please ask at your local library or write directly to:

Magna Large Print Books
Magna House, Long Preston,
Skipton, North Yorkshire.
BD23 4ND

This Large Print Book for the partially sighted, who cannot read normal print, is published under the auspices of

THE ULVERSCROFT FOUNDATION